JACK'S TALE

JACK'S TALE

David Randall Hill

Cover art by Cari Tobin, based on original design by Andrea Burke—used by permission.

Acknowledgments

Every good gift I've ever received, I owe to God. In writing this book I was ever reminded of His mercy and kindness. If anything praiseworthy is found in this tale, all the glory should be His alone.

He also provided me with many people who have supported me along the way. Chief among them is my daughter Andrea, who was always encouraging me to keep writing. My wife Fran and my other children—David, Elizabeth, and Matthew—have found many ways to help me. I also want to thank Andy Meisenheimer who provided many helpful suggestions on ways to improve the text. There are many others who have read the books and provided helpful comments and to them I am very grateful.

Author's Note of Thomas O'Ryan

I need to point out a couple of things. First, I'm not proud of all the things I have ever done and specifically some of the things recounted in this story. Second, I can't say that I approve of all that my friends have ever done either. When I decided to write this down I realized that I needed to tell it as it happened and to add things which explained what characters were like and why they acted like they did. If I had cut out everything which was arguably objectionable about the behavior of the characters I would have been left with a very short story. There's probably a lesson there about life generally. That reminds me of ... no, that can wait. Let's just get on with Jack's tale.

Chapter 1

April, 2003

The first time I met Jack I was near the end of my rope. Okay, so maybe that's over-the-top. Still, the day had turned pretty rotten, especially since it began with me thinking about Amanda Hollister and our upcoming date, which would be my first real date in a long time. Unfortunately I was still daydreaming about her during first period which is why I got a zero on a Latin III vocabulary test as I missed word one when the teacher called it out which meant that all the rest of the words were out of order. Yeah, that's right, Latin—I'm a nerd, or a geek if you prefer. Anyway, the real problem came at lunch when Amanda broke our date for Saturday night saying that she still liked me but Brad Elliott, our high school's starting quarterback, had just dropped his girlfriend and instead was asking Amanda out. Amanda apparently thought this an opportunity not to be missed and she was sure I understood as we were, after all, "just friends." While reflecting that "just friends" rarely caused a zero on a vocabulary test, I thought better of saying so to Amanda, subtlety not being one of her strong points. So I just said sure, of course I understood, adding, with a touch of sarcasm, how could anyone expect her to choose me over a guy as spectacular as Brad? Regrettably, she missed the sarcasm and instead saw my statement as an acceptance of reality, so we parted amicably, at least on her part.

After that, my day continued downhill. During sixth period my guidance counselor called me in to find out why one of his star students had made a zero on a vocabulary test. Word gets around fast at our high school. Mr. Olsen meant well, though I suspect his original interest in me was related to my test taking ability which gave our high school the chance to break our school's two year drought in the National Merit Scholarship tests. This test is used to provide scholarships for students who are adept at taking standardized tests and also for providing bragging rights for many school officials and parents. Results of tests like these were important to Mr. Olsen as he felt he needed to show improvement at his school if he wanted to move up from guidance counselor to being an assistant principal. It sometimes seems to me that guidance counselors are teachers who had escaped teaching and school administrators were guidance counselors who had escaped counseling. Something about this always bothered me and I had considered mentioning it to Mr. Olsen, but had decided against it. Subtlety was not one of my guidance counselor's strong points either. Anyway, I have always been sure that Mr. Olsen had argued so forcefully against my whimsical desire to try out for the baseball team because he didn't want any ninety-five mile an hour fastballs thrown at his ticket to a better job. As it had turned out we had three National Merit Scholars my year so he had no reason to worry.

With that last ordeal out of the way the school day was over, but the trip home had its bad points as well. Mainly it was the fact that Brad Elliott, the star quarterback, and I carpooled to school whenever we could, understandable since we have been practically best friends since first grade. Whenever sports didn't conflict, Brad would drive us to school in his family's eight-year old minivan one day and the next I would drive in my dad's blue, twenty-three year old Olds Cutlass. Not that any of my friends would understand, except maybe Brad, but I always felt a sense of pride in coming out and seeing the Cutlass there. The fact that my dad trusted me to drive it meant a lot.

Today being my day I got to the Cutlass and waited for the almost always late Brad. Finally he came, and there was Amanda with him. But at the last minute I was spared additional torment as she and Brad parted (without a kiss thankfully, as that would have been too much) and she went over and got in Gina Walker's car.

Brad climbed in and immediately began to apologize. "What's with you? You datin' Amanda Hollister and not tellin' me? Does she really like all those big words you use? I need to know by Saturday to get out my thesaurus." Okay, so it wasn't really an apology and I did note that he was still going out with Amanda. I let it pass. As for the 'big words' comment, Brad knows as many as me, especially in the sciences, but he always claims I talk more like my dad than my dad. Maybe he's right. At least I come by it naturally. At a little league game many years ago I wasn't running very fast and my mom yelled, "Don't meander!" I still hear about that every now and then.

"Well, we hadn't actually gone out yet, Brad," I said. "Saturday night was to have been the first time. Why are you going out with her anyway? What about Laurie?" Laurie Arnold and Brad had been dating off and on since the seventh grade. I liked Laurie a lot in spite of her temper which led to a breakup in their relationship every three or four months. The breakups were resolved in the same way each time. Laurie and Brad would briefly date someone else, then they would reconcile with each other, apologizing for what the other person had done wrong and so everything would be fine until the next time. Mostly, when they were broken up, Laurie would date me. This arrangement worked out reasonably well for all parties. Laurie got a nice, polite guy with whom she would always feel safe, Brad would know he could count on me never really trying to move in on Laurie, and I, well I could at least be seen dating a special girl, even if one I never had a chance at kissing; regrettable, since from what Brad had once told me, kissing Laurie could be pretty spectacular.

"You know how she is, I mean, how she always wants to argue and how she always has to be right," answered Brad as I pulled out into traffic. He launched into an explanation of their latest spat, to which I paid no attention, trying as I was to think of a way to say no to the request I knew was coming by the time I turned into Brad's driveway. Sure enough. "Look, how about you call her and take her to a movie? I don't want just anyone calling her up. You're really her best friend, at least she says so. What d'ya say?"

I guess predictability is one of the things we value in friends.

"Okay," I heard myself saying, "but this time I'm serious about dating Laurie—I'm not gonna walk away when you want back with her." I said all that, knowing it was nonsense.

"Sure, sure," said Brad, knowing exactly the same thing. "Hey, can I come over after supper, maybe lose a few games of chess?" he asked. This in part was Brad's way to make amends. Though he likes chess and is a decent player, I'm better, and our record shows it. Offering to come over and lose a few games of chess was no small concession on his part, given how competitive he is.

"Great," I said cheerfully; cheerfulness being a learned attitude, not a natural one.

Brad slid out the door, saying, "See ya' later, sorry about Amanda."

I waved as I pulled out of the driveway, thinking that Brad was really all right, and that I would probably forgive him in about six to nine months.

Then I thought of Amanda—the long honey blonde hair, the big green eyes, the ... —maybe I would forgive him in six to nine years.

Having driven the half-mile from Brad's house I parked the car and walked around back to the kitchen door. Mom was giving Angela, my ten-year old sister an afternoon snack. Mom is a part time attorney with a small local firm. She plans to go back full time when Angela finishes high school.

Angela's bus normally beats me home by fifteen minutes. Fortunately, Stephanie, my fifteen year old sister, was at soccer practice. She would be home just before dinner. I could be civil with Mom and Angela but in the mood I was in I would never get through five minutes with Steph.

I gave Mom a kiss and she handed me a glass of milk and a plate of warm cookies. I suppose when I'm fifty I'll wish she had always given us carrots and celery for snack time but for now I'm happy with the warm cookies we get every couple of weeks.

"How was school today, Thomas?" she asked.

"Fine, Mom," I said, as I subscribe to the general principle that parents are helpful in times of crisis but otherwise they have their own problems and there is no sense in bothering them with things we should be able to take care of ourselves.

"How is Amanda?" was the next question. The problem with the above principle is that parents are not always cooperative, especially caring ones. Mom has a way of selecting the very subject I most wish to avoid.

"Oh, she's all right," I answered, "but, we're not going out Saturday night after all. Brad and Laurie have broken up again, so I'm asking Laurie out instead." Note that I was not saying anything inaccurate to my mother; rather I was putting a positive 'spin' on the news.

Mom, who at almost five-seven is just four inches shorter than me, gave me a serious look. "Now Thomas, are you sure you should break the date you've been talking about for three weeks just to ask Laurie out? After all she always seems to get back together with Brad." This conversation was not going well and the tactic called for was an abrupt change of subject.

"Don't worry, Mom, I know what I'm doing," which is the closest thing to an outright lie I hope I would ever say to my mother. "How's planning for the picnic going?" Our church has an annual spring picnic in late May and this year Mom was in charge. After this the conversation went better and I actually had one or two helpful suggestions.

All this time Angela was appearing to ignore us while she finished her cereal—she didn't like chocolate chip cookies, causing us often to raise the issue of switched babies at the hospital. After Mom left to do something upstairs, Angela said, without looking up, "Sharon told me that Amanda was breaking your date so she could go out with Brad."

Now you have to understand. Many sisters, Stephanie for example, could be expected to make a statement like that precisely for the pain it would cause. This is not true of Angela, who was merely asking for a clarification of the apparent discrepancy between her brother's statement and that of her friend Sharon who happened to be Amanda's sister.

"That's correct, Angela, but it's probably all for the best as she evidently was never really interested in me to begin with."

Angela wiped the milk from her lips and pushed back her chair. "Yes, that's what Sharon said." With that she got up and left the room going off to do her homework. I stared at the door she had walked through for a few moments in silence and then, realizing there was nothing else to do, I reached for some more chocolate chip cookies.

Wanting to avoid further conversation given my present state of mind, I called to Mom that I was going out for a walk, which meant, like it usually did, I was going to my favorite spot.

I live in a little neighborhood in northern Montgomery County, Maryland, a part of the extended Washington, D.C., metropolitan area. Our house is a two-story and looks like a farmhouse with a big front porch. It sits on a quiet cul-de-sac (my dad always calls it a dead end street which makes my Aunt Jean, who is a real estate agent, mad). The neighborhood was built thirteen years ago and we were the second family to own our house, moving in just before I started first grade. Brad's family (Brad, his parents, and Bobby, his younger brother) already lived there, in the gray colonial on the corner next to the main road. Laurie's family (Laurie, her parents, her grandmother, and a sister who died four years ago) had actually been the first in the whole neighborhood. Their house was the big brick two-story at the end of the street. All the land in our neighborhood used to be part of the old farm that had run all along the south side of Smithtown Road between Burdette Road to the southwest and West Hancock Road to the north. Now the farm had been reduced to just some woods, a creek, a falling down barn, and a big old farmhouse.

I walked to the gate in the fence at the back of our yard and passed into the woods which ran between our neighborhood and the old farmhouse just barely visible through the trees on the other side of the creek which ran down to the nearby lake. Most of the trees were oaks and wild cherry, with a scattering of beech and maple, though the springtime showed through with redbuds and dogwoods here and there. Some of the trees were quite old, especially right along the creek which had originally separated two large pastures before the farm had been broken up. Someone long ago had planted clumps of daffodils which continued to spread in drifts along the woods' edge. Later in the spring, iris, or 'flags' like my grandma called them, would show bursts of purple and red and be joined by daylilies as spring turned to summer.

Even though it wasn't part of our yard I had come to think of it as mine. My favorite spot was a clearing along the creek bank where the surrounding trees were dense enough that on a bright April afternoon you couldn't see any houses at all. It was as if you were alone in a wilderness. I loved to spend long hours there.

I sat down and leaned back against the big flat rock that always seemed as if it had been put there for that purpose. The day was very warm—more like summer than spring. Some squirrels were scampering through the trees and a cardinal was showing off his bright colors in the low branches of a nearby oak. Often I'll see deer in this clearing, drinking from the cool water of the creek. On this afternoon I sat and thought about the day I was having and what I was going to say to Laurie when I called her later. Nearly an hour had passed when I noticed a rabbit on the other side of the creek. The rabbit was considerably larger than most I had seen in the neighborhood and gray, not brown. I watched as it hopped along. It turned and with one great leap crossed over to my side of the creek. I leaned forward to get a closer look. The rabbit came up to within six feet of me and seemed to be looking at me with curiosity. Just as I noticed that it had the most incredibly blue eyes, the rabbit said, "I think you are the one to help me."

Chapter 2

Have you ever thought what you would do if something totally outside your experience happened to you? You know, if one of the space aliens from those tabloids landed in your backyard or if a million dollar prize patrol from the magazine publishers showed up at your house? Well I suspect that I would do the same thing that I did when the rabbit first spoke to me. I would faint.

Now I realize that this was not a heroic response to great stress, but in my defense I must point out that I am no hero. At any rate, as I began to regain consciousness the rabbit was rubbing my forehead with one of its front paws and saying, "There, there. I know this is a shock, but you simply must come out of it. I have come to ask for your help and you must give me an answer."

I scrambled to my feet, still somewhat unsteady, and backed away, looking down on the rabbit. Now that it has been some time since I last heard it, its voice is hard to describe. It sounded, well, like you might expect a rabbit to sound if it could speak; neither high nor low, but soft and gentle.

"Now, now. It is quite unfair of you to tower over me. Sit down so that we might discuss things evenly. For I am a human being like you, though my form is not. You should pay me respect for that, no matter my appearance."

This seemed a reasonable request to me; at least as reasonable as anything seemed under the circumstances. So I sat down in front of the rabbit and asked, "What do you want?"

"You must help me destroy an evil sorcerer and break the spell which condemns me to an eternity in this form," came the reply.

As I might have expected, I thought.

"This is really crazy."

The brilliant blue eyes conveyed understanding. "Still, it is real, Thomas. Yes, I know your name and your sisters Stephanie and Angela. I know of Brad and Laurie and many others. But I have come to you. Your imagination is great. I know you will be able to accept this reality. Even as you have grown up to be a fine young man you have retained, in just the right measure, a child's heart."

That last was meant to be a compliment I'm sure, though one could debate whether, if true, it is such a good thing.

The alarm on my cellphone went off to remind me to get home for dinner. "Look, I've gotta get home." I said. "Can I give you an answer tomorrow?"

"Oh, yes," said the rabbit, "come here at this same time and we can talk further. By the way, you may call me Jack." Without another word the rabbit turned and swiftly bounded away.

I sat there for a few minutes trying to decide if it had been a dream; hoping, in fact that at any moment I would wake up. When it became obvious I wasn't going to, I started for home. I had enough problems without being late for supper. Scrambling to my feet I barely stumbled at all as I walked home in a daze.

My parents really enjoy dinner with our family. As for their children, there were good days and bad. We, by this I mean especially Stephanie and me, did not always enjoy one another's company, or at least we often understood the pleasure of one of us to be directly proportional to the discomfort of the other. The origins of the situation are lost in the dimness of time though Stephanie believes it began with the incident of the frog and her glass of lemonade when she was five. I am not so sure.

This time however luck was with me as Stephanie's day had been as wonderful as mine had been distressing. She had received the itinerary for her French Club's tour of Europe. Though the trip was fifteen months and innumerable fund raisers away she was overcome by thoughts of "La Belle France." While my father said the blessing I was especially grateful for this and any other distractions that might focus attention away from me.

Stephanie's great day had continued through her select team soccer practice. She became the first freshman to score on the star junior goalie— one Laurie Arnold.

"She was really spaced out," said Stephanie, "I guess it's 'cause she and Brad broke up again."

"Yes, Steph, I heard that," said Mom. "Thomas is planning to ask her out for Saturday."

Uh, oh, I thought.

"But, Thomas, weren't you ..." began Steph in a puzzled voice before Dad cut in.

"Don't attribute your success to others' problems, Princess," he said. "You are a fine soccer player who can compete with anyone."

"Thanks, Dad." She was radiant from our father's praise. Which was due, I had to admit. Steph had already been earmarked for stardom by her coaches. She had always been the best at each level on which she had competed.

"That's right," I agreed smiling and, as she smiled back, we shared a moment of happiness. This also served to deflect her from what could easily have been an investigation of what happened to my date with Amanda. The rest of the dinner went well though I had to force myself to eat my normal two servings of chicken cacciatore just to make sure things seemed routine to Mom and Dad. With my mom's cooking it wasn't that hard.

At the first moment it was diplomatically possible to do so I excused myself and went to my room. I tried to prepare myself mentally for calling Laurie.

I talked to a rabbit.

The thought exploded in my mind like the Fourth of July fireworks near the Washington Monument. For a while I could think of nothing else—just that one fact.

I talked to a rabbit.

It was like being in an unending whirlpool, grasping for something to hold fast. Oddly, the first thought that formed in my mind was that if this got out I could never be President. After all, I had read about the grief Jimmy Carter had gotten years before I was born for fighting with a rabbit. If a "killer rabbit" means bad press, a "talking rabbit" is death.

Gradually I became able to accept the new reality. Though my political and theological beliefs run to the conservative side I still am pretty flexible. A world with sorcerers and talking rabbits? Sure, why not? The only alternative was that I was hallucinating and somehow, as between the possibilities, I preferred believing in the rabbit. At least it wasn't six feet tall and invisible like the one in "Harvey" or wearing a vest and carrying a pocket watch like the one in <u>Alice in Wonderland</u>. This was just a nice, big rabbit with bright blue eyes. And it talked.

15

And as Jack had said, I really could imagine it. But is that all it was—just my imagination? No, it was real. Wasn't it? I desperately focused on what I knew was real. I had a chance to get another date with Laurie. With the greatest of efforts I pushed the rabbit out of my mind—well, not really out of my mind, more just to one side.

Okay. I still had to call Laurie. Brad was probably on his way over and he would be asking. Like usual she didn't answer her cell so I punched in the shortcut for her home number and let the phone ring.

Her grandmother answered, "Hello, this is the Arnold residence." Different generations—nowadays we're taught not to give out any more information than is necessary.

"Hi, Mrs. Jernigan, this is Thomas O'Ryan. May I speak to Laurie?"

"Why certainly, Thomas, I'll call her," said Mrs. Jernigan. I heard her call "Laurie!" and then, even though she had muffled the receiver I heard "It's that nice O'Ryan boy." I always have been good at impressing grandmothers, except for one I'll mention later.

"Hello, Thomas," said the sweet voice that I'd known for almost eleven years, "Guess I know why you called."

"Hope springs eternal, Laurie," I said, and we both laughed. I remembered Brad's comment that afternoon about the way I talked. At least Laurie never objected. Maybe it's because she often talked the same way, at least to me. Someone at school had once been listening to our conversation at lunch and suggested we were parents in disguise. I took it as a compliment but Laurie seemed offended.

"This time I think it may be more serious than before between Brad and me," she said. Sure, I thought, but I tried to listen politely, wishing now that I had paid attention to Brad's side of the story so I could compare notes.

To understand their quarrel you need to know that Laurie is passionate. She's not necessarily romantic—passionate and romantic not being the same things. But she is very passionate and not just about things like kissing which I've mentioned before, but everything in her life. In soccer she is the best goalie in the state because she is absolutely determined to be. Where the word for Steph is talent, the word for Laurie is intensity. She has the ability to will herself to play at a higher level. It would be a long time before Steph got another ball past Laurie because of a lapse in concentration. Her passion carries over to other interests as well, like politics, and, not for the first time, politics had been the source of her quarrel with Brad. It wasn't that they had even disagreed about whatever the issue was; he had just made the mistake of saying it wasn't that important. You don't say that to someone who's passionate. Their longest break-up had been back in January when Laurie led a group of students to the annual March for Life on the Mall in downtown Washington and Brad refused to come because it was too cold.

Her story about the breakup complete, she paused for me to comment. This was tough as I wanted to be supportive to Laurie without speaking harshly of Brad. Not too harshly. Besides, once I realized the nature of their fight I had stopped following what she was saying. I decided on a different approach. "Maybe it's time we tried this without bringing up Brad. How about going out with me Saturday night? We can go get pizza and then see a movie."

Laurie laughed brightly, "You didn't hear a word I said, did you?" She knew me pretty well, except for the fact that I now was talking to rabbits.

"I refuse to answer—Fifth Amendment," I answered. "What about Saturday?"

"Okay, but, I really mean this—I want it to be different this time."

"Great," I agreed, with a hopefulness in my voice that I found surprising. I kept thinking I had gotten over Laurie. It's not that I worship her, but like I think it was Charlie Brown who once said of the little red-haired girl, I'm quite fond of the ground on which she walks. "Look, I gotta go, but I'll pick you up at six on Saturday and we'll have lots of time to talk then."

She said fine and we hung up. So far, so good. Now I just needed time to think. I wished that I had arranged a night time meeting with the rabbit as the next afternoon seemed so far away. Do rabbits move around at night? The Internet might tell me but would the websites discuss this type of rabbit? Unlikely.

Heavy footfalls on the steps cut short my reverie. Brad knocked on my door; polite as ever.

"Come in," I called.

Entering, he plopped down in the big easy chair I had asked Mom to let me have. She and Dad were preparing to throw it out, a decision she was more committed to than my father. When he heard I wanted it in my room, he became the idea's chief advocate. Mom finally gave in and I had my chair. Shortly thereafter Dad started letting me drive his Cutlass. I guess he liked that chair a lot.

"You call her?" asked Brad.

"Yeah, I did. And we're going out. And this time you're not getting her back so easily."

"Super. How about some chess?"

Brad is blonde and gray-eyed and, according to more than one girl I know, "ruggedly handsome," whatever that means. Full grown at six-four, weighing two-twenty; he can bench press routinely twice as much as I have ever been able to lift. If I were to hit him, which was on my mind to do, I would need to hit him awfully hard, or he would clobber me. Or maybe not. Brad is a very mild-mannered guy with his friends. He would probably laugh, repeat his not quite an apology about Amanda, and start setting up the chessmen. Maybe this comes from having your life so well-planned. Growing up in Montgomery County can be very focusing for kids like us. My mom once told the story of consoling a friend who was sure that her failure to get her daughter into a certain pre-school would doom her chances to reach Harvard. Anyway, Brad had long ago decided he wanted to be an aerospace engineer and he had set his sights on Stanford to get his education. Convinced that he needed an edge to get accepted, he was pleased to find he had a knack for throwing the football. This past season he had set almost every single season passing record for Maryland high school athletics. His four touchdown passes, including one with eight seconds left to win it, had made him the star of the state 3A championship game. While naturally happy about everyone's compliments, the most important thing was the letter from the Stanford coach saying that he hoped Brad would sign a national letter of intent with Stanford at the next national signing period. Brad already had the pen picked out to use.

"Instead of chess, how about a walk?"

"Whatever you say."

Playing chess would not have been a good idea. Mainly because in my condition I might have lost.

We stopped downstairs to tell Mom where we were going and then we set out. Next to Laurie's house was one of several trails that led into the county park which surrounded our neighborhood in a sweeping arc behind the houses on the opposite side of our street down to the causeway across the lake and then back up on the other side of Smithtown Road. Technically, the park is closed at dark, but for the kids who lived on the street before the park opened it would always be "our woods" and so we mainly viewed the rules as applying to outsiders. The main change which had come to "our woods" in recent years had been the artificial lake which had finished filling up just three years ago. Some of our favorite places were gone under several feet of water but I had to admit the lake was awesome. We walked along the shore, ducking behind some large rocks when a ranger's truck came by, there being no point in entering into a discussion of whose woods these were. Within a few minutes we emerged onto Smithtown Road. We crossed the causeway which cuts across a narrow part of the lake and walked to the general store which will likely give way within the next decade to convenience stores and fast food chains. For now we can each get a can of Orange Crush and pretend to be growing up in the country instead of one of the most rapidly expanding suburban areas in the nation.

Throughout the walk we had spoken hardly a word; not uncommon— when you are really good friends you don't always need to talk. Besides, I was thinking about my afternoon encounter and Brad was sure I was still bothered about Amanda, so there really wasn't much to talk about. When we got back to Brad's house we stopped.

"Thanks for going on the walk, there's really no hard feelings," I said, truly meaning it.

"Good. Amanda's not worth that. See'ya at six; gotta get there early tomorrow."

"Sure thing," I replied, skimming quickly past the thought that it would be easier for me to say the same thing if I was the one who still had the date with Amanda.

I walked back to my house and sat down in the swing on our big front porch. In a few minutes my mom came out.

"Oh there you are," she said. "How was your walk?"

"Great," I answered with some forced enthusiasm. "It's nice out."

"Yes it is." She paused for a moment. "You like Laurie more than you let on, don't you?"

I sighed. This was one of my mom's favorite tactics; come out of nowhere with a question you would prefer not to answer. This time I did not feel like being evasive. "Yeah, Mom, I guess I do."

"Try not to ...," she began, before stopping herself. 'Let her hurt you again' was what she had started to say.

"Well, I better get up to bed. Big history test tomorrow." I started for the door.

"And you went for a long walk tonight?" she asked.

"Mom, there's always ...," and we both said "homeroom" together, then we laughed.

As I was starting up the stairs she called out, "Oh, by the way Thomas, one of your friends I don't know called tonight. He said his name was Jack and wanted to remind you of your meeting tomorrow. He had a very unusual voice."

"Yes, uh, yes he does, Mom. Thanks," was all I could say.

I didn't sleep well that night but at least I knew that if this was a hallucination it was one I was sharing with my mother.

Chapter 3

Fridays are usually hectic at John Clark High School. This in turn usually makes the time pass quickly. That particular Friday was the longest school day of my life. At least the test on the Civil War went well. My dad had interested me in American history when I was a kid. Antietam was not a place in a book to me. By the time I was ten I had walked Bloody Lane, crossed Burnside Bridge, and huddled in the Dunkard Church during a lightning storm so fierce it almost made me feel the terror of McClellan's army pounding at Lee that September day in 1862 when 25,000 Americans fell—13,000 wearing blue and 12,000 gray. By the time eleventh grade history came along I had developed a genuine love for the subject. This love is not shared by many of my contemporaries. Unfortunately, our teacher, Mr. Spruill, who only had the chance to teach this AP class because Mrs. Hastings had left suddenly, had suffered through too many students saying "who cares?" and "how boring" and so he had about given up. Still, he encouraged me to pursue history as a career, though he was quick to say that almost anything would make me more money. He had little encouraging to say about teaching in high school; he was burned out. I know that many companies have programs to loan employees to schools as teachers. Maybe they should set up programs to borrow teachers for a year to give the teachers some time away from their students.

There were only two other good things that happened that day. The first was lunch which I got to share with my Saturday date. To me, Laurie Arnold is very special. Some guys would call her cute, some pretty, but many would say she wasn't their type. She rarely takes much time with her appearance and almost never dresses to show off her figure, so she usually wouldn't get noticed if standing next to someone like Amanda. Of course, I decided that

Laurie was beautiful the day I met her at age six, so I may not be an unbiased judge. Still, she has long brown hair with just a touch of red, gorgeous brown eyes, and a perfect smile (thanks to braces which had come off just before the beginning of ninth grade). Of course, what makes real people most attractive is what comes from the inside, which in Laurie's case meant intelligence, compassion, and a fiery determination. I realize I'm not sounding objective. Does she have flaws? Oh, sure. I'd list them in some detail but she might someday read this.

Normally she has a much earlier lunch time than I do, but a special Students Against Drunk Driving (or SADD) program meant she had to eat late because she's one of the club's officers. The cafeteria's Friday special—spaghetti—while normally good, was better than ever. We talked and kidded about light things—nothing serious; only once did I let my mind wander to the question of whether Laurie would want to be having lunch with someone who got phone calls from small furry animals. It was also satisfying to notice Amanda walking by and looking a bit irritated that I was having a good time the day after she had broken a date with me.

The other good thing was a student-faculty committee meeting. The subject was the use of computers in the classroom. Mr. Chambers, the head of the English Department, and I had an informal agreement—we were committed to a guerrilla movement to disrupt the use of technology in the classroom. Needless to say we were in a minority.

George Chambers had been on his way to obtain a degree in civil engineering, at the specific instruction of his parents, when, in early 1950, he decided to enlist in the U.S Army just in time for the beginning of the Korean "police action". Having been too young for World War II, he did not ask their permission before enlisting. He served in the Twenty-fourth Infantry Division, holding the line at Pusan; then participating in the breakout following the landing at Inchon which would take him almost to China before the icy retreat to the thirty-eighth parallel. Few faculty members and practically none of his students knew of the list which followed his name in his unit's history- "Chambers, George E., M. Sgt. —3 Purple Hearts, 2 Bronze Stars, Silver Star." The only reason I know is because I looked up the book once in the Library of Congress. When asked about it, he politely said that he preferred not to discuss it. He said it brought back memories too painful, even now. He asked that I mention it to no one and I never did.

After the war he came home and went to college to study English literature and the classics. If his parents approved, he never said. He began teaching in Montgomery County in 1958. Now in his early seventies, though he looked fifteen years younger, it would take more than a few generations of students saying "boring" to burn him out. Teaching was what he lived for. He never understood faculty members for whom teaching was a job, not a calling.

He disliked computers. Not that he disliked what they could do. Instead he hated the fact that many people expected them to do things they could not—especially to take the place of real teaching. As for me, I love computers. My family, courtesy of a very generous grandmother who has seen too many commercials about the danger of children growing up without a sophisticated computer in the house, has two advanced ..., oh, well, what's the point? No matter the specs it will not sound near so impressive by the time someone reads this.

Nevertheless I know what Mr. Chambers means. Besides, rooting for the underdog is what made America great. Also, Mr. Robinson, the assistant principal, was the committee chairman and he was not one of my favorites, ever since the time he sent Doug Whitmyre home just because he put up a sign calling for a heterosexual awareness week. Political satire from the right did not please Mr. Robinson. He also wasn't too thrilled when he found out that some of us had established a student Bible study contrary to his wishes and were meeting, thanks to Mr. Connelly, the head custodian, in the furnace rooms in the school's subbasement, which we had taken to calling the Catacombs. Even Mr. Robinson understood that historical allusion. He was once overheard to be calling us "reactionary Neanderthals." Several of us had t-shirts made up with the letters RN on them and a picture of a caveman on the back. Mr. Robinson would be very glad to see the class of 2004 graduate. How Mr. Chambers and I came to be on Mr. Robinson's committee was always something of a mystery, though I guess it had something to do with the fact that Mrs. Barnes, the principal, didn't have much use for the assistant principal either.

The topic for this week's meeting was the use of computers in teaching foreign languages. The session was intended to be for "brainstorming." In my limited experience such occasions normally consist of several committee members putting forward their own agendas while everyone else wishes they could be elsewhere doing something worthwhile.

The argument boiled down to Mr. Chambers, who speaks three languages fluently and can translate several classical and medieval languages with only occasional use of a dictionary, matched against Mr. Robinson and Mrs. Endicott, the Spanish teacher, who, it is generally agreed by her students, should never risk being stranded in Madrid.

While entertaining for a time, I eventually started looking at my watch, worried that I might miss my woodland meeting. At a break in the action I quickly moved to table the proposal, not really sure if there actually was one. Miss Johnson, the American government teacher, quickly seconded my motion. Mr. Robinson's objections were drowned by cries of "Vote! Vote!" Following the passage of the motion there was little to do but adjourn. I returned Mr. Chambers' wink before hurrying out the door.

Brad had hung around to lift weights and to wait for me. He was ready to go when I met him in the lobby. He asked if we could drive over to the Jimmie Cone in Damascus for some soft ice cream but I told him that I had some things to do. He dropped me at the door and I hurried to put my books away. Mom was downstairs so I asked Angela to tell her that I'd gone for a walk. Since it was starting to cloud up I grabbed my rain jacket on the way out the door.

When I got to the clearing there was no sign of Jack. Distant rumbles of thunder made me put the jacket on. Just as the first big drops began to fall, Jack appeared on the far bank.

"Hurry!" called the rabbit, "you must follow me!" Turning before I could say anything, Jack bounded through the trees. I crossed the creek by way of the fallen tree (which had been where Brad and I had played Robin Hood and Little John fighting with staffs when we were ten—with me as Robin only I didn't do as well as Errol Flynn in the classic movie) and tried to follow as quickly as I could. Rain was falling more heavily. Every so often Jack would stop to let me catch up, before hurrying on ahead.

It quickly became apparent that we were making for the old farmhouse. As kids we had called it a haunted house and every Halloween we dared one another to go up and look in the front window. One year, I forget exactly which one, Brad took the dare. The caretaker, who was really a kind-hearted lady, was evidently expecting us. When Brad bravely raised his head above the window he saw a green face with a harsh red mouth that said, "Who's looking in my house?!" Laurie and I found that out the next day. That night all we saw was Brad running home as fast as he could. We heard his door slam just before a spooky wail from the house sent us flying as well. Now that I'm older I realize what a good joke it was but I've never recaptured my interest in late night surveillance.

I reached the porch just as the skies really opened up. It was, as my dad liked to call it, "a real Kentucky frog-strangler", though of course it was in Maryland. Jack ducked through a small panel near the front door. I walked up and tried the knob but it was locked. Before I could raise my hand to knock, the door swung open to reveal Mrs. Donnelly, the kindly caretaker who had scared us so badly that Halloween.

"Come in, Thomas," she said smiling, "no green faces this time, I promise. Let me take your coat." After she hung it in the closet she led me down the hall and to the left where there was a cozy den, with two big wingback chairs and a fire burning briskly in the fireplace. There in one of the chairs was the rabbit. In front of the chair was a low table the height of the chair seat. Mrs. Donnelly indicated the other chair was for me. Her presence was very reassuring. It meant that I wasn't the only one who could accept talking to a rabbit.

"Hot chocolate, Jack?" she asked.

"That would be wonderful, Helen."

"And you, Thomas?"

"Yes, please." Mrs. Donnelly left us. The room was decorated with flowers—paintings of flowers, floral prints on the furniture, and bouquets of cut flowers in vases scattered about the room. I waited silently. Jack did as well until the housekeeper had brought the hot chocolate. The aroma seemed to fill the room as she sat a steaming mug on the table next to my chair and a bowl on the low table in front of Jack's. We murmured our thanks and she left. Then I listened.

"I have decided to tell you my story; all that you need to hear. When you have heard it, I hope you will decide to help me. But if not, we will part as friends, not enemies, and I will continue to look for one to come to my aid.

"'Twas in the year of our Lord, ten sixty-five. William of Normandy was preparing his bid for the English throne, waiting only for Edward the Confessor's death, when there came to my father's house in what is now France a tired and sick man. We took him in and gave him such care as was within our ken. When he regained his strength he returned our good deeds with evil. He took control of our house and our lands. My father he enthralled completely, and he put me to work in his service. None could withstand him, for he was a sorcerer. Thomas, you must understand this well, our world was not meant to have sorcerers. Merlin and all the rest are legends; fables wrought of one part fact and one hundred parts imagination. But this sorcerer was real. His name was Antalan, and even now I cannot speak his name without anger. For he did not belong here. He came from beyond the stars; from a world he called Merindelon."

Space aliens after all, I thought, but had the presence of mind not to say so out loud.

"When all seemed hopeless," Jack continued, "Another stranger arrived; one who seemed to have some ability to withstand the sorcerer. He had been sent to take the evil one home. The struggle was hard, but at last good won out and the sorcerer stood before us bound in chains we could not see. His captor stood at his side with sword drawn and spoke words in a tongue I have never heard elsewhere. There came up a mist about the pair, then a burst of rainbow colors, and they began to fade. Next a breeze blew the mist away. And they were gone."

The rabbit paused for a moment and lapped the chocolate which had cooled considerably.

"The evil the sorcerer had done began to evaporate like the mist. But not all." Again a pause; Jack seemed sad, burdened with memories undesired, but which could not be surrendered. "For the sorcerer had selected a helper from among the servants—a scribe who kept our accounts, cheating us I suspect, though perhaps that charge is unfair. The night before the sorcerer was defeated this helper had stolen an amulet. A mere trinket it must have been to the evil one, and so it must have been in any world where there was much magic. But with the sorcerer gone it was all that was truly magical in our world. And it was beautiful. Gold, with an etching of the Lion's Crown and the twin moons and ... ," Jack's voice had grown almost wistful, but changed abruptly. "And it should not be here!" Suddenly quite angry, the rabbit stopped to regain control before continuing.

"He tried to use it for his own purposes but he failed; or at least he did not accomplish all he desired. He never acquired great powers but he did weave one great spell. I do not think he knew what he was doing. Still, it is why I am here as I am. I had just discovered that he had the amulet. I was on my way to my father that we might gather enough strength to wrest the amulet from him. Using words beyond his understanding, some only half-remembered from spells of the evil one, he wove a spell intended to silence me. But instead of making me silent it changed my form to that which you see, and it bound me to this form until the spell is broken. But since he lacks the cunning to break the spell it has given me an unending life. One more thing—he bound himself as well. The limited powers he had developed were locked inside the amulet and with that, he too gained what may be immortality.

"Out of fear he ran away. When my father came looking for me, and found the evil which had been done, he wept bitterly. He kept me safe and shared my secret with one whom he trusted greatly. So it has been ever since that I have sought the love and protection of others. In this I have been blessed with one unintended result of the spell. Often, though not at will, it is as if I can see tomorrow as today. The sight comes and goes but I have often traded on this unsought talent. The years have brought me many who have served me well. Great wealth is now held in my name, though only Mrs. Donnelly and three others know my story. Four others now, Thomas."

"Why are you telling me this?" I asked. "How can I help you?"

"Because for nearly one thousand years I have searched for the one who did this to me. Now I have found him. And I believe I know what must be done to break the spell. You will help me; at least I hope you will. Based on what I've observed of you—yes, I've watched you as you've grown—and what I have learned of you from Mrs. Donnelly's investigations I believe you will help me. My judgment has grown keen concerning people. Oh, and in return I shall attempt to give you any one thing which is your heart's greatest desire."

This was going way too fast for me. There were so many questions to ask that I did not know where to begin. The first thing I grasped was the offer of a reward. I guess that could be expected since I am the type who always asked my grandparents "What did you bring me?" by the time they had been in the house fifteen minutes.

"My heart's greatest desire?" What in the world would I most desire? It was dumb to think that a wish could come true, but ... . Thoughts of the past day filled my mind. "A girlfriend," I heard myself saying, "Like Brad has Laurie even when he doesn't have her."

For a moment it seemed like the rabbit was chuckling, though it was hard to tell. "I see what you truly desire," Jack said thoughtfully. "Help me break the spell and I will do what I can. I have learned much in a thousand years, perhaps enough to help you. Now, will you help me?"

I had much more to ask, but I just said, "Yes, I'll help you. How?"

Jack told me.

Chapter 4

I agreed to meet Jack to talk some more about the plan on Monday afternoon, although to me it was less a plan than a hope. Anyway, by then I intended to have some information of my own to share.

When I got home, quite late for Friday dinner, I expected to find two hostile and cross-examining parents. Happily, I was wrong.

"Boy, are you lucky," said Stephanie, as I walked into the family room where she was curled up on the couch watching television. "Any other time and you'd be in big trouble for being an hour and a half late for supper."

In answer to my puzzled expression she handed me a note. It was from my mother and it read:

> Thomas and Stephanie,
>
> Your father called. He needs me to come meet him to look at some furniture before the store closes. I'm taking Angela with me. We'll get dinner   while we're out. I've put your meals in the refrigerator, just warm them in the   microwave.
>
> Love,
> Mom

My mom is such a good sport. Dad is always getting her to go look at this or that and she does, though not with a great deal of joy. Typically the outcome would be for her to suggest they go home and think about the purchase which eventually results in Dad losing interest as well. Mom has saved the family a lot of money that way without actually being non-supportive to her husband.

"She meant for you to be in charge," Steph said. "Though why she would want an absentee brother to be in charge, I'll never know."

While it can sometimes be entertaining to exchange insults and other pleasantries with Steph, this time I decided to ignore the comment and try to pick up on the happy theme of last night's dinner. "How did soccer practice go?"

She looked cross. "Laurie told you, didn't she?"

"I haven't talked to Laurie this evening. What happened?"

"She knocked me in the mud."

I looked genuinely shocked. "She hit you?" I asked incredulously.

"No, stupid," said Stephanie, "I was trying to score on her like I did yesterday and I thought the rain might slow her down. I was wrong," she added ruefully. "She got to the ball just before I did. When she grabbed the ball she stayed down. I tried to stop, but she hit me like a football block and I flew over her and landed face first in a puddle. My hair won't be clean for a week." She looked up to see my response.

This was quite a test. As a brother I wanted to laugh and say "Wish I'd been there," but as someone who might require Stephanie's understanding at various times in the near future I decided to be more understanding myself.

Keeping my face straight with no small effort, I said brightly, "That's a compliment."

"What do you mean?" she asked suspiciously.

I sat down next to her on the couch. "Laurie respects you as a player. She knows you can play with anybody. She won't ever cut you any slack."

Steph began to look happy. "Really?"

"Sure. If you get the chance to knock her down fairly she'll respect you for it." Which was absolutely true, though it would also mean that Steph might spend more practice time in the mud.

With my sister in better spirits we talked for a while, laughing together at Steph's latest Mr. Robinson story. As I've mentioned, our assistant principal was not the most popular of fellows.

For some time Mr. Robinson had been getting calls at school from a woman, not his wife, and he had supposedly tried to get her to stop. Eventually he was able to persuade her to call him only on a cell phone which he kept in his office. This was all common knowledge to those of us in the Anti-Robinson Underground (it includes some three dozen students and several faculty members serving *ex officio*). We found little humorous about it. Several of us knew Mrs. Robinson, who taught at the local elementary school, and wished she had found someone worthy of her. Still, Mr.

Robinson's problems could bring out the sadistic side of high school students. One of them, Roger Avery, is an electronics and computer whiz. He could have gone to the gifted program in the sciences but chose to stay with his friends, saying college was soon enough to do advanced college work.

Roger's problems with Mr. Robinson started the first day of his freshman year when the assistant principal made the mistake of assuming that my friend is liberal because he is black. Roger, who is a big fan of Thomas Sowell, the conservative economist, and has a picture of Ronald Reagan in his locker, came upon the assistant principal having an argument with Doug Whitmyre, whom I have mentioned before, concerning the t-shirt Doug was wearing. It was a pro-life message comparing abortion to slavery. Seeing Roger, Mr. Robinson asked Doug if he thought it was appropriate to offend the African-American students with such a debatable comparison. Before Doug could respond, Roger instantly sized up the situation and said, "Great shirt, man! Can you get me one?" Then he and Doug walked off together getting acquainted leaving Mr. Robinson standing alone taken aback by the turn of events.

Back to the cell phone. Roger had somehow, we won't get into how because I don't want anyone else to try something similar and also because of some statute of limitations concerns, discovered the frequency upon which Mr. Robinson's cell phone received calls. I suspect that's not the precisely correct way to explain it technically but then I'm planning to be a history major. In any event it was then a fairly simple thing, or so Roger said, I doubt it really was, to rig a receiver/transmitter arrangement which would allow Mr. Robinson's cell call to be shared with a wider audience, in this case a tenth grade study hall of students who had not gone on a class field trip. When a call came in that afternoon an office messenger notified Roger who slipped out of the study hall, made some adjustments on a piece of equipment in his locker and returned to find chaos. Mrs. Brewster, who was supposed to be in charge of the study hall, but who in fact was allowing the students to run the place, was oblivious at first to what was happening. When she realized what her students were hearing over the loudspeaker she panicked. Torn between running to the office to stop the call and also wanting to stop the class from hearing the call, she finally ordered the forty-seven students out of the room. It took the rest of the period to restore order. Meanwhile Roger had moved his control box to his brother's car, where it would take a search warrant to find. As for the extra attachment to the speaker system, it would have no fingerprints, Roger being eerily thorough. Mr. Robinson, I found out later, received a tongue-lashing from the principal—it was the last call like that he ever received, at least at school. If I'd known about all this I might have wished Mr. Chambers had been easier on Mr. Robinson at our after school meeting. But I doubt it.

Thinking of Roger made me realize that at some point I might need some help. "Could you get Roger to do me a favor, Steph?" Roger was known to be partial to my sister—his only character flaw from my view.

"Maybe. If I wanted him to," she grinned. "What is it?"

"I'll think about it and let you know." I said. I really wasn't sure what I might need him for, but Roger is a great guy to have on your side.

The rest of the evening went quietly. After I had gone to bed I found myself wide-awake. Finally, after reading (for the third time) most of The Black Mountain by Rex Stout, I fell asleep.

The next morning I was up early to help my father with the spring yard work. My father absolutely loves gardening from late March through early June. However, our two acre yard looks like thirty during August when it needs mowing. As my father has many hobbies (at least four too many by my mother's count) there are numerous pleasant distractions after the weather gets hot. But in April, with the joyous spring flowers and new buds on the roses, there is much to do. Especially cleaning out the flower beds.

One of the things my father likes about gardening has nothing to do with the plants. It is the fact that as he is gardening he gets to talk with his kids who invariably end up helping—his decision, not ours. Often, our conversations are wide open, about whatever is on our minds—sports, politics, religion. Dad is pretty well read and interesting to talk to. Sometimes, though, it becomes obvious that Dad has been asked to pursue a particular line of conversation to gain information for Mom. The reason why this is so obvious is that Dad almost never, on his own, will ask us about our personal lives. His stated reason is that we need room to develop without our parents looking over our shoulders. If children receive the proper guidance and are given the correct examples, then they should be expected to turn out well. If a crisis comes they will most easily turn to parents who have not been obsessive micromanagers. I don't know if this theory will actually work as the only crisis I had been in was the current one and I don't think Dad's theory was made for talking rabbits. Anyway, while I know he holds to this theory, it's also true that day to day matters of growing up don't particularly interest my father. He has a fairly demanding and not terribly interesting job in the government and looks forward to having thought-provoking conversations with his kids. For example, we once had a long talk about love after I had read some poems by Keats and Shelley for an English lit class.

But I'd never dream about bringing up Amanda or Sarah Gilvain or Jeana Tonawitz or any of the other girls I'd considered trying to date. Especially not Laurie.

My mom, on the other hand, feels like a little micromanaging never hurt anyone; a position that appeals to me from a managerial standpoint but not so much when I'm on the receiving end. Sometimes she attempts to maintain surveillance through others, most often, and most clumsily, through Dad.

On this occasion we had worked about ten minutes when Dad said, "I hear you're going out with Laurie Arnold again tonight."

"Yes, Dad," I said, with resignation, as I thought that this was going to be a long morning in the flower beds.

"Well, as you might know, your mother isn't too happy about this, and, as you might expect, she asked me to talk to you about it."

This was an unusually direct approach, I thought.

"So instead of talking to you about it," my father continued, "I am going to tell you about Carol Holliday." Suddenly I had no idea where this conversation was going so I just kept quiet and listened.

"Carol and I were seniors in high school together and I was in love with her," he began. "I've often considered this and upon reflection I am sure that was the case. It really was love. However I never could get up the nerve to tell her. She liked me but she had a boyfriend—Billy Knox. He was a few years older than we were, out of school, working as a carpenter's apprentice. I thought he was as stupid as they come and it always infuriated me that Carol could see anything in him at all. After graduation I went to college and they got married. For several years I wished I had told her how I felt. Not that I'm not happy with the way things turned out. There's no finer woman than your mother and no one has ever had more wonderful children. It's just, well, like something has always been incomplete. I don't think it would have made any difference anyway." He sighed as he returned to his raking and we were both silent.

Finally, I asked, "What happened to them—Carol and her husband?"

He stopped raking for a moment. "Well, I don't know much about the personal level—we haven't talked in recent years. But I know they had two kids. Carol was teaching an aerobics class for a time there. Billy is now a custom home builder, one of the best in town so I understand. I saw his picture in the Louisville paper your grandmother brought last Thanksgiving. He had just been elected state representative to fill out someone else's term." Dad laughed. "Guess he wasn't so dumb after all."

After a few minutes of silent raking, Dad asked, "What do you think about the new pitchers the Yankees have?"

Gardening really can be fun in April.

I have serious problems with timeliness. My papers are turned in on time, but at the last moment, with the computer printer still warm. Appointments are viewed as goals, not absolute requirements. However, I have never been late for a date in my life. Not that I've actually had very many. Normally my plan would be to arrive in the neighborhood of the girl's house fifteen minutes early and drive around, hoping not to be seen. With Laurie this is impossible since we live so close to each other. On the two earlier occasions since I got my license that I took her someplace I just paced in my room hoping the clock would move and then I still arrived at her house early. For this date I came out of my door at five minutes to six and was starting down the steps when I heard her call, "Where ya' goin'?"

I turned to see her sitting on the front porch swing wearing jeans and a dark green sweater which went beautifully with her reddish-brown hair. I sat down next to her. "I thought I was supposed to drive over to pick you up. Why the change in plans?"

"I thought it would be more ... umm, expedient for everyone," she said and it dawned on me what she meant. My mom and Mrs. Arnold agreed on only three things that I was aware of. First, they were both Baptist—which I guess includes agreement on a bunch of other issues; second, they both loved the Washington Redskins; and third, they believed Laurie and I should not date one another. In Mrs. Arnold's case it was because she felt Brad was obviously right for Laurie and I was someone who occasionally appeared to get in the way. This would have been all right; after all, how many parents truly like the boys their daughters drag home? The problem was Mrs. Jernigan, Laurie's grandmother who I've already mentioned, who lives with the family. She was unabashedly in my corner and never failed to mention it on evenings when I dropped by, provoking a heated discussion with Mrs. Arnold. Of course, the real problem, as I viewed it, was that all three generations were as alike as could be but I had never had the right opportunity to discuss this idea with Laurie. Since Mrs. Arnold and Mrs. Jernigan had been having these quarrels since the days Mrs. Arnold, then Miss Jernigan, had been bringing boys home, it wasn't for either of them that Laurie had left the house to meet me. Instead, it was with the hope that her father might be spared the difficult task of trying to avoid taking sides. I think he has always favored me though he has never said.

We walked to the car, my dad's Cutlass, and waved to Angela who was looking out her bedroom window and making funny faces at us. Opening the door for Laurie I asked, "Why didn't you knock and come in? You know I've been ready for half an hour."

"Just didn't think Stephanie would be in the mood to welcome me," answered Laurie.

I laughed like I had wanted to Friday afternoon when my sister had told me about their soccer encounter. "Steph told me. I think I smoothed things out for you. Just watch yourself in practice next week."

"What?" she asked warily.

"Nothing, nothing," I said and closed the door. Getting in on my side I changed the subject and we talked happily all the way to Martinelli's.

Pizza is a subject about which reasonable men and women may differ. What to one person is a culinary delight, to another is a waste of calories. It is helpful on a date if both parties like the same style. Personally I like pizza thin and crisp, light on the cheese, while Martinelli's is Chicago style, thick and chewy with lots of cheese. It was however Laurie's favorite and she thought it was one of mine. I always thought I should tell her she was wrong someday, say after we had been married for ten years or so.

At any rate the company was wonderful and time passed quickly. We still refrained from talking about anything serious, as if we had made an agreement in advance to avoid such matters. Talking about a relationship is often a good way to end it. A summer ago a good friend of mine whose family was preparing to move out of state in the fall was out with his girlfriend when she asked simply, "Where is this relationship going?" His reply, that "My part of the relationship is going to Atlanta in September," was accurate, but not particularly helpful. He had a lonely August.

Looking at my watch, I said, "Guess we'd better get over to Germantown for the movie." I paid the check and we left.

On our first date after several months and with the firm desire in my heart that this time things would be different you might expect I would push for a romantic love story. Instead I let Laurie choose and she selected "The Two Towers". Nothing like a climactic battle scene with several thousand dead orcs to set the stage for me to finally get up the nerve to try to kiss her good night.

After the movie I offered to get some ice cream but she declined. Instead she suggested we check out some new houses. This was not as strange as it sounds. Laurie's dad sells real estate, lots of it. We occasionally helped her dad scout the many new neighborhoods going in all around us.

"Have you seen the new development off Black Rock Road?" she asked.

"No. The one called the Refuge?" I replied.

"Right. Let's see how much they have done," she suggested.

"Sure," I agreed. Black Rock Road was just off our route home so we could swing by there and still get home at what Mrs. Arnold would consider a reasonable hour. Laurie never, or at least rarely, has an actual curfew. Her parents want to know where she is and with whom. But they don't want her rushing home to make an arbitrary deadline.

The Refuge at Black Rock Estates seemed a pretentious name for a collection of distantly spaced concrete foundations, but they were big, at least as best I could tell on the moonlit night. When we reached the end of one dark street Laurie asked me to stop. We had a great view of Sugarloaf Mountain in the distance.

"Thomas, please turn the engine off, we need to talk."

I complied, then turned to her with a sinking feeling, knowing she was about to give me the same "I like you as a friend, but my heart belongs to Brad" speech that I had heard several times before.

"Thomas, I meant it when I told you that this time things are going to be different." Just her saying that made it different already.

"I'm all for that," I said cheerfully. "How can we start?"

Laurie pulled us close together and said softly, "Like this."

Brad was right. Kissing Laurie Arnold is very spectacular.

Chapter 5

It occurs to me that in all fairness to Laurie I should make sure that no one draws the wrong conclusions about her. Kissing Laurie is spectacular but it is also the absolute limit for a physical relationship before marriage. She has spoken on the subject at youth activities often enough that it is absolutely clear what was allowed of anyone she permitted to take her out on a date. So far as I know Brad and I are the only guys who know how she kisses. Oh, except maybe for the one guy she went out with instead of me one time when she had broken up with Brad in tenth grade. He came to school on Monday with a black eye. I suspect he was not aware of her standards. She would never talk about it.

Black Rock Baptist Church is modern Southern Baptist, with chairs instead of pews (that was a wrenching change according to my parents; I was too young to be involved), a long center aisle to make future brides and their moms happy, and songs—including the occasional hymn—on overhead screens. There aren't assigned seats at our church but you wouldn't know that considering how we always sit in the same places. Each of my close friends sits with their respective parents. Stephanie, on the other hand, is always off with her friends. Brad's family and mine take up one row on the piano, or left, side of the church. Laurie's family sits closer to the front on the organ side. Twice during the service she turned and caught me gazing at her, and she smiled, happily I hope.

We had decided to avoid each other as much as possible on Sunday as Laurie had not arrived home until twelve-forty-five in the morning which meant that my stock was continuing to decline in value with her mother. As far as my own mother was concerned she apparently had reconciled herself to living with a depressed son following what she saw as Laurie's and Brad's inevitable reconciliation.

After our regular Sunday dinner of roast beef, potatoes, and carrots I went for a walk near the old farmhouse. I caught sight of a rabbit but it didn't have blue eyes and showed no interest in conversation. The idea that this was actually a case of insanity, driven from my thoughts by my date with Laurie, began to come back. I wished that Jack would come out to see me but no such luck. Knocking on the door was tempting but Jack had said not to come by unless requested.

At youth praise team practice Laurie sat next to me and occasionally held my arm. Stephanie snickered with her friends. Nothing bothered me. After evening service I broke our less than one day old rule about Sunday and asked Laurie to go for a drive and get some ice cream. Though expecting her to turn me down, she surprised me, and maybe herself, by saying yes. Technically, I was inviting her to take me to get ice cream since she was the one there with her own car, a red Mitsubishi Eclipse Spyder GT convertible.

Laurie's family has plenty of money but they are not, as a rule, ostentatious. While Laurie could have almost anything she wanted just by asking, she doesn't have flashy tastes. That made it all the more surprising when her dad took her car shopping and she fell in love with the red sports car. She didn't select it though, instead choosing a sensible used car for a fourth of the price. Her father told her he would go back the next day to negotiate a deal for the used car. Instead he drove up to the house in the Spyder. Brad and Laurie went for a drive in the new car leaving me standing next to her dad. "You sure made her happy," I said.

Turning to her dad I saw he was crying.

"I know it's too much for a sixteen year old but she's the only little girl I have to buy for now," he said, then walked inside the house. His older daughter had died four years earlier. It must be hard to ever get over the loss of a child.

We drove down to the Baskin-Robbins in Gaithersburg and ordered two hot fudge sundaes. This was always one I had up on Brad since he only liked soft serve. For the first time since I began considering girls as people to spend time with I was close to having what I wanted—someone special who might really care about me. Best of all it was Laurie, the only girl I ever really wanted it to be. This was not the time to be thinking about sorcerers and amulets; it should have been Laurie exclusively. For just a moment there was a flood of anger at Jack for the way my world had suddenly changed. I didn't like the introduction of the unknown. Still, it merely reminded me that there is always an unknown out there. And as far as unknowns are concerned, talking rabbits have nothing on girls, at least so far as I can see. So my anger quickly passed as I found myself under a far different spell than the one Jack was experiencing.

When we got back to our neighborhood Laurie drove past my house and into her driveway. I accompanied her to the door and she gave me a quick kiss goodnight. I walked home in a daze.

That night with considerable effort my mind switched gears and focused on planning the intelligence work that was to begin the next day. There was much ground to cover and from what Jack had told me we might have reason to hurry. Checking my watch and realizing it was only nine o'clock I came to a decision. Help was needed and it was only a text message away.

At that time on Sunday night I knew where she would be. I texted— "Need to see you urgent someone needs research willing to pay."

Within moments the response came, "Long time no hear gate in five."

Chapter 6

To explain why I reached out for help with research requires some background, starting at my high school and then going backward in time several hundred years.

The faculty at any school is bound to be an interesting set of characters, the teachers at John Clark HS being no exception. One of the more unusual examples was Mr. Edward Pierce. According to Mr. Pierce's personnel file, a copy of which was made available to me by an associate who has special need of remaining nameless, he had been born in California in 1952. He had graduated from the University of Wisconsin with a degree in chemistry along with teaching certification, followed by a master's degree from Purdue. He moved to Maryland in 1980, beginning a teaching career with the Montgomery County Public Schools. Unmarried, he had no children or other relatives. His teaching record was excellent. Around school he was known as a demanding yet fair teacher who knew his subject well and ran a highly disciplined classroom. In extremely good shape for a man of fifty-one, he looked much as he had in the picture attached to his file from 1984.

All this was interesting, even more since I now had reason to doubt his entire history. According to Jack, Mr. Pierce was nearly ten centuries old and the world's only true, if not particularly adept, sorcerer. Well, at least sorcerer's helper.

The story, as Jack explained, began in Normandy, near Rouen, in the year 1065 with the arrival and subsequent departure of the other worldly sorcerer. But the story continued for a millennium. Jack's encounter with the amulet and the resulting transformation was just the next chapter. Jack's father realized that, as a rabbit, Jack would require special protection. He made an arrangement to bring Jack under the protection of a minor Norman noble who took the rabbit to England in the early days following the Conquest. The nobleman began a secret society dedicated to the rabbit's safety. The society, which never reached over ten in number, provided a stability to Jack's existence which endured for nearly seven hundred years. It was a period of relative contentment for the rabbit as there seemed no way of escaping fate.

In early July of 1723, Jack was perched on the shoulder of Sir Geoffrey St. John-Quincy as they made their daily walk along the Portsmouth waterfront. Much to their pleasure, many children and adults were quite used to seeing the tall, gaunt, elderly man in the clothes of an earlier generation with the large gray rabbit being carried along. Despite an occasional remark, like "Ho, Cap'n whyn't ya' get ya' parrot?" these outings were quite agreeable to Jack.

The rabbit saw him. The sorcerer's helper, known to Jack as Charles, emerged from a shop looking first away from them, then turning back toward them. Now he brushed past Sir Geoffrey and hurried up the gangplank to a merchant ship.

"Sir Geoffrey," Jack whispered urgently, "That's the man who did this to me!"

The old man was astonished that Jack would risk speaking in public and muttered, "Shhh, Jack, not here." He made his way to a pub he knew, the Crescent Moon, and asked for a back room, "So as to collect my thoughts," he said. The tavern keeper, who recognized eccentricity when he saw it, but liked Sir Geoffrey nonetheless, was happy to oblige. He brought him the usual tankard of ale before returning to his regular customers.

"It's him, I tell you. It's him!" Jack cried.

The old man was confused. "How can you possibly be sure? Seven hundred years have passed. Certainly there must have been other occasions when you thought …"

"Yes, yes," Jack interrupted excitedly, "But this time is different. I knew him before he turned toward me. I knew as surely as if he had worn the sorcerer's amulet about his neck. The amulet. He must still have the amulet. He would never let it get away from him. If we could get the amulet, I know we could break the spell. Sir Geoffrey, you must help me catch him."

But despite his best efforts this proved impossible. The ship was the Mary Whyte and it sailed that week for America. Jack observed Charles standing along the railing as the ship left the dock.

Sir Geoffrey, a kindly man who had made a small fortune many years before in trading and who had retired early due to poor health, cursed his own ineffectiveness. "If only Sir James had been here," he said. Sir James Angleterre was one of Portsmouth's most prosperous merchants and the chief of Jack's protectors. He was in London on business.

"You did your best, Sir Geoffrey," consoled Jack, disappointed but wanting to reassure the old man. "Now we must wait for Sir James to return." Jack's mind was now set. Charles must be pursued and Sir James would surely help.

When Angleterre returned from London he called a meeting of the seven members of the society that could easily attend. There Jack presented his plan. The society must find someone to take the rabbit to America. While there was hope it must be pursued.

Sir James and the others were undecided as to what should be done. For over six centuries their society had preserved Jack as their treasure—now the treasure was bidding to act on its own. John McAlister, the youngest of their group at age forty-one, spoke up. "At last I am decided. My partner and I have long thought to open an office in the colonies but it has been hard finding a man to trust. I shall go myself and bear Jack to his new destiny."

Thus all was arranged. Jack set out aboard the Golden Eagle barely one month after the Mary Whyte had sailed. John McAlister, his wife Hermione, and their five children accompanied the rabbit. Tragedy struck mid-voyage as McAlister fell gravely ill. With death nearing, he called upon his eldest son, David, and charged him to care for Jack. He could not have chosen better. David accepted the responsibility along with the leadership of the family. His father died the day before landfall in America.

David McAlister lived until 1805, dying at the age of ninety-four, survived by children, grandchildren, great-grandchildren, and a new, this time American, society to protect Jack. Through David's long life he had led a search for the elusive Charles.

The search had failed, though at times the quarry seemed almost within reach. Jack had provided a detailed description of a trim, moderately athletic man, with thinning brown hair and a distinctive scar which stretched across his chest, the result of an encounter with an angry swordsman. The Mary Whyte had arrived in Boston only weeks before the Golden Eagle but young David's questioning determined that Charles, known to the ship's crew as Edward Holden, had left the ship. No one had been close to him and no one knew his plans. Detective work spanned decades. At one point he was believed to have run a store in our area of Maryland. That was during the Civil War. But after the detectives came close, he rarely settled down again. The closest they came was in 1922. A picture of a Sacramento mining engineer named Francis Weldon, Jr., appeared in the Boston newspaper. Though the image on the photograph was not clear, Jack knew it was Charles with absolute certainty. When the society's detectives arrived at the Sacramento mining office they found that Weldon had resigned only two days earlier leaving no forwarding address.

At this time Jack lived in a comfortable home in Boston attended by a series of trustworthy servants. But by 1962 the rabbit had grown weary of the increasingly urban setting. That year one of the society's last five members had died and left a house and one hundred twenty-five acres of fields and woods in rural northern Montgomery County, Maryland, to the society. Jack moved there the next spring. Settling in with a housekeeper and despairing of ever becoming human again the rabbit sought solace in the peace of the Maryland countryside and stopped the hunt once and for all.

The current housekeeper, Mrs. Kate Donnelly, was a childless widow in her mid-fifties. She was beginning her fifteenth year with Jack. One of the many things Mrs. Donnelly did for the rabbit was to take Jack out for drives to see how the area was changing. On one such drive in early March the housekeeper stopped for some groceries leaving Jack inside the van. That day, just a month before the rabbit spoke to me, Jack again saw Charles.

As Jack peered out the window at the traffic and the people, a man emerged from the Giant grocery store and crossed to his car. The chilling tingle of recognition came again. At the moment Charles was recognized, he may have felt something as well, for he turned, even as he was about to put his key in the car, and looked about peering intently most especially in the direction of Jack's van. A sudden terror came over the rabbit, who shrank into the shadows of the van's interior. The moment must have passed quickly for Charles as he turned back to his car and drove away.

By the time Mrs. Donnelly returned with the groceries, Jack had calmed down slightly and told her what had occurred. As they drove home Jack settled on the only plan that seemed to have any promise. They would stake out the Giant.

Five days passed before Charles reappeared. Mrs. Donnelly followed him into the store to get a good look at him and returned to the van to be ready when he made his exit. When Charles drove off, Mrs. Donnelly followed him. Happily, Charles seemed in no particular hurry and traffic was unusually light. Within ten minutes they were entering a townhouse development less than five miles from the old farmhouse. After noting the address Charles had entered, Mrs. Donnelly drove them home. Jack had asked to be alone for a while to consider the next move.

Within the next week the intrepid Mrs. Donnelly was able to discover that Charles was now calling himself Edward Pierce and teaching chemistry at John Clark High School. While this information was useful, Jack remained uncertain about what to do next. Of the society's three remaining members, two were now elderly and in poor health while the third, a noted attorney, had accepted an international engagement which would keep him out of the country for several months. Mrs. Donnelly could not be expected to take on challenging Pierce by herself. But time might be running out. Mrs. Donnelly had uncovered a rumor that their quarry was considering putting his townhouse on the market the coming summer.

The rabbit's thoughts turned to those closest at hand. Jack had indeed watched the neighborhood children grow up. Rabbits can be silent observers of much that goes on. Laurie, Brad, and I were just a few of the people familiar to the rabbit. The fact that we were students at John Clark suggested a plan, or at least a first step in a plan. The rabbit would, for the first time, speak to someone outside the small circle of protectors. By some thought process which Jack did not explain, the rabbit chose me.

The theory of the plan of action was fairly clear. Verify Pierce as Charles, find the amulet, take it, and destroy it. As to the last the rabbit was unwilling to discuss details but seemed convinced the destruction could be accomplished. In any event Jack was certain the destruction would end the spell. But what then? Might the end of the amulet mean the end of both Charles and Jack? The rabbit was determined to take the risk.

The first part of the plan was unnecessary from Jack's point of view but I wanted confirmation before I began an assault on one of my teachers. I still had hopes of going to college. Even in a tolerance obsessive culture like early twenty-first century America I suspected there would be a reluctance to embrace an applicant whose record included an explanation with the words "But I thought the man I was harassing was a thousand year old sorcerer." Upon further reflection I suspect that such a statement might have been okay with the Ivy League but I wanted to go to Duke. Well, maybe it would be okay there, too.

Identification was to be by the distinctive scar which I would see running across Mr. Pierce's chest. How to see him without a shirt? Since Mr. Pierce always wore a coat and tie to class, and even to all extracurricular activities I could remember, this posed a problem, but one which I thought could be solved. In fact, an idea came immediately to mind which I would implement on Monday. Fortunately, my plan to check for the scar would provide an answer to another question as well. The most obvious place to keep an amulet is on a chain around one's neck.

So, as I sat in my room on Sunday night my problem seemed relatively straightforward. I would have to investigate a teacher from my high school, find where he was keeping an ancient and otherworldly amulet, steal it—rather, appropriate it—a fine distinction which made me somewhat more comfortable, and get it to Jack. Sure, a piece of cake.

So I sent the text asking for help. I needed to learn everything possible about Mr. Pierce, realizing that it was unlikely to show him to be one thousand years old. The one person who could best help was Erin Shea, one of the three or four brightest people I know. A small, red-haired junior, she was one of the two female reasons why I would never be valedictorian of my high school class. Laurie was the other; she was even better in class than on the soccer field. Of course, no one would actually be valedictorian. To protect the students' sensitive self-esteem John Clark, along with other high schools in our area, eliminated such blatant displays of competitive accomplishment several years ago.

Erin's parents had broken up when she was quite young. She lived with her grandparents along with her younger brother and her mother. At least her mother was there occasionally, the rest of the time it was not clear where she was. That Erin and her brother were as level-headed as they were was a tribute to the grace of God and the determination of her grandparents. Mr. and Mrs. Shea were in their early seventies. At a time when some would begrudge the responsibility of two grandkids, they embraced it. Their son had abandoned the family before Erin's brother was born. Then, when Erin was nine her father was killed in a car accident. Erin's mom had apparently really lost it then, and had been in and out of the kids' lives ever since.

Erin had many strong values. Her only major flaw was that she kept having crushes on some of the most disreputable members of our class, most recently on Jamie Schiller, a star lacrosse player with an overblown ego. Other than that she had a sterling character. She was absolutely trustworthy. The grandparents had instilled a strong faith in the kids. Every Sunday as we left for Sunday School we would see their family returning from Mass. Her family did not have lots of money so she worked after school to pay for her cell phone and most of her own clothes.

I slipped a folded sheet of paper which I had prepared into my pocket, then left quickly, whistling as I went down the stairs. I understand that whistling is a lost art. I have worked at it for several years, starting the day

Stephanie made a passing comment about whistling bothering her. She says she likes it now, but I've kept whistling anyway.

"Mom, I'm going for a walk! Be back soon!" I called out, then left quickly, only pausing to grab Dad's telescope from the study on the first floor. Mom would be happy as she always wants us to get exercise, but I wanted to be out of earshot before she realized what time it was. Dad didn't like us to be out late but he was still at a church stewardship meeting. For most children, the idea of forum shopping—finding the best court to give you the outcome you desire—comes naturally, long before attending law school. Dad is more generous with money but Mom could be counted on to say "yes" to requests far more often than her husband.

In recruiting Erin there was a practical problem. Mrs. Shea was the one grandmother I had never impressed. She would not like to see me around. Not that she had anything against me personally, it's just that she's fiercely protective of Erin. She would like Erin to become a nun. While I think that may be a noble calling I can't see Erin going in that direction, especially since Erin was already giving some indication she was looking at other churches to attend.

So Erin and I occasionally met at the back gate of their house. It's a small, well-kept older home, the last house on our side of Smithtown Road before turning into our neighborhood, if you're coming from Clarksburg.

Ours is a relationship which would have seemed unusual to many. We have been friends since Erin moved in with her grandparents and we respect each other greatly. We never do anything together except, on occasional cloudless nights, we go stargazing. That might sound romantic to some but it's never been for us. We both like astronomy and Erin could never afford a telescope like my dad's.

Behind her house, separating it from our development is a strip of parkland along a ridge. There on top of the ridge is a clearing where a house had stood long ago. Around the edge of the clearing are pine trees grown so dense that you have the best view of the sky in the whole area.

Erin was already at her back gate and smiled a quiet welcome. We were silent by habit until we got to the clearing. The night was crystal clear. We set up the telescope and as she was looking at the constellation Orion she asked, "Okay, so what's this big business deal about?"

"Someone wants to know everything there is to know about Mr. Pierce. He wants to know his likes, dislikes, personal history—everything."

"Mr. Pierce? The chemistry teacher?"

"Right. I know you've had him for class. He can't know he's being investigated. Absolute discretion is required."

"Less than absolute discretion is pointless," she said matter-of-factly.

"My friend also wants you to research some names from the past." I gave her a slip of paper on which I had written the names and locations in place and time of Mr. Pierce's other identities which Jack had tracked down.

She looked at the paper and said, "This isn't much to work with."

"With which to work," I corrected. It was a private joke about a ninth grade teacher who had tried diligently to keep us from hanging prepositions. "I know if anyone can find useful information, it's you."

Erin grinned at me, "Flattery will get you nowhere. What's in it for me?"

I hadn't precisely thought of an answer to that question. But Jack seemed to have plenty of money. "Five hundred bucks," I replied confidently, "and another five hundred if the information solves the problem."

Erin stared. "Are you serious?"

"Absolutely. Is it a deal?"

She eyed me carefully. "Why?"

This question I was ready for. "Someone thinks Mr. Pierce has something which doesn't belong to him. I can't tell you any more than that. These other names and places are related to the problem. You shouldn't be in any danger."

She looked startled. "Danger?" She thought some more. "It's a deal." I really do know Erin.

We spent a relaxed half hour talking about constellations and galaxies. Only once did I find myself wondering if we were gazing in the direction of the distant planet from which the amulet had come. Then Erin had to get back before her grandparents missed her and I had to go home and try to avoid my parents telling me not to be out so late on a school night. I managed to make it.

There remained some planning which interfered with my usual sleep when my head hits the pillow. Sleep did come eventually, by which time I had decided on a definite course of action for the following day.

Chapter 7

First period Monday was English Lit with Mr. Chambers. He and I shared several strong interests in life other than making the assistant principal's job more difficult. One which mattered to me that morning was our common interest in golf. The last three summers a friend of Dad's from church who was a club pro at the nearby Monocacy Golf Course in Urbana had given me a job helping out with the grounds. He had also thrown in a few lessons and some complimentary greens fees. I play well enough to challenge for a place on the school team but I just don't have the single-mindedness to give up on all the other activities in which from time-to-time I would prefer to engage. Mr. Harper, the school's golf coach tried to recruit me after I won the ninth grade fall tournament by four strokes. I offered to play if I could still have spring break off to go to Florida on a family vacation. He seemed offended that I should ask. He then told me that there was no point in my ever coming out for the team until my attitude changed. As my mom said to my father upon hearing the story, Coach Harper might as well wait for the sun to rise in the west. I thanked her for complimenting me on sticking to principle. Her attempt to hide a smile made me suspicious that she had not precisely meant it as a compliment.

Though a man of modest means, Mr. Chambers always bought an annual pass at the Monocacy course as one of the two big splurges in his life. He loved golf. He played regularly and is a fifteen handicapper. After the bell rang to send the students to second period I quickly stepped to his desk.

"Played much golf lately, Mr. Chambers?" I asked.

"Just a little so far this spring, Thomas," he replied. "How about you?"

"Oh, I haven't played since last fall," I told him, "but I thought this Saturday might be a good time."

"That sounds like fun," he said, taking the hint, "how about joining me up at the club—say about eight?"

"That would be great, Mr. Chambers. Can I bring Brad?"

"Sure Thomas. Any ideas for a fourth?" he inquired.

"Well," I hesitated. This was what I was working up to. "How about Mr. Pierce? I've never had a chance to play a round with him before." The chemistry teacher had won the faculty tournament six years in a row. Which shouldn't be surprising, I thought, since I now knew that he may have played the Royal and Ancient in St. Andrews when it was royal and recent. Mr. Chambers had twice finished third and respected Pierce's ability. On the downside was the fact that the two teachers did not like each other much on account of an incident several years ago during a teachers' strike. Someone had slashed Mr. Chambers' tires because he refused to stay out of school. The story was that Mr. Pierce had seen the incident and recognized the slasher. However, he denied it and refused to discuss the matter.

When the English teacher looked unhappy at my suggestion, I quickly added, "You and I could team up against Brad and Mr. Pierce." With that, Mr. Chambers brightened considerably and said he would see if the chemistry teacher was available.

I hurried along to second period hopeful things would work out.

By lunch I had arranged for Brad to join us for Saturday. He didn't really want to do it, so I twisted his arm a bit by reminding him that he owed me for ruining my date with Amanda. He finally agreed to play. I thought this was not a good time to tell him how well my date with Laurie had gone and that for ruining my date with Amanda I owed him instead of the other way around.

Laurie. The Saturday date had been one of the best things to ever happen to me. Now circumstances intervened to keep us apart. The principal circumstance was soccer. As I mentioned before, Laurie is the best goalie in the state and one of the best on the east coast. She had been selected for almost every special soccer team in Maryland the past two years. Her next few weeks were loaded with tournaments meaning her afternoons were filled with practices. My sister, who was already receiving college recruiting letters as a freshman, and was the other John Clark player to make the all-state team, would be the only member of the O'Ryan family to spend much time with Laurie for the next month. At least I could see her at school and talk to her via cell phone from time to time.

I had never actually dated a girl like this. By which I mean that while I had gone out with Laurie before, this was different. How much attention was right? I had no idea. But I was supremely confident that I would get it wrong. That may sound more negative than it was meant to be. Still I could not help but have a sense of disaster that circumstances relating to Laurie were headed for a collision with circumstances concerning Jack.

That evening I showed up at the old farmhouse fifteen minutes early. Mrs. Donnelly let me in and escorted me to the study. She said Jack would be with me shortly. While I was waiting I looked at the books that lined the study. It was the most incredible collection. I selected one with a leather binding and was surprised, though I suppose I shouldn't have been, that it had been printed in the late seventeenth century.

"It is a fine collection," said the rabbit from the doorway. "It would be better still but Mr. Jefferson insisted on some of the finest to replenish the Library of Congress after the fire."

Startled, I almost dropped the book. "The fire?"

"In 1814. Surely you know the history."

"Well, yes, but—then you mean Thomas Jefferson?"

The rabbit sighed. "Thomas, I will be happy to satisfy your curiosity later. But first, will you please tell me how things are proceeding?"

I recounted the day's events. Although Jack was not happy about having to wait till Saturday for more information, at least the plan itself seemed acceptable. Then the rabbit humored me by telling several stories which I had never read in any history books. Pulling away to go home was not easy. I said I would drop by Thursday evening.

That night, continuing a pattern which would last for a while, I did not go to sleep quickly, and the sleep was fitful at best.

Chapter 8

Tuesday morning I ran into Marnie Meachem which gave me an idea. Generally, running into Marnie made me unhappy because her voice affects me like fingernails on a chalkboard. This time I forced myself to make an exception. Marnie was a sophomore and the vice-president of the science club. Mr. Pierce had been ordered to take on club sponsor responsibilities when Mrs. Barber had to go on leave with a problem pregnancy. Perhaps Marnie could provide some information about my target.

After forcing myself to make some small talk I brought up the subject of the science club. That opened the floodgates and I forced myself to listen to the screechy whine for several minutes. What caught my interest was when Marnie mentioned that they would be meeting at Mr. Pierce's house the following Tuesday.

"But Marnie, that's during spring break," I objected.

"Thomas, the science club doesn't stop for such things. The big state competition is coming up and we have to strategize about which projects to enter and how best to deploy our resources," she said. Somehow, even if she actually goes into science I suspect she will end up on the business side of the company. My dad rarely has anything bad to say against anyone but after meeting Marnie he commented that she sounded like a Power Point briefing prepared by a consultant. "This meeting is very important. After discussing an approach to one big project we'll be going to a biotech firm before returning to Mr. Pierce's house to analyze what we've heard. They wanted us to come in the evening when less was going on." That really caught my attention.

"Does he go with you on these visits?" I asked casually.

"Oh, yes. He's not as supportive as Mrs. Barber," she went on, "but he tries his best. And he's not at all as standoffish as some say. He's not what you would call warm exactly ... ." She provided an extensive analysis of the chemistry teacher which unfortunately provided no additional insight into how to find the amulet.

"Marnie," I said, stopping her in mid anecdote, "Would it be okay if I dropped by to see what the meeting is like? I can't go with you on the plant visit but it would be interesting to hear how you plan for a project."

"Why, Thomas, we'd be happy to have you. Everyone knows you're just about the brightest kid in school. Except for Erin and Laurie, of course. I thought you were mainly interested in the humanities."

Shrugging off being relegated, deservedly, to third place in intellect behind my two friends I assured her it was important to be well-rounded. She gave me the time and said she would call if plans changed.

The middle of the week went by without incident. I barely saw Laurie at all though she did have a big smile whenever we met, which was encouraging. The upcoming spring break meant that not only would there be a weekend tournament but it would be followed by a week-long tour with her getting back late Saturday evening just in time for Easter. It occurred to me that, thinking strategically, I should be finding some way to firm up our newly redefined relationship but I couldn't figure out what that strategy would be.

On Thursday evening I reported in to Jack. The rabbit was extremely interested in my conversation with Marnie.

"This is exciting news, Thomas. As I am sure you have planned, this will provide a wonderful opportunity to search for the amulet while Charles is out. I am certain we will find it if it is there."

I noticed the pronoun. "'We'?" I asked.

"Of course," came the reply. "You will carry one of those backpacks and I will be inside. We will hide, wait for him to leave, and then see what we can find. I am certain that if the amulet is there I will be able to perceive its presence."

I did not like this very much, though I had to admit it made considerable sense. Still, I raised a number of objections. It took almost an hour before Jack convinced me there was no point in discussing the matter further.

That night I had a text from Erin. It was very brief. "Mission begun no early success will see Joey Friday." Joey was her cousin who worked at the Library of Congress. Erin had told me that he was viewed as a preeminent researcher. So, I would just have to wait for results. Patience was not something for which I had ever been known.

Chapter 9

On the way to the golf course Saturday morning Brad was unusually quiet. This was fine for me in that it gave me plenty of time to get mentally ready for the encounter with Mr. Pierce. Unfortunately, just as we were arriving at Monocacy I decided it would only be polite to ask Brad what was wrong. This was a mistake, because he proceeded to tell me.

"Nothing," he said as we pulled into the parking space. "It's just that Amanda and I won't be going out any more after last night. She took me to a party and started drinking. I told her I had to go 'cause of the athletics code's rules on alcohol. She said she wasn't going anywhere. Her cousin Bill was there and he offered to be her designated driver. So I left. When she wakes up she won't be very happy with me." Brad made it sound casual, which to him it was, at least with respect to Amanda. But it had other implications for both of us.

"Gee, Brad, sorry to hear it," I said, rarely meaning anything more. A strong sense of what I understand Yogi Berra called "déjà vu all over again" came upon me. In fact I had been through this several times. If the past was any indication, within days Brad and Laurie would be back together and my soaring spirits were due for a crash landing with me home on date nights. This time, though, it was different with Laurie, I told myself, not really believing it. Brad certainly didn't expect things to be different which explained why he had been so quiet. Losing Amanda was no blow to Brad. He just hadn't wanted to disturb me by putting me on notice that my days of dating Laurie were numbered. Well, we would see.

Meanwhile, my confident mental preparations were shot. The faculty members were waiting at the first tee. After we paid our greens fees we joined them to wait to tee off.

Unlike Brad, I never had Mr. Pierce for a class. He mainly taught Advanced Placement and honors chemistry classes. I had just barely managed an A in first year and that was plenty for me. Still, he had seen me around enough to recognize me.

"Brad, Thomas, good to have the chance to golf with you today." Mr. Pierce greeted us like old friends. Perhaps he was only distant around school.

Mr. Chambers also came up and shook hands all around, a grim smile on his face. Apparently just a little of his fellow teacher was proving too much.

After some inconsequential small talk about clubs and balls it was time to tee off. I hit last—let's just say Brad's news had disturbed me quite a bit. By the time I steadied my game, we were three holes down and heading into the back nine. Only a twenty-five footer by Mr. Chambers at four and Brad missing a three-footer on the par five seventh had kept us this close.

On the other side of the ledger I was finding out lots of trivial information about Mr. Pierce, some of which might be true and none of which was likely to be useful. We were bantering like old buddies. Brad was puzzled but not saying so and Mr. Chambers was fuming.

After halving ten and eleven I started to square things with my partner. My first shot on twelve was perfectly placed in the middle of the fairway. I followed it with a five iron that bit and spun back to six feet away. The birdie pulled us to within two which became one after the par three thirteenth. I hit first and nearly made it, rolling it up three feet short. Brad and Mr. Pierce both found traps and made bogies before I even had to putt. We pulled even at sixteen when the English teacher holed a chip for a par and our adversaries again had sand problems.

By seventeen I was really pumped and even outdrove Brad. My second shot went fifteen feet past, but my birdie putt was dead center. We held on at eighteen. Given my distractions it is no wonder that it was sometime later before I realized it was the best back nine I had ever shot at Monocacy.

In the clubhouse we sat around and chatted about golf among other things. The faculty members had iced tea while Brad and I had Cokes. Mr. Chambers was more comfortable now; beating Mr. Pierce made it easier to tolerate him. During the round the chemistry teacher had denied ever playing St. Andrews or any other world famous golf course. Now I steered the conversation towards travel, specifically France. I knew Mr. Chambers had been there and I asked the target of my investigation if he had ever traveled there.

"No, I'm not much of a world traveler," he replied.

"Really, well I've wanted to see the small towns and countryside ever since a friend described them to me. He comes from a town in Normandy called Bayeux." My eyes were directly on Mr. Pierce as I said the name and I thought I caught a flicker of surprise, but maybe not.

Whether my mention of Bayeux had upset Mr. Pierce was not clear. Still, just a few minutes later he excused himself, saying he needed to shower before a dinner engagement. Mr. Chambers arose, too, saying that he needed to do the same. As the two pass holders went off to the locker room, Brad and I went to the car and loaded our clubs. Brad was ready to go but I held back trying to guess how long to wait. This was the point of the whole morning. The chemistry teacher had a reputation for neatness and I had guessed he would shower and dress before leaving the course.

"What's with you? Get in," he urged.

"Wait a minute," I replied, "I just thought of something I need to ask Mr. Chambers." I hurried back into the clubhouse leaving an irritated Brad at the car.

The locker rooms were around back so it took a couple of minutes to get there. I hoped my timing was good. As I came in Mr. Chambers was emerging from the shower room with a towel wrapped around his waist.

"Something wrong?" he asked.

"No, not wrong," I hesitated. What I wanted to do was walk up and down the rows of lockers looking for my quarry but I realized that would be at least curious if not downright strange. I mumbled some questions I had developed for just such a situation about an upcoming English literature assignment.

The English teacher answered them and added with a laugh, "Since when are you worried about a semester project a month before it's due?"

I smiled back and answered with a deflecting question, "Isn't it time I turned over a new leaf?" We both laughed and I reluctantly turned to go.

Then Mr. Pierce came out of the shower. For a man supposedly in his fifties he looked in remarkably good shape. Trim and muscular, he had only one obvious blemish. A scar, nearly a foot long, stretched diagonally across his chest. Jack told me the swordsman had never intended to kill him.

Any lingering doubts about Jack's story vanished.

But he wasn't wearing the amulet.

Back at the car an exasperated Brad demanded, "What's goin' on?"

"I wanted to ask Mr. Chambers about a project I'm doing on Jane Austen."

"When's it due?" he asked coolly.

"Umm, next month sometime," I answered evasively. After a moment I turned to Brad who had not started the car. "Any time now."

Brad's eyes are a dark gray and he was using them to stare at me. They were hard to meet. He gazed at me with a look I have seen him use before with people who have challenged him about something. I did not recall him using it on me and I found it unnerving.

"Thomas, at best you won't start that assignment until the weekend before it's due. You'd get an A even if you waited until nine o'clock the night before, which, come to think of it, is more likely. I'll repeat my question, what's goin' on?"

One of the difficulties about having very close friends is that they know you so well. I have ethical problems lying to anyone, especially to someone like Brad. So I said, "As soon as I can tell you, I will. Can you accept that for now?" When he didn't respond except to start the car, I tried to change the subject. "Let's talk about something else. I suppose, now, we could both discuss how great Laurie can kiss but that would be ungentlemanly." I looked away. That was meant to serve two purposes, first, to deflect him from pursuing the line of questioning and second, to let him know that getting Laurie back was no sure thing. I am not sure if that part worked but we didn't speak the rest of the way home.

Chapter 10

Sunday was a quiet day. Laurie was playing soccer in Pennsylvania. Brad wasn't at church. That was suggestive. His brother Bobby told Angela that he had ridden up to the soccer tournament with Mrs. Arnold. That was conclusive. Brad thought everything was going to be normal.

I guess I did, too. It's funny, because I don't consider myself fatalistic in any other area of my life. But as much as I might hope otherwise, nevertheless, the cold light of reason told me how this story was going to end. Like a Greek tragedy from my perspective. That's right, self-pity. But sometimes self-pity is the only kind you can find.

That evening though, I pulled myself together and called Laurie to ask about the match. She had been named the MVP. She was leaving the next morning for a five day tournament over spring break in New Jersey. Still, we actually set a date for the Monday after Easter to go somewhere together.

But then—disaster.

"Uh, Thomas, there's something we need to talk about."

"Sure," I said warily.

She seemed to be hesitating for a minute. "I mean it. It won't be like before. But ..." My heart began to fall. "I do have a standing commitment to Brad about prom."

Prom. A four letter word which cut straight to my heart. The fact that it wasn't on my radar screen shows not only how much I had been preoccupied with Jack's situation but also how I had never allowed myself to even consider that I would ever go to the prom. Groups of happy people traveling in limousines to fancy dinners and then a big dance with the girls in beautiful dresses and the guys in fancy suits. Sigh.

We talked on for a while. At least I suppose we did because when I hung up it was a lot later than when I called Laurie. But I don't remember clearly any of the rest of the conversation. I hope I was somewhat coherent.

Monday of Spring break was rainy, from dawn till late at night. Normally that makes me feel happy but this time my spirits were as gray as the skies. Erin had nothing to report. Jack was not receiving callers apparently; my calls were unanswered. I didn't feel like trying to do anything with Brad. There was nothing else to prepare for my Tuesday night visit to Mr. Pierce's house. But there had been one noteworthy incident that day.

A little before noon I wandered in to the rec room where Angela was watching television. Sitting down beside her I got the feeling she was sad.

"Rain gettin' to you?"

"No," she answered curtly. After being silent another minute she asked, "Thomas, will you believe me if I tell you something?"

I thought about that for a moment. "Yes, Angela. If you tell me something is true and that you aren't kidding then sure I'll believe you."

"Do you remember when I was six and I told everybody that a rabbit saved my life by fighting off the Corcoran's Doberman?"

"Yeah, I remem-," I stopped talking mid-word. She was looking at the television while we talked which was a good thing because had she looked at me she would have seen me with my mouth hanging open.

"Everybody laughed at me. They said I was making it up. But I wasn't. There really was a rabbit. He was a very big gray rabbit. And after he drove the dog away I was crying and he really did talk to me. He said everything would be all right." She turned to me and looked to see what I was going to say.

"If you say that happened, then I believe you," I said.

Her green eyes widened. "You do?"

"Yeah." Of course I believed her.

"I've seen him a bunch of times but he never talked any more. Till this morning."

"This morning?"

"Right. I went out early to get the newspaper for Mom. 'Angela,' he called. 'I have something to tell you. I may be going away soon so you must be very careful without me to look after you. But you're old enough to do that now. If you need something, ask your brother.'"

"I told him that I would miss seeing him. Then he said goodbye and ran away. Do you still believe me?"

"Every word." I then did something which surprised her because normally I'm not a very demonstrative person. I reached out and hugged her tight. "Every word. I wouldn't tell anyone else just yet. But always know that I believe every word."

After dinner I called my friend Prajwal Anand to see if he was free for a movie. He said sure, he would be happy to go. We settled on the details—movie, place, and time. Now I had something to look forward to—Praj was always good at cheering up anybody he was around.

Chapter 11

There are a number of ways to get into someone's house when you want to look for something. If you tell them what you want, they may say no. I didn't think the direct approach would work with Mr. Pierce. Alternatively, getting into someone's house without his or her permission has its own set of problems, ranging from its questionable morality to the fact that the practice is frowned upon by the Montgomery County Police Department.

I had examined the problem in some detail. To be honest I first looked at the question of feasibility. Mr. Pierce lived in a two story townhouse in a slightly upscale complex in Germantown, about eight miles from our high school. It was an inner unit with a walkout basement. It had double cylinder deadbolts made by a company known for high quality locks. I have an acquaintance very familiar, perhaps too familiar, with such matters.

No. I would have to find a way to be invited inside, which of course was what Marnie had provided. So, when the time for the meeting of the science club took place I was there carrying a particularly large, and well-stuffed, backpack. Marnie, as hostess, let me in. I placed the backpack just inside the door so that when I went to look for Mr. Pierce to say hello he would not get too close to the contents of the backpack.

"Well, Thomas, have you come to join the science club or just to give me a hard time about the golf on Saturday?" he asked jovially.

"To check out the club. I let my clubs do the talking about golf." We both laughed at the stupid joke.

The meeting, which included a last run-through about the visit that night, lasted almost an hour. Mr. Pierce seemed genuinely committed to encouraging the students to take a real interest in science. Finally, as the meeting was breaking up I headed for the door. I went in and out a couple of times to confuse the issue about who had seen me leave and when no one was looking I ducked down the stairs to the basement, all the while holding my backpack. At last it seemed all was quiet, but I waited another five minutes before silently pushing the door open. Walking along the hall I called out softly, "Jack?"

The rabbit had not been in my backpack when I picked it up. That did not surprise me as we had a difference of opinion about what to do while in the house. It was my opinion that if Jack was so sure about perceiving the presence of the amulet just from proximity then the time for the meeting should be enough to resolve the issue. Besides, if Jack came with me and then left with me when everyone else did then it was easier on my conscience to argue that I hadn't done anything wrong. By Jack not being in the backpack when I picked it up, my hand was forced.

"In here," Jack called from the living room. The rabbit emerged, looked right and left before darting down to the basement. We started there. Jack seemed to want to get as close as possible to every part of every room in the house. The rabbit was nothing if not methodical. After the basement came a revisit to the first floor. Finally, we reached the second floor. The first step creaked loudly enough to have awakened the household had there been one and had we been burglars. Again the meticulous back and forth across the rooms. Through the closets, under and behind the furniture. Jack was moving silently in the near dark. The task almost seemed complete when I heard voices on the front porch. Moving silently to the doorway I pushed the bedroom door almost closed and listened. A key turned in the lock and the kids poured into the house. They seemed quite enthused about their evening field trip and they were making a lot of noise. I was crushed. The company had promised a two hour visit—obviously it had been shortened to less than an hour and a half. I made a mental note to write a letter of complaint to the company's public relations department if I got out of this mess intact.

Then matters got worse. The talking had died down as the club members went to the big family room at the back of the townhouse. I was almost prepared to descend the steps with Jack when I heard Mr. Pierce's voice.

"Marnie, I'll be right back. I need to get something," he said, faintly but clearly to my ear. Listening carefully I heard him come down the hall.

Then I heard the creak of that first step.

Chapter 12

Mr.Pierce was climbing the stairs. We were doomed. I motioned Jack to hide under the bed while I tried to come up with a convincing story about being in the teacher's room when I was supposed to have gone home much earlier.

Then I heard a sound I will never be irritated by again. It was Marnie's voice, that wonderful screeching whine, yelling "Mr. Pierce, come here! Ted and Malik are wrestling and I think they're going to break your lamp!" The steps descended in a hurry and were followed by a peremptory "Stop that, boys!" directed toward the family room.

I gasped for breath. That had been entirely too close. The people on television never properly convey how nerve-wracking it is to be almost caught in someone else's room, looking for something which you knew they did not want you to find. Maybe Jack had picked the wrong guy for this job.

In any event I still had to hurry. Mr. Pierce was unlikely to be distracted by Marnie and the wrestlers for long. With Jack returned to my backpack I quietly but quickly edged down the stairs and with the students in the family room at the back of the townhouse still in an apparent tumult I quietly let us out.

When we reached Jack's house we went in for a few minutes. The sheer lunacy of the effort was beginning to sink in. What had we expected to find anyway? Surely not the amulet itself. Mr. Pierce must have hidden it well and, with all the places in the townhouse, it would have taken a crew of searchers several hours, if not days, to find it. And that presupposed that it was there to find. There were lock boxes, rental lockers, a hole in the back yard—the possibilities were limitless. At least now I knew how impossible this undertaking actually was. Hopefully Jack and I had managed to learn this lesson without creating any suspicions in my target.

Unless of course Jack was right and the mere presence of the amulet would have been noticed by the rabbit. If that was true then we had learned something useful. I was sure Jack would insist that we assume that to be the case. All things considered I had no real reason to suggest something different.

Jack had hardly said a word on the trip home. Now, sitting in the study, the rabbit said, "That was so exciting! I know we are closing in. But the amulet was not there. I am sure I would have felt its presence. The entire way home I have been trying to devise a plan to have him bring it into the open. Do you have any ideas?"

Jack might as well have asked me if I had any contributions to make in the field of quantum mechanics. All I wanted to do was go home, go to bed, and try to forget about all that was going on. Instead, we stayed at it for a good two hours with no success. When at one point Jack became cross with me I actually started to walk out. Suddenly, Jack was repentant.

"I am so sorry. Thomas, you are doing wonderfully. Please do not allow my outburst to cloud the fact that I am forever in your debt for what you have already done. And if we succeed I will try to fulfill your heart's greatest desire. I even have an idea that on preliminary examination appears promising. But first things first."

I accepted the apology and continued talking but we were not any further along when I left.

Mom was still up when I got home. She had baked apple bread and was watching one of my favorite musicals. If I had not cut three slices and sat down to enjoy the snack and the movie with her I would have been out of character. So there I was watching and eating, knowing that a trap was about to be sprung. Sure enough.

"Didn't you and Laurie have a nice time the other night?"

"Oh, yeah, Mom, it was great," I replied with a smile and no small amount of caution.

"Well, you haven't seen much of her since. Don't you think you should strike while the iron's hot?"

I paused to consider my mother for a moment. I knew she liked Laurie even more than she disliked Laurie's mom. But she always thought Laurie was wrong for me because I would continuously let her hurt me. Mom, I always knew, considered Laurie out of my league in a high school dating sense. Mom had been a cheerleader in high school and had dated the star quarterback until the relationship came to a tearful end. In college she finally turned her attention to my father, to whom, they both agreed, she would never have given the time of day in high school. She actually expected Laurie to dump Brad for a college guy. There were several at church who would have happily pried her away from Brad, but for it looking difficult and the fact that Brad can be rather intimidating when he wants to be. In some respects, Mom trying to give me pointers about Laurie was rather sweet and somewhat encouraging. Unfortunately, nothing else about the circumstances warranted encouragement. She meant well though and so I played along as best I could for a while before heading up to bed.

Wednesday passed uneventfully. I spent the entire day doing yard work. Dad took the day off and led me through more work than I ever expected to accomplish in ten hours. I went to bed before dinner.

The next day was something of the same, except with Dad not around the pace was decidedly slower. That Thursday was Maundy Thursday, the day the church remembers the last moments of Jesus before he was led away in custody. The service our church has that night is one of the most meaningful of the year. I'm one of the few of the under-twenty crowd to come. But ever since I was really little I've been drawn to the tradition we have that night. At the end of the service of scripture readings and meditations, all delivered by lay people instead of the pastors, we take a small piece of paper, inscribe on it the sins or problems with which we need God's help, and then we physically nail them to a cross which is in the front of the worship center. That night I wrote only the word "worry".

Chapter 13

Friday I received a fairly big surprise first thing. Mr. Pierce called to ask if I would like to play golf with him Saturday morning. While I didn't, I thought I should, so we arranged it for seven o'clock.

I kept at the gardening for most of the morning as requested by my father, then cleaned up and set about my plans for the rest of the day. Unfortunately I didn't have any. Jack and Mrs. Donnelly were going somewhere. Laurie was playing soccer, her team was winning, and Mrs. Arnold had invited Brad to go up for the championship. Erin was not at home—she may have been downtown at the Library of Congress. Stephanie had gone shopping and to the movies with her friends—my parents had refused to let her go on the New Jersey trip. Mom and Angela were off on some set of errands. Dad would be home from work about six.

There were several books on my list to read but they all seemed unappealing at the moment. Cable, videos, internet—they all seemed more pointless than normal. Then I remembered a commitment I had made back in March so I picked up a different book.

Carrying it, a notepad, and a hastily assembled lunch I walked back to the clearing where I had first met Jack. I dropped down next to the big rock, got comfortable, began munching on some chips, opened the book and read, "But the fruit of the Spirit is love, joy, peace, patience, kindness, goodness, faithfulness, gentleness, and self-control. Against such things there is no law." The Bible study to which I had committed was a review of the fruit of the Holy Spirit that Paul mentions in his letter to the Galatians. I should have been on week six. Instead, I was on week three—peace. The first thing to come to my mind in considering the idea was to reflect on how little peace I had been feeling lately. The study guide pointed out that the inner peace of a

Christian is often inversely proportional to the turbulence around us. For outside reading it suggested a text from C.S. Lewis. I knew Mom had a copy so I made a plan to read it later that day.

The afternoon was beautiful, in marked contrast to the first Good Friday so long ago. By the time I welcomed Mom and Angela home I was feeling better than I had for a long time.

I dropped by to see Jack in the evening. We spent very little time talking about Pierce or the amulet. Instead we talked about matters of faith. Jack had been born to a Catholic family in Normandy. The rabbit had experienced the Reformation in England and the Great Awakening in New England. It was an interesting conversation. When I look back on it now it was a very special time and one more way my spiritual resources were being built up. I was going to need them soon for many reasons.

Chapter 14

The day before Easter began cloudy but warm. I was up very early for my second golf date with Mr. Pierce. When I arrived at ten till seven he was already at the first tee. I took care of the fees and joined him for some practice swings.

He seemed more intent this morning. Always on the serious side, today there was a different tone to him. Could he be determined to beat me after the previous golf date? Or could his change of mood mean that he sensed something concerning our search for the amulet just as Jack sensed his presence? In any event I was more on guard for what he might say and what I might inadvertently reveal.

We started talking only about golf as we matched stroke for stroke over the first four holes. Then at five I hooked my tee shot into some woods along the fairway. I had to play short and when my chip flew past the green he easily earned the hole. We both parred six and bogeyed seven and eight. Still only talk about golf. At nine I misplayed three shots in a row and so was down two holes at the turn.

After Mr. Pierce drove out into the center of the fairway at ten, I stepped up to hit. The chemistry teacher said, "You seem off your game today, O'Ryan. Something troubling you?" The way he said it was unnerving. It was a different voice than I had ever heard him use. Cold, very cold. An edge, sharp and dangerous. His eyes were hard to meet. This was a different man from the polite, but correct, science teacher from school

"No," I replied, trying to appear oblivious to his change of tone. "Just playing more like my game. I was really on last week." At least the nerves were not apparent on this swing as I outdrove him by about ten yards. We walked along toward our balls. Then he spoke again.

"Sometimes we lose our focus. A young man like you has so many things on his plate. It's hard to do all things well. Sometimes you can be tempted to take on something that is beyond your understanding. Do you know what I'm suggesting?"

All that he had said could have been delivered by a kindly father, but I heard him and there was nothing fatherly about his tone. If I had been a betting man I would have given ten to one that he knew, though it was impossible to see how. I held at ten, threw away two more holes at eleven and twelve, and managed to halve thirteen. Throughout, Mr. Pierce had remained silent, which now appeared even more menacing. He closed out our match by winning fourteen to go up five with four holes to play. I congratulated him and he merely gave me a shrug.

We halved fifteen through seventeen. As we were reaching the eighteenth tee, he spoke once more. Only this time he held my shoulder and stared into my eyes. "What I am saying is that there are significant risks to fighting for lost causes. For everyone involved." I stepped back from him, brushing off his hand. He turned and hit a decent but fairly short drive to the fairway's center.

I was really steamed about Mr. Pierce's words. I didn't like threats, even if I am no hero. Besides, if he knew I was working with Jack, why wouldn't he deal directly with Jack? The answer to that seemed obvious at any rate. He could guess my connection to the rabbit, but he was handicapped by not knowing where Jack actually was. I would have to be careful about approaching the old farmhouse in the future. Analyzing that little question made me quite pleased and reminded me that Mr. Pierce might well be wrong about which causes are lost.

The eighteenth at Monocacy is a fairly straight four hundred thirty yard par four. It's my favorite hole, in part because I got my first birdie on a par four there. Suddenly calm, I took my time before teeing off. My follow-through was just about perfect for me. I outdrove him by fifty yards. His second shot came up short. My second headed straight for the stick. It hit ten yards short then rolled to four feet from the pin. The teacher got down in three. I dropped my birdie putt, the only hole I won all day, but an important one for my outlook.

He was marking his scorecard in silence. I said, "Some causes just look lost for a time." I walked straight to my car leaving him staring at my back.

That afternoon I recounted the morning's disturbing events to Jack via telephone. "Perhaps I should have waited until Hal was here." Hal Andrews was the rabbit's attorney protector who had gone to Europe on the international court case. "I cannot put you in danger, Thomas."

Trying to say what I thought was called for I replied, "That's okay. We'll just keep a sharp lookout." Hopefully that sounded more confident than I actually was.

Everything was quiet until eight o'clock when my cell phone rang. "Hello?"

"Thomas, I have to see you. Big news." One thing about Erin, she was not very excitable. But Erin was excited, which meant so was I.

"Okay could you come … ."

She interrupted. "Do the lights in the clubhouse still work?"

"Yeah," I replied, "That would be a good idea. Meet you there in fifteen minutes."

We have about two acres of property, the back fourth of which are woods, thanks to the trees which were there when we moved in and to my dad planting too many additional ones too close together that first year. In a corner of the backyard my grandfather from Kentucky built a small twelve-by-twelve shed which we called our clubhouse. He and Dad ran power to the building a couple of years later to give us an overhead light. Mom loved it because she said it was just like one she had read about in some teenage mystery stories when she was a girl. The trees, especially a cluster of pines, now hid the house from view until you got quite close. When it was first built all the neighbor kids came over for our 'secret' club. Steph and her friends had met there for years; now Angela's friends were the most frequent visitors.

The night was very warm for April and there was almost no wind. The moon was clear of clouds. I arrived before Erin, unlocked the door, and turned on the lights. The locks had been a fairly recent addition, the result of finding evidence of uninvited guests. In the center of the room was an old trestle table that had been in my parents' first dining room. It was surrounded by a motley collection of mismatched chairs.

"Everything looks great," said Erin with a smile, standing in the doorway with her arms filled with papers. She had walked along the equestrian easement before entering our yard through the back gate.

"Okay, what's the big news?"

Erin paused. "I'm wondering if I should bargain for more money," she said with a serious look on her face, before laughing. Crossing to the center of the room she placed the pile of papers on the table and then began to spread them out.

"Wait," I said suddenly. She stopped motionless. I touched her left arm at the elbow and pushed it up into the light. There were bruises at two places on her forearm. "Let me see the other one," I ordered. She meekly complied. There were matching bruises there. It looked like someone had grabbed her and held on as she was trying to get away. Someone fairly strong. "Erin," I began, but she cut me off.

"It's all taken care of, just a misunderstanding really," she said. "Hey, forget that, let's look at what I brought."

I let it drop but I was concerned. Throughout the years I had known her, as I mentioned earlier, Erin's only major flaw was that she had fallen for guys I would never have let spend time with my sister. That had not been a problem before because Erin had always been so shy that the crushes were always at a distance. But recently she had gotten contacts and a new hairstyle. Someone besides me had noticed that the little bookworm was quite pretty. Someone that she had no business with. I would take it up with her another time.

"You won't believe the incredible luck we've had, because of my cousin Joey. The first thing I did was put together a file of everything I could find out about Mr. Pierce. See, I pulled these photos from each of the yearbooks in the school library." She had copied the pictures and then blown them up to the maximum before too much resolution was lost. Ten years at John Clark and he still looked the same.

"There really isn't much there. But I took the file with me when I went to visit Joey at the LOC. He's responsible for a lot of the microfilmed newspaper holdings.

"I showed him the list of names I was researching along with the timeframes. I kept talking but then I noticed he kept looking at the list. When I asked him about it, he said that a couple of the names were familiar but he couldn't remember why.

"As I took the list back from him and was putting it in the folder he asked about the pictures. I handed them to him and then he said, 'That's why the name was so familiar.' I said, 'What do you mean?' Then Joey pointed to the pictures and said, 'That's Edwin Harper.'"

I interrupted, "You mean Edward Pierce? Edwin Harper was the name from the 1880s."

Erin grinned her most patronizing. "If I had meant Edward Pierce I would have said so. Joey named him as Edwin Harper, a man who had been doing extensive research at the Library of Congress off and on for the last eight years. Unless Mr. Pierce has a double, he is researching matters at the LOC under the name of a man who lived in the 1890s. And what matters you may ask?"

"I do."

"Thank you. The same ones you were asking about. What was going on while Edwin Harper, the nineteenth century one, that is, was living and working in Colorado in the 1890s. Over time he focused his search for information on a man named Ben Davis and then, most interesting of all, Samuel Clemens."

This was fascinating. "How'd you find out all this?"

"Joey broke some rules. I explained that we thought our man had taken something which didn't belong to him and we needed information to try to confirm it. Joey will do anything for me. He blames himself for my dad going off the deep end. It's a long story." A cloud passed over her features. Brightening she said, "Anyway, he let me have the information about which materials Pierce, AKA Harper, had checked out over the last several years."

"This is amazing. Well, I know Sam Clemens but who was Ben Davis?"

"An outlaw. Straight out of a western. Not one of the big name criminals like Butch Cassidy or Billy the Kid but a guy who was pretty well-known in Colorado in the 1880s and 90s."

"What kind of things did he do?"

"Alleged to do for the most part. Bank robberies, stage coach holdups, and at least one train robbery. He went to prison for that last one in 1893, though the papers say he always claimed he was innocent. Twelve years with time off for good behavior. He was released in 1901."

"You got a lot of this fast."

"Like I said, Joey got me the same materials Mr. Pierce had checked out. It was easy to figure out the common thread. To get back to the story. The robbery was in the spring of 1893 near Sublett, Colorado. The other two suspected train robbers were shot and killed by a marshal trying to arrest them in Wyoming. They each had a small amount of the money traceable to the robbery on them. So did Davis when he was captured in Deadville, Colorado, while he was playing cards. His story was that he had won it from the train robbers in a poker game but the jury didn't believe him. The rest of the loot was never found. After leaving prison there isn't any more mention of him in the local Sublett papers for years. He does turn up again but I'll get to that in a minute."

"Wow," I was very impressed, "This is great stuff but where does Sam Clemens fit in? And why was a chemistry teacher researching wild west history?"

"All in good time, young Thomas. What was that?"

There had been a sharp crackling of a branch out in the woods. I went to the door but didn't see anything. Erin came and put her arms around me and whispered, "Oh, please protect me, maybe it was a fox!" Then she laughed. This little joke went back to a time when we were ten and playing in the same clubhouse. Erin noticed a fox through the window. I had insisted on keeping the door closed, but was conflicted because I wanted to run for home. Erin, on the other hand, had gone within five feet of the fox and came back talking about how pretty it was. I would probably hear that story at our fiftieth class reunion.

We returned to business.

"Okay," she resumed, "Look at this. It's a photoprint of the Sublett Intelligencer from October 18, 1893. Read the next to the last paragraph out loud."

"The next witness against the accused was ..." I stopped and looked at Erin in wonder before continuing, "Mr. Edwin Harper of Denver. Mr. Harper confirmed that he had been robbed of over one hundred dollars and several valuables. Mr. Harper had been singled out by the robbers to be searched and was made to take off his shirt for the robbers to remove a money belt and a small medallion that he wore about his neck." I whistled admiringly.

"Elsewhere you read that none of the valuables ever turned up."

I had to talk to Jack.

"Okay, where does our friend Mr. Davis turn up again? But first, why would Mr. Pierce need to research this, surely he knew all about this without ..." I broke off, realizing I wasn't making sense to Erin who had no need to know the entire story.

"What makes you think that, Thomas? This Mr. Harper may have been an ancestor. Anyway, the reason he didn't find this years ago was because this collection was only made available for microfilming to the Library of Congress three years ago by a private collector. Mr. Pierce seemed especially interested in the papers from 1901 on. My guess is that he was looking for mentions of Davis after his release. The last Sublett papers he reviewed were from 1913. I took a look at them and found this on October 8, 1913:

"Famed train robber visits town

"Ben Davis, the notorious train robber, visited our fair city this past Tuesday on his way to California. He declined to be interviewed by this paper but indicated that he had made a good life as a tavern keeper in New York City. He said he counted among his many acquaintances the famous author Mark Twain. Mr. Davis was on his way west to spend his last years in Los Angeles."

"Fascinating," was all I could say.

"Really," replied Erin. "Mr. Pierce's research then shifted to the New York and Hartford papers. About two years ago it expanded to include Mark Twain broadly. Mr. Pierce spent last summer in California."

I asked, "Why is that so interesting? Was he trying to find out about Davis' last years?"

"I don't think so. He was in the Bay area, not Los Angeles. The greatest collection of Clemens' papers is held by the University of California-Berkeley."

"I see," which I thought I did.

"Does this help, Thomas?" she asked.

I startled her by giving her a hug. "So much so that it is almost certain you'll get a bonus. But, next we'll have to find out why the switch in focus. It must have been something to do with what he read in the Hartford papers."

Erin saluted. "Yes, Captain. I have already started. I'm going back Monday. I will let you know." She picked up the papers and smiled, "It does help when all you have to do is follow after someone else's research trail."

I praised her again and she headed home. I stayed there for a while thinking before going up to the house.

Chapter 15

Easter Sunday dawned beautifully. We all looked for the baskets my parents continued to make up for us. After a breakfast of chocolate candy (I couldn't eat the bunny for some reason) we got dressed for church. Just after arriving I saw Laurie talking to Brad. Even though my heart began to sink I made myself join them for small talk. Laurie seemed a bit distant.

When we sat down before the service began Mom spoke to me. "I forgot to mention to you that Laurie dropped by last night. Did she find you? I told her that you had gone out back somewhere and I thought she was going to look for you."

"I didn't see her. When was this?" I asked, suddenly seeing what might have happened.

"Not long after you went out there." The praise team got up to their mikes to begin. I looked at Laurie from across the church. If she had seen Erin ... the thought was too horrible to imagine. The only girl Laurie was ever jealous about; though, until now it never had anything to do with guys. It had to do with academics. Laurie was the very best student throughout elementary school and middle school. During that time our neighbor Erin was attending Catholic school. But starting in ninth grade Laurie had a competitor. Laurie still got straight A's but often Erin's grades were slightly higher. On the PSAT Laurie beat me by twenty points. Erin beat her by ten. When it came time for the SATs, same result, Erin by ten. It drove Laurie crazy. One might expect that Laurie should have perceived the stereotypes and cut Erin some slack. Laurie, the super popular, well-to-do sports star vs. Erin, the quiet, relatively unnoticed, lower middle income kid who had to work after school. Laurie's competitive side was not always pretty to behold.

After Brad had left with his family, I did have a moment with Laurie. And she asked the question I dreaded. "Who was that you were with at the clubhouse?"

"Erin. She and I are working on a research project together. Why didn't you come on in?"

"The way she had her arms around you that didn't seem a good idea," Laurie's voice was cold.

What was she talking ab—, oh, I remembered; the crackling branch must have been Laurie—what bad timing. "Laurie, I'm not interested in Erin. Whatever you saw it was likely us kidding around. We have been friends for a long time. There is only one girl I want to date—you. You are the one who has always had her eye on someone else." She was somewhat mollified by that though she failed to appreciate my point that, if she could debate between Brad and me, what would be wrong about me debating between Laurie and Erin? Admittedly, for me, it would be a short debate.

She had to go then but I reminded her we were going to do something Monday afternoon and she smiled, saying she remembered.

That evening I finally was free to go see Jack. The rabbit insisted I go over all the details of my golf date with Mr. Pierce and my suspicions that he knew of my assistance. I then told Jack about Erin's report. "If I'm right he knows you're here. He knows you are looking for him and that I'm helping. Which leads us to this question, with you so close, looking for the amulet, why hasn't he left?"

Jack replied, "And your answer is?"

"Because he's looking for it, too." We looked at each other intently for a moment. The rabbit slowly nodded in agreement.

We talked on for some time. It wasn't clear if we were actually making progress but at least we were now seeing the true picture. Jack seemed pleased Erin was continuing research on Monday and agreed that a significant bonus was indeed in order. Jack also thought Laurie's reaction to seeing me with Erin was extremely funny. I had to admit there was some humor to it but it was hard for me to laugh.

There was one topic I had decided to broach with Jack and this was as good a time as any.

"What's the real reason you picked me? You could buy all the help you want. I'm just a guy in the neighborhood. Why?"

This was the first time I had really perceived Jack as uncomfortable.

"Come on, Jack. Why? I deserve an answer."

The rabbit sighed, "Yes, I suppose you do." Jack considered a moment before saying, "You may remember that I told you that from time-to-time I see, unbidden, a vision of something which has been or of days which may yet come."

I nodded.

"I saw you first just after the neighborhood had been built and the first few families moved in. You were playing in the backyard with your new friend Brad. I watched you for several minutes and then, using some sticks you had found, the two of you began to pretend that you were fighting with swords. As I watched you play, Brad remained Brad, but to my eye you were transformed. He was still a little boy but you were a young man with a gleaming sword. It was so real that I was about to intervene to protect him when the vision changed. You, as a young warrior, stood in a great hall lit only by candles with two others. One was a towering man of mighty strength with hair of coal black. The other was slightly less in stature but very handsome with a well-trimmed beard of brown tinged with gray. You each held swords at the ready. And you were waiting. For what I do not know, for the vision passed."

I swallowed hard. "You say things which 'may' come to pass?"

"Yes, sometimes a decision changes what seems the otherwise inevitable course. One dear friend refrained from a sea voyage at my request when I saw a vision of him lost at sea. The ship went down with great loss of life.

"In any event, I have long remembered that vision. Whether it was of something real or only metaphorical I cannot say. But as I have watched you and your friends these years I have only seen visions of you. They have always been brief. But you have always been a young warrior facing grave danger.

"As you grew older I observed you had developed a quick mind, a kind heart, and a noble character. When the need arose you were the obvious choice." The rabbit's tone abruptly changed to what I took for amusement. "There was one other reason why it should be you and not another. I may tell you one day or I may not. In any event the visions were conclusive."

The vision of a warrior made no sense. I may not be a pacifist, but a warrior? Unlikely in the extreme.

I was up early Monday. The idea of another date with Laurie probably affected my sleep. I was particularly happy that Montgomery County had the tradition of extending vacation through the Monday after Easter. We hadn't made any definite plans. She was going somewhere with her mother in the morning and would call me when she got back, probably around noon.

Then at ten o'clock the phone rang. It was Erin.

"I'm downtown and I've found something you need to see. You've got to come now. Joey is going to let us look through some materials and I need your help."

'But I'm going out with Laurie,' I wanted to say. Instead, I said, "I think I can get down there by eleven thirty." I knew it was the right decision but it wasn't easy. A line from Jane Austen kept running through my mind— "The one thing a man can always do is his duty." Yes, well, but it wasn't always easy. And I guess in one sense I didn't owe Jack anything. But when I committed to coming to the rabbit's assistance I knew I was taking on a job which had to be seen to completion.

First, I tried Laurie's cell, then her home number. No answer. Even Mrs. Jernigan must be out somewhere. I sent a brief text to her cell. "Laurie, sorry about today. Something's come up so I've gotta go downtown. I'll call later. Bye."

Mom was willing to let me go downtown but I had to explain that I was going to help Erin on a research project at the Library of Congress. That would come back to haunt me but there was no helping it. I drove to the Metro at Shady Grove and took the train to Union Station. The day was cloudy and a bit cool, great for walking quickly to the Jefferson Building which is just to the East side of the U.S. Capitol, next to the Supreme Court.

As a would-be historian, the Library of Congress is one of my favorite places, even though I don't get down there often. With the support of my high school principal I had gotten an ID card some time before to allow me to check out materials.

Erin was waiting in her cousin Joey's office. I had made it in eighty-seven minutes from receiving her call. Very quick.

"It took you long enough," she said with a note of exasperation in her voice. She could be impatient.

"I had to leave a message to break a date," I explained.

"Oh, I'm sorry," she said genuinely. "Who with?" When I didn't answer immediately, she guessed. "Not with Laurie? This project must be important to you. If she finds out that you're here with me she'll really go ballistic."

I guess Erin understood Laurie pretty well. "Unfortunately, that has already come up." I went on to explain about the misunderstanding from Saturday night.

After Erin stopped laughing, which she did when she realized I wasn't joining in, she said, "I'm going to have to set that girl straight sometime."

I wasn't sure that would be helpful. "So what have you found?"

Taking the cue that we did not need to spend any more time discussing Miss Arnold, she said, "As you will remember from our last episode, Mr. Pierce, after reviewing several years of the New York papers, switched from research concerning Ben Davis to research concerning Mark Twain. Do you suppose this was the reason?" She handed me a photoprint of a newspaper from 1911.

Local Tavern Keeper Takes on Partner

Mr. Benjamin Davis has announced plans to sell fifty per cent ownership in his popular establishment, The Liberty Inn, to Mr. Herman Everett of Brooklyn. Mr. Davis has welcomed many famous patrons to his establishment including the late Mr. Samuel Clemens who lived in nearby Greenwich Village from 1904 to 1908.

Mr. Davis recounts how, at their first meeting, he displayed to Mr. Clemens a peculiar medallion he had acquired long before. Mr. Clemens proposed a bet over a game of billiards with the medallion put up as a stake against the author's watch. Mr. Davis, who fancied himself a fine player, accepted the wager to his later regret. He had possessed the medallion for many years and was sorry to part with it.

I looked at Erin in amazement. "Did you find this today?"

"In all modesty, yes. I read quickly." In fact her speed reading was legendary to those of us who knew about it. "I concentrated on those years when Twain lived here and then kept going till I found this. I could tell which newspaper Mr. Pierce had been focusing on."

She gave me an intense look. "Thomas, you've shown no surprise about these references to a medallion. Is that the key to what we are looking for?"

"Yeah," I said, there being no point in denying it.

"Okay, then it's clear that Mr. Pierce is seeking information on the medallion as well."

She leaned back against her cousin's desk. "We know that Mr. Pierce has spent the last two summers researching something at the Mark Twain Papers Project at Berkeley. But he's been back here recently, not looking at newspapers. He has been looking at collections of letters. I am going to make a suggestion."

"Go right ahead," I certainly didn't have any.

"The Berkeley collection provides access to almost everything Clemens ever wrote. Note I said almost. Let's assume that he didn't find anything about this medallion. His hope is that there is something somewhere by Twain or someone who knew about the medallion. My suggestion is that he is searching archives of letters to find some mention of what he is seeking."

"That's seems pretty desperate."

"Yeah," Erin agreed unhappily.

We were quiet for a while, both trying to find a way forward. I didn't want to return to Jack with such a disappointing result. This might mean that the amulet was lost forever. But how to find a break?

There was one thing about the article from the New York paper. Just maybe. An incredible long shot. But something seemed forcing this to a conclusion. So ... .

"Erin, was this the last of the papers Mr. Pierce reviewed?"

"I think so. Let's see," she went through some papers. "Right. This is the very last day of the last roll of microfilm he checked out. He gave up on Davis and immediately began exclusively to research Clemens' papers."

"Then let's get the microfilm for the next month."

"Okay, but what are we looking for?"

"This article contains a reminiscence about a recently deceased famous man. If someone read this and had something to add about Clemens—"

"And a medallion!"

"And a medallion," I repeated.

"They might have written a letter to the editor!" She moved off quickly to get the microfilm.

She wasn't gone long.

"I brought the next three months, just in case." Erin led me to some microfilm viewers and handed me several rolls. Quietly we began to work.

I always love to look at old newspapers and magazines. Each is a window to a time just as important to the people living then as ours is to us. In my grandparents' attic in Kentucky there is a collection of National Geographic from 1910 to the present. It was begun by my great-grandfather when he was very young. I've been told it will be mine someday. The advertisements tell you as much as the articles about the world of those now distant days.

I was probably quite distracted by such detail because I had barely gotten through three days when Erin exclaimed, "Thomas, it's here. You are a genius. Well, maybe not a genius," she added with a grin as she printed copies of what she had found.

To the editor:

This is in response to the article of the thirteenth which tells of Mr. Everett taking an interest in the Liberty Inn. I was delighted that Mr. Davis will have help as he enters his declining years. I am grateful that he reminds us of the days when Mr. Samuel Clemens lived in our midst. He was a wonderful gentleman. He was also a fine billiards player as others besides Mr. Davis would learn once it was too late.

I will inform Mr. Davis as to one matter—the whereabouts of his medallion. Shortly after Mr. Clemens won the prize he bestowed it upon my daughter Amelia, then age ten, who fancied it. Do not expect to wrest it from her as she will always treasure it and with it the memory of the good-hearted man who gave it to her.

Sincerely,
John Parker

"The longshot comes through," I said softly.

She looked at me and smiled, "We're ahead now."

I nodded. We discussed our finding and determined that the next step would be hers. She had done genealogical research in the past for several people and would now look for a John Parker from New York City with a daughter Amelia born around 1895. Since she would begin on the Internet we could now go home. I asked about thanking Joey and she said that wouldn't be necessary. We turned the materials in and headed for the elevators.

There he was. Directly facing us as we prepared to get off the elevator was Mr. Pierce. He was obviously surprised and not happily so. When it didn't appear he was going to move, I said, "Excuse me we have to get off," and started to brush past him. He grabbed my arm. His grip was quite strong.

"I thought I warned you about continuing to be involved in affairs which are beyond you," he hissed.

"Why, Mr. Pierce," Erin spoke up, "Thomas is down here helping me on a research project. What can be wrong with that?"

He turned his fierce scowl to her. "And what kind of research is that, Miss Shea?"

"Research which is my business, Mr. Pierce," she answered defiantly. Her spirit would get her in trouble one day.

"You need to let me go. Others are noticing," I said.

He let my arm go as if it was suddenly too hot to touch. Glancing around, he noticed that several people were watching us closely.

"Mr. O'Ryan, if you persist in your efforts, there may be consequences you cannot manage. Warnings grow few." He stepped away abruptly and boarded an elevator.

"Whew, Thomas, what is this all about? I thought you said there was no danger."

"That's what I thought, Erin."

The trip home from the LOC was uneventful. Since I had a car at the station I dropped Erin at her house. I knew Jack deserved a call to be brought up to date. But I had something else to do first. I needed to try and right things with Laurie. When she didn't answer her cell phone, I called the house number. Mrs. Arnold answered. I identified myself and asked, "May I speak with Laurie?"

"Laurie is not here, Thomas. She was very disappointed when she got your message. She called to ask about when you might get home. Your mother said you had gone out with Erin Shea." I suspect that was not precisely how my mother had said it. "Laurie was upset about that. But Brad called and they have gone somewhere," she said triumphantly. You may think I'm paranoid if you wish, but I heard her voice and "triumphantly" is the right adverb.

I thanked her, my good upbringing coming through, and hung up.

Jack was home and invited me over. My continual going for walks pleased my parents but then they had no reason to suspect I was going to have chats with rabbits.

Jack was even more excited about the news from this day's research. "We are getting closer, Thomas. It is almost within our grasp. But we must be very careful not to underestimate our foe. He must be getting desperate. From now on you must be cautious as to what you tell me on the phone. If I ever call you Mr. O'Ryan you will know I am in trouble. Then approach my home with utmost care."

In spite of Mr. Pierce's words and behavior I wondered if all Jack's fears were warranted. I would soon find out.

Chapter 16

Laurie started to brush by me at school but I blocked her path.

"Please forgive me. I'm really sorry for breaking the date. I'm sorry I had to help research something with the friend I cannot name without getting you upset. Let me take you out Friday to make it up to you." Silence and a fairly cold stare. "I'll grovel. I promise. I would here and now in the hallway but it would be embarrassing for both of us." Finally she relented and laughed.

"I can never stay angry at you. Okay. Friday night. What time?"

"How about eight? I know you have practice."

"Eight it is. Hey, I've gotta' run now. Talk to ya' later.

"Bye, Laurie."

The rest of the day went happily until Mr. Chambers motioned to me as I was walking by his class, "Wait a moment. Mr. Pierce asked if you would stop by his classroom before going home."

"Thanks, Mr. Chambers. I'll do that."

After one last check of my locker I walked down the long corridor to the science wing. Brad had driven to school by himself so I didn't have to be in a hurry. Most of the school was already clear of students and teachers. I came to the door of the honors chemistry class. The sulfur was overpowering. The smells of chemistry were one more reason for me to be a history major. Mr. Pierce was at work setting up an experiment. I stood in the doorway and he motioned me over.

"Sit down," he said, motioning to a nearby chair. "I'll be through in a few minutes. It seems to me I've made a mistake in the way I've approached you till now. I'd like to explain things from a different perspective."

He seemed very intent on setting up his equipment properly. He began to explain the procedure he was using. I sat down. As I've mentioned before, I had not slept well for some time and it was quite warm in the chem lab. I began to have trouble following the details of the complicated procedure. In fact, I felt quite dizzy to the point where Mr. Pierce seemed in a haze and I began to slip sideways off the ch—.

Chapter 17

When I came to I was gagged and bound hand and foot. It was quite dark. I tried to think about what had happened but my mind was not working too clearly, probably because of whatever Mr. Pierce had done to knock me out. Eventually I worked out a likely plan that he had arranged some kind of gas cylinder under the chair which he operated by remote control. The sulfur smell had masked any other odor. He would have moved quickly to lock the door and cover the window. At that point he could do whatever he wanted to me.

Which also suggested where I probably was—the storage closet of the chemistry department. If this seems like I figured a lot out in a short time then I am leaving the wrong impression. I was there quite a while. At some point I realized that someone in the movies would have found some way to free himself. He would have managed to stand, hopped to some beakers which he would have found in the dark, broken one, and cut the bonds which held him. As for me, I could barely move.

Although I didn't know what Mr. Pierce intended, I was still somewhat relieved when the door to the storage closet opened and he began to drag me out by my legs. He really was a stronger man than I would have thought. With me as dead weight he easily hoisted me up onto the chair I had been sitting in earlier. Aside from the corner of the counter I caught with my forehead, that didn't go too badly.

"Well, O'Ryan, I'm glad to see you're awake. Hopefully this has given you more time to think. Here's what I want to know. Where's the rabbit? And this is the deal—tell me and this kind of thing stops happening. No negotiations. In a few minutes I'm going to let you go." His voice was steady, his face serious, but not angry. "I want you to think about this and give me an answer soon because time is running out. I'll remove the gag if you promise not to yell so you can ask any questions. If you agree not to yell nod your head."

I complied though not without some pain.

He removed the gag, rather more roughly than I would have thought necessary. "Questions?" he asked, probably just like before a chemistry lab.

Surely I must have some. Why wouldn't any come to mind?

"Wh-why are you doing this?" I finally said.

He laughed. "Immortality isn't a good enough answer for you? It's not the only one but it will do."

"Why didn't you get the amulet back from Ben Davis when he was let out of prison?" While a good question, I have no idea how it came out. My mind really wasn't focusing too well.

The question actually startled him enough to provoke an answer. "Your friend's detectives. They happened to be running around town looking for me in the days before they let Davis out. How the rabbit came up with my identity at that time I'll never know. But they kept revisiting some of the places I had been. It was a good plan and almost got me that time. I had to clear out for a few days and when I got back Davis was gone. He had left some stories that he was going to California but he was a liar in addition to being a crook. I spent many years in California trying to find him. But these aren't the kind of questions I meant. Do you understand what I want? Do you understand how serious I am at getting what I want?" I nodded yes to both questions.

"You're tougher than you look, O'Ryan. But not tough enough. Next time I take someone it won't be you. Maybe the Shea girl. Maybe that hotshot sister of yours. Most likely, though, it will be the other girl—now what is her name?" he said it almost playfully, "Oh, yes, Miss Arnold." He laughed as my muscles tensed up and I moved as if to get up.

"Easy, easy. I'm going to set you free. Stay absolutely still until I give you permission to stand or I will have to hurt you again." He undid my bonds while I sat very still.

As I rubbed my wrists I said, "So you're just going to let me get up and walk out of here?'

"Why not? I'm certainly not afraid of you. You won't tell anyone about this and even if you did, who would believe you? The rabbit will never come forward."

In fact, all that had occurred to me as well. What could I do? I thought about asking why had he gone to so much trouble for such a short conversation but it was really obvious. He wanted to make clear that I shouldn't doubt his resolve. There was no denying his words about Erin, Stephanie, and Laurie had really stung. And one other thing—he wanted the amulet and he thought there was a one in a million chance I just might find it.

I noticed that it was five-thirty. I had been tied up for nearly three hours. I staggered a bit as I stood up. To avoid giving him any more satisfaction I forced myself to walk as normally as possible past the teacher, out the door, and down the hall. He had a slight smile as he closed the door behind me. Still a bit light-headed I wondered what kind of gas he had used.

Nevertheless, all was going fine until the final corridor when I heard the dread voice of the assistant principal.

"O'Ryan! Who gave you permission to be in this corridor at this time? Follow me to the office at once." This day risked going downhill, which, if you think about it, is pretty bad since I had already been gassed, tied up, and gagged.

"Mr. Robinson, I was looking for someone and then I got to feeling bad and lay down for a while. I'm still a bit dizzy." All true, though I admit I left out some fairly significant details.

We finally made it to the office; I had forgotten the hall was so long. There were still a few people there, which surprised me until I remembered this was faculty meeting day. I collapsed into a chair.

Mr. Robinson noticed and said sternly, "No, O'Ryan, back to my office. Be prepared to tell me who you were supposed to meet or we'll have to have a conversation with security."

I tried to stand up again but my legs were too wobbly.

"Have you been drinking or doing drugs?" the assistant principal demanded.

"Of course he hasn't," came an irritated voice. It was Mr. Chambers, who must have walked in from the hallway just in time to hear Mr. Robinson's demand. "I'm glad to finally find you, Thomas." He sat down next to me. In a very low voice he added, "I heard you're looking for someone. Will I do?"

"You sure will, Mr. Chambers," I said gratefully. I knew it wouldn't mean as much as the others he had but I was prepared to give him a medal myself.

Louder now, he said to Mr. Robinson, "Now that I've found him, Gil, I can relieve you of your burden. I'll see that he gets home safely." He smiled at the assistant principal.

An angry Mr. Robinson, robbed of what would have been a major prize and realizing he had been outflanked, retreated to his office to lick his wounds. I realize those are a lot of mixed metaphors but I was dizzy at the time. I did notice that Mrs. Warren, one of the art teachers, was trying to hide a smile.

Mr. Chambers began giving me a mini-lecture on Keats, as if in answer to some question I had previously asked. It was quite interesting and gave me more time to catch my breath and let my head clear. Then he said, "Are you feeling better? Perhaps I should drive you home."

"That might be a good idea," I agreed.

The seventy-plus teacher steadied me as we walked to his car. It was the second splurge of his life, the season pass at the golf course being the first—a Porsche Boxster S which he leased.

"Thank you so much, Mr. Chambers. I can get my Cutlass tomorrow."

Before he started the car he turned to me and asked, "Do you suppose your rescuer deserves some answers? Why *were* you there?"

I knew that was coming. "It was my meeting with Mr. Pierce. I'll tell you what I can but please let me handle this." My head was clearing now, but I hadn't regained full control. I realized that as I heard myself explaining. "Someone I know believes Mr. Pierce has something that doesn't belong to him. He wanted me to find out some things about our friendly chemistry teacher. Unfortunately, Mr. Pierce didn't take too well to that so this afternoon he invited me to his classroom. He knocked me out with some gas, tied me up, and then made some threats if I don't tell him where my friend is. I know I'm taking a big chance telling you such a crazy story about another teacher. I want to take care of this myself. I need to." I waited to see how he would respond, grateful that at least I hadn't mentioned talking rabbits.

Mr. Chambers studied me carefully for a few moments. Then he started the car and drove out of the parking lot. We were half way home before he spoke, "I don't know which is worse—that wild story of yours or the fact that I find it credible. At least it explains to me why you were trying to ingratiate yourself with that scoundrel earlier this month. I know Pierce and I believe I know you. Before you ever got to Clark I had heard about you from your middle school principal. He described you as the straightest of straight arrows. 'If Thomas O'Ryan tells you something you can take it to the bank,' he said. I've found all that to be true."

We were at a light. He turned his head to study me for a moment. "Assuming this is true, why not walk away from this? Why not try to charge him?"

"How, Mr. Chambers? Even if I wanted to, where's the proof? Gone by now, I'm sure. No, I think there are better ways to deal with him. This is my fight now."

He drove in silence again for a time. He knew the directions because he had taken me home on other occasions. At last we came to my house. He stopped the car and without turning his head he said, "I remember when I wasn't much older than you, deciding something was my fight. I've never regretted that decision. Not for a single moment." He glanced my way and smiled. "If you need me, let me know."

"Thanks for everything. If we could keep this between us I would appreciate it."

"Certainly, Thomas."

We got out of the car. "Let me handle your mother," he said. Which he did. Mom was very solicitous and offered to bring dinner up later. I said that would be fine, though it proved unnecessary. I collapsed on my bed and was asleep almost instantly.

The next morning I woke up fine except for a dull headache which lasted most of the morning. I saw Laurie briefly but I wasn't in any mood to talk and it seemed that neither was she. Thankfully I was able to avoid Mr. Pierce all day long. Until I walked to my car.

Brad had driven me to school so I was able to drive home in the Cutlass. Mr. Pierce was waiting for me. "Do you have an answer for me, O'Ryan?"

He was giving me a hard look and for once I was able to match it. "What do you think it is?"

His frown deepened. "I suspect you will have reason to regret your decision." He strode purposefully away.

Throughout the day I had spent time considering a most important question. Was anyone else really at risk? Erin, Stephanie, Laurie? He was right—Laurie would be the most obvious target to gain total control over me. How clear was it to the world that I was totally gone on Laurie? I would think about that later.

But how could she be at risk? The only reason he took me captive at school was because he had no intention of keeping me. It would be too hard to get someone out of school unseen. He couldn't have any real idea how to capture her. In spite of Laurie's days being pretty scripted, how would he know enough about her schedule to find one of the few times she wasn't with people who would make her capture impossible? Of course, I knew how I would do it, but then I knew as much about her as almost anyone.

Something still bothered me. But I couldn't clearly focus on the one point I seemed to be missing. What was I forgetting?

Chapter 18

That's it.

I woke up abruptly, before the alarm—totally awake. I flipped on the light by my bed and hurriedly made my way to the file cabinet in the corner of my room. The top drawer. At the back. In a plain manila folder—no markings. I took it back to my bed and began to flip through the pages. They were clippings and printouts off the internet. Washington Times, Washington Post, Gazette, Baltimore Sun, some specialty soccer magazines and papers, and even one from Sports Illustrated. It was one from the Post I was looking for and I found it toward the bottom of the stack. The folder contained every article I had ever found featuring, or at least mentioning, Laurie Arnold. I had another for Brad but I hadn't bothered to keep it so carefully.

The article I had suddenly remembered was a profile of Laurie when she had made the preseason all-metro soccer team. My heart sank as I read the opening paragraph.

"Every morning, Monday through Saturday, the alarm clock rings at five o'clock. Laurie Arnold is out of the house in ten minutes, dressed and ready to run. For the next half hour she runs the streets of her neighborhood. ..." The article continues at some length to tie her success to her dedication to fitness. But I didn't bother to read that part this morning. I was too busy dressing. As I hurried from my room I noticed the clock reading five fifteen.

She always followed the same course. That way she could easily compare her workouts from day-to-day. She had convinced me to go running a couple of times. The first day she was frustrated that she had to go so slow. The second day I was so tired I fell back asleep and was late for school. But for all that my experiment in exercise was a failure it did mean that I knew the course she followed. She left her house and ran to the corner of Smithtown

Road by Brad's house, a moderate incline which she handled easily. Then it would be down and back the two side streets of the neighborhood and back to her house. She would repeat the course in its entirety and then do as much of the course as she could one more time before her thirty minutes were up. It was along the second of the two side streets that she would be most at risk. The spot that came immediately to mind was where the street ran immediately by the edge of the park. At that point the woods were fairly thick. Less than twenty yards away a park road ran by. To the right it led behind the houses across the street from my home and toward the park warehouse and a dead end. To the left was the boat landing and the way out of the park.

It was foggy that morning. I ran toward the place that worried me. This was probably ridiculous but I couldn't just ignore the possibility. It would have been easy for Mr. Pierce to find the article in the Post online archive. An early morning drive through our neighborhood would confirm that Laurie did run and would allow him to see what her route was. Even if he didn't know that she always ran the same course he could still see where his best chance to attack her without being seen would be.

I cut off our street and down toward the park road by the Harrimans' house. The Harrimans had followed my dad's example and planted dozens of different trees when they first moved in. By now their yard was a veritable forest. I moved more slowly, trying to be as quiet as I could. If Laurie had started on time and I had guessed correctly about her pace, I still had some time before she got to the second side street.

I pushed through a tight opening between two old wild cherries and emerged on the park road. There was Mr. Pierce's car.

I forced myself to calm down. The route from the car to the neighborhood street would lead up a small creek bed that was normally dry. Following it as quietly as possible I saw a camouflage clad figure, his back to me, in position to observe the street. I was sure my pounding heart would be enough to disclose my presence. I was within ten feet when I caught a brief glimpse of Laurie passing by on the way to the cul-de-sac. He was ready to seize her as she came back by. Like normal, Laurie was wearing earphones and wouldn't hear him coming. I was about to make my move—whatever that was going to be—when there was a sudden movement to our left.

Jack's attack was amazing for its rapidity and its ferocity. Rabbits generally are fast but there was something almost, well, magical about Jack's movement. Mr. Pierce tumbled over and fell backward down the little ravine. By the time he stood up and got his bearings Jack jumped at him from behind and down Pierce went again. When the teacher stood up again he began to retreat toward his car and of course he ran right into me since I had been too stunned to try and get out of his way. We tumbled several more feet down the ravine. We both managed to stand up at the same time and he took a swing at me. Unfortunately for him the gravel beneath his feet caused him to lose balance again and his swing went wide.

I've sometimes worried that I have an inner problem with anger. The last fight I was in had been in second grade when Billy Forester tried to take my lunch money. As I recall I hadn't been hungry that day anyway. But since I've gotten older I've wondered how I would respond to some sort of physical challenge.

I responded with a right fist to the pit of Pierce's stomach. I actually intended it to be slightly lower but my aim was off. It was effective nonetheless. He dropped to his knees. I said, very softly, "Get out. Now." He managed to get back to his feet and, after flashing a look of what I have to admit appeared to be hatred, he stumbled down toward his car. We had made a good bit of noise. I dropped to the ground to avoid being seen if Laurie came to investigate. That's how I was when I heard the teacher's car drive away. A very small noise nearby was followed by Jack's appearance.

"What a fine team we make." the rabbit said.

"Is Laurie…?"

"Gone? Yes, she stopped a moment to look in but I ran past and she shook her head and went on her way."

"Have you been watching over her like this …?"

"Every day. It occurred to me that Charles probably knows of your interest in Laurie and might use it against you. Hurry home. You'll be late for school."

I made it by two minutes.

Chapter 19

Thursday at school proved eventful, but less physically challenging than my before school activities. Still, I felt great. Even better when I saw Erin at lunch.

"Thomas, we're getting closer. I need to see you tonight. I think I've found Amelia Parker—her genealogy that is."

I was very excited. But then I remembered something I had failed to do. "That's super. But before we talk about that there's something else. Until this is over with Mr. Pierce I want you to be very careful. Never go anywhere by yourself. Tonight, I'll come to your gate and walk you back to my house. We can go over the information in our dining room."

Erin didn't argue about my advice but she did say, "Are you sure that's a good idea? I don't think Laurie will like it if she finds out. She didn't like the look of us sitting together at lunch."

"What?"

"She just came into the cafeteria and was walking this way when she saw us. She got a funny look on her face and turned and walked out."

So much for feeling great. At least I had one more chance with Laurie the next evening. How could she be jealous of Erin? Then I took another look at Erin. I had realized before that she was taking greater care in her appearance. Her red hair was pulled back and tied in a ponytail. Her complexion was flawless. With her contacts her pretty blue eyes could be plainly seen. She was wearing jeans and a sweater which showed off a great figure. So I guess it did make sense for Laurie to be jealous.

"Thomas, are you okay?"

"Hmm, uh, yeah. I'm fine. I'm an idiot, but I'm fine."

Erin looked at me with a very puzzled expression.

I did see the chemistry teacher later that day, but since I was walking with Brad I supposed he would not want to speak to me. I was right.

That night Erin was very happy when I met her at her back gate.

"I can't be out long. My grandmother wants me home early this evening. I have a date tomorrow."

Although I expressed happiness about her date, inwardly I had serious reservations. I did say, "This isn't with the person who had something to do with those bruises, is it?"

She brushed aside my concerns, "Really, I told you not to worry about that. You'll be very interested in what I've pieced together," she said, changing the subject quickly.

We walked back talking mainly about how she did genealogical research on the web. She had made some good money from several projects and thought it might prove better than the library job she worked at several days a week. We talked about pros and cons, and perhaps I helped her analyze the problem.

Arriving at my house we commandeered the dining room. After I removed the candlesticks and centerpiece Erin unrolled a large chart made by taping many other charts together.

"I thought you'd like larger print since you're so much older than I am," she said. It was another old joke between us since we had been born on the same day, February 15, at the same hospital—me at eleven-fifteen in the morning, Erin an hour and a half later.

I examined the genealogy. Then sat down. Quickly.

Erin was immediately concerned. "What's wrong?"

I goggled at the genealogy because I actually knew a name on the chart.

Penny Bradford. Of all names. I had to admit that it was one more sign that forces beyond me were pulling things toward a conclusion but why this way?

"Are you okay? You look sick." Erin was very solicitous.

As well she might be because I suspected that I looked pretty bad. Afraid of talking rabbits, sorcerers, evil chemistry teachers? For me, all paled by comparison to Penny Bradford.

It was William Congreve, not Shakespeare as I used to believe, who penned the lines:

"Heaven has no rage like love to hatred turned

"Nor hell a fury like a woman scorned."

I looked that up in Bartlett's once and it led me to a quote from the Lysistrata by Aristophanes:

"There is no animal more invincible than a woman, nor fire either, nor any wildcat so ruthless."

While I take no position on these sentiments generally it is my suspicion that each of these gentlemen knew one of Penny's ancestors. And now Erin was suggesting that the amulet had been in the hands of at least one of those ancestors.

"So, do you want me to tell you about this, or do you want to spend the rest of the evening in a daze?" I suddenly was aware that Erin was speaking.

"Umm, what? Oh, I'm sorry. Seeing a name I know is ... a shock. This is wonderful. Please tell me all about it."

She began to describe the meticulous effort she made to produce the genealogy. She wasn't showing off, just certifying its quality. She had traced multiple John Parkers from New York City through census data from 1900, 1910, and 1920. She couldn't find one with a daughter named Amelia. She then expanded her search and found a John Parker who lived in Hartford, Connecticut, in 1900, and in Bayonne, New Jersey, in 1910. I suppose he was making his way southwest. He was married to the former Elizabeth Osterhaus and had one daughter, Amelia Marie who had been born in 1894.

Erin then traced Amelia Marie to her wedding in 1919 to one Averitt Amery of Bordentown, New Jersey. They had four children, the oldest of which was Evelyn Elizabeth who was born on May 5, 1921. Evelyn had married William Garlington in 1947. Their one daughter, Deborah Susan, had been born in 1954. Deborah had married Frank Bradford in1980. And that led to the birth on January 4, 1986, of their one child, daughter Penelope Evelyn, known to me as Penny.

This is just a small, but relevant, portion of what Erin told me, quickly, because she was in a hurry. When she finally had to leave, I drove her home to save time, hoping that Laurie would not be coming in and see us driving out together. A 1980 Cutlass is not inconspicuous.

Back home, I looked over Erin's work and reflected on "What next?" It seemed obvious the way forward was through Penny. She might even have the amulet, or maybe it was in the possession of her mother, or grandmother. The reason I was sure this was where to look had nothing to do with Penny. Instead it was the growing conviction that some will, other than mine, was being exerted on the process. Maybe someone else wanted the amulet or maybe Jack and Mr. Pierce, both being so intent on the search, had some influence on the circumstances which they did not realize. That meant I had to have something to do with Penny. I was not pleased.

My troubles with Penny Bradford started when we were fourteen. And the person I will always hold most responsible is Bradford Edward Elliott, my good friend and competitor for Laurie. He is also Penny's cousin.

It all started innocently enough, at least on my part. It was the fall of the ninth grade. Brad and Laurie had broken up temporarily and I was "dating" Laurie, which consisted of dropping by her house after her soccer practice to watch television. This at least made me think I was dating Laurie. Even then Mrs. Arnold wasn't too happy to have me around but Mrs. Jernigan would bring us some cookies and milk. Inevitably Brad and Laurie reconciled but that left an unfinished piece of business—the fall homecoming dance. Unlike prom where only juniors and seniors can buy tickets, the homecoming dance allows freshman and sophomore guys the privilege of being dateless for a big dance. I should stop for a moment and admit that it is worse for girls than guys about missing out on such events. I have been assured this is true by my mother and I accept her opinion as definitive. Still, the five girls who turned me down for a chance to go to my junior year homecoming dance did not seem too upset about losing out.

But in my freshman year, when I was even more naïve than now, I was under the impression I was going with Laurie. While true that I had not asked her, we had discussed the dance while watching television. But when suddenly Brad and Laurie were back together I appeared headed toward what would later become a rather routine night at home. Brad and Laurie had other ideas, however. They were determined to find me a date so we could all go together. Mom and Dad were prepared to let me go since it was "in a group" though double dating was a more accurate description. My parents did not have precisely the same standards about dating. For example, I could go watch television with Laurie because that didn't meet Mom's definition of dating. In theory both parents held to a "no one-on-one dating until sixteen" policy but in actuality my mother, the part-time attorney, applied the rule with numerous exceptions and caveats. I suspect this is because Mom dated routinely from thirteen on while my father didn't have a date until he was fifteen. Still, I've seen enough of my peers caught up in relationships beyond their maturity level to realize that there is considerable reason to have some controls in this area of life. In any event Brad and Laurie agreed the perfect person for me was Brad's cousin Penny Bradford. They were wrong.

Penny lives with her parents in a mansion on fifty acres of land in Howard County, the county which is suburb to both Baltimore and Washington. They have horses, I don't know how many, and Penny is an expert rider. Her father, the brother of Brad's mother, is a well-known plastic surgeon who makes very good money. But the real wealth in the family comes from Penny's mother's family.

Penny is also a knockout. At fourteen she could pass for a Washington Redskins cheerleader. Already at that age she had a maturity, both physically and otherwise which left me far behind. But for some reason she took a fancy to me.

We were going together to the dance in a big white Cadillac, rented and driven by Brad's father, who was wearing a suit for the occasion. Mr. Elliott rarely wears a suit for anything, so he looked out of character to us who knew him. But to outsiders he would appear one impressive chauffeur. Unlike his son the quarterback, Mr. Elliott had been a college lineman—six-five, two sixty. Now approaching his late forties there wasn't an ounce of fat on the man.

On the way Brad and Laurie were happy as was Penny, while I was merely intimidated. Penny, who had shoulder length black hair to accompany her vivid violet eyes, was wearing a teal dress that was cut precariously low in front and was non-existent in the back. I couldn't keep my eyes off her and she probably enjoyed that too.

Now, at some point you may be asking exactly what was the problem? Well, the best way I can express it is that Penny was wildly too mature for me. Her parents were indulgent, materialistic, and agnostic. That reads harsher than I mean it. I'm not trying to be judgmental, merely descriptive. Her values were greatly different than mine. Don't get me wrong, she would no more do drugs than I would. Our lines were different, it's not that she didn't have one.

But as I'm suggesting, I was in no way ready for a date with Penny Bradford. Most threatening, she was very physical. She always had her hands on me, especially when dancing. Actually I think it was the dancing which attracted her to me. I had learned to dance for a couple of middle school plays and I think Penny enjoyed dancing with someone who didn't just sway back and forth.

I had never seriously, okay, actually, kissed a girl before Penny. After the trip home from the dance that was no longer true. In fact I must have demonstrated some flair for it because she seemed pleased. All this amused Brad greatly but Laurie seemed taken aback, if not actually shocked. As to Mr. Elliott, he was very business-like throughout the evening until he dropped me at my house. After I thanked him for driving he said, "Think nothing of it, Casanova."

Penny called me every day for the next week and invited me out for a Saturday to ride horses. I was flattered and a bit troubled. While our date had unquestionably been fun I was still uneasy. But my unsuspecting mom, who saw going riding as falling within another exception to her "dating" definition, was willing to drive as she had to go to Columbia for some church meeting and she would be going right by Penny's home. So it was arranged.

Penny and I actually did go for a ride which was quite enjoyable. I learned to ride when I was little while visiting my grandparents. When we got back she showed me around the estate. It's quite a place. She set up a movie in the spacious video room and we settled down to watch it. It became quickly apparent that she had seen the movie before and was not inclined to let me pay too much attention to it either. If I had been willing, I suspect I could have had even more of an education that afternoon.

While I found aspects of the time pleasurable, my main reaction was one of fear. Penny scared me. If I really fell for her she would be hard to resist, and she would be able to give or withhold favors at whim. What bothered me most about the whole business was that, in spite of her many positive attributes, I wasn't really interested in a relationship with Penny, with whom I had almost nothing in common. Nor was she interested in me—I was just a passing fancy. We were really just using each other for entertainment that afternoon. Everything I had ever been taught at church and at home said that was wrong. What Penny was for me was a major temptation. Again church and family agreed but now I was being asked to decide, "What do you believe, Thomas O'Ryan?"

So I called Penny and explained that I didn't think it would be a good idea to see her again. I even told her why. Her reaction, confused at first, resolved itself into a very cold anger. I think I may have been the first person, at least the first teenage male, to ever say "no" to Penny Bradford. This is not a distinction to which I had ever aspired.

In the nearly two and a half years which had passed I had run into her about half a dozen times. She would invariably snub me, with a hostility which was frightening for its depth, and then spread various unflattering stories about me with whoever was there to listen. The funny thing, and the real reason for my continuing fear, is that every time I saw Penny the physical attraction I felt for her was stronger.

All the above is intended to explain why I had to enlist Brad to get to Penny's grandmother assuming she was still alive. My own chances were slim and none, unless I totally abandoned principle and found Penny willing to accept an abject apology. I'm sorry to say I actually considered this course first but I decided it would be wrong. Admittedly I also decided that I didn't think it would work.

I picked up my cell phone. Fortunately, Brad was available.

"Brad, do you know if Penny's grandmother Evelyn Garlington is still alive?"

There was a pause on Brad's end before he said, "I think we've got a winner in the strangest way to start a conversation contest."

It had been rather abrupt at that. "Let me back up. I have a friend named Jack. You've never met him. He's asked me to track down some information about an old amu- er, medallion. Penny's great grandmother owned it many years ago. I want to talk to Mrs. Garlington, assuming she's still alive, to see if she remembers the medallion and if she knows what's become of it."

Another pause. "You're crazy. But I'll answer your question. Mrs. Garlington is alive, or was two months ago. I think I'd have heard if she'd died. She lives in a big house in Northwest D.C." This was good news, but also consistent with the theory that everything was coming together to either free Jack or permit Mr. Pierce to reacquire the amulet. Brad was continuing, "My family went down there about three years ago for some charity event. It's huge. But let me guess where this is going. To get to Mrs. Garlington you gotta go through my cousin Penny. Hmmm. You could call Penny—you know the number. I wonder why you're calling me?"

Brad can be hard to endure when he tries to be clever.

"Look Brad, you know I'm uncomfortable in dealing with Penny."

"You mean you're scared to death," responded Brad.

Ignoring his accurate statement I said simply, "I need your help."

"You'll get it. You know you will. Anything except with Laurie. Okay, what do you want?"

I told him.

Chapter 20

Laurie's Friday morning run went off without any sign of the chemistry teacher. Jack had followed her most of the way. I had kept watch from the woods near the park.

The only thing of significance that happened on Friday at school was that Brad informed me he had reached Penny rather late the previous night after our conversation.

"It's all set for Penny to try and get you a meeting with her grandmother. It wasn't easy. It may have to be the spur of the moment 'cause Penny said her grandmother is goin' out of town soon. What exactly did you do to get Penny so angry with you? You never told me."

"It's not what I did, so much as what I wouldn't do," I replied.

He looked surprised. "Oh."

"Wait. What I mean is, I think she enjoyed pulling my chain. She wasn't happy that I took the chain off before she grew tired of me." Now it was my turn to ask a question. "Why'd you and Laurie ever set me up with her in the first place?"

Brad laughed. "That's really my fault. I knew she's great looking and that she'd make a spectacular date for you to take to the dance. Which I thought would make up for you losing out on Laurie." He grinned. "After all, I've always been more superficial than you are. I convinced Laurie that she might be good for your confidence with girls. It never occurred to me that she would ever really want you." A thoughtful look crossed his face. "That didn't exactly come out right."

"That's okay, Brad," I said ruefully. "I know what you mean."

Laurie has a weakness for chocolate. She wouldn't give into it often but occasionally, if it was something very special, she would make an exception. After school I drove down to the mall and picked up a small box of Godiva chocolates, one of her absolute favorites. Then I stopped by Giant and bought some flowers. This was probably overkill but even as pessimistic as I was about the ultimate turn of events, it seemed a good idea to give it my best shot.

My parents and Angela had gone out to dinner so at least my Mom would not have to watch me be so nervous.

The day had dragged on interminably. I kept close watch on the clock. It was seven forty-five. The phone rang. I could barely make out the voice on the other end. It was Erin and she was crying. My first thought was of the chemistry teacher.

"What's Mr. Pierce done?"

"No. It's not him. I'm at a party with Jamie. Please, Thomas, come help me," she sobbed. "I don't know who else to call. I don't have much time. He'll expect me back."

Jamie Schiller. The 'I'm great and you're not' lacrosse star. 'Erin, why him?' I thought, but said, "Don't worry; stay calm. What's the problem?"

She sounded a little more in control, "Jamie's taken me to a party at Joe Franklin's house." More bad news. Franklin was said to be into some pretty bad stuff. "He was ... he was very rough with me. He wanted ... but, I wouldn't ...," her voice trailed away."

"Erin, where's Joe's house? I'll call the police."

"No, Thomas!" she was nearly hysterical. "It would kill my grandparents! Please come and get me!"

"Do you know the address?"

She told me. I took it down and said I would be right there. She said she would call me back if she could. I looked at the clock. Seven fifty. Ten minutes. I looked at the chocolates. If the call had come ten minutes later. But that might have been bad for Erin. I shook my head and hurried down the stairs. Stepping out on the front porch I saw Roger sitting with Stephanie on the swing.

"Roger, come with me now; this is important," I ordered.

He was startled, but said, "Uhh, okay, sure, if you need me. See ya', Steph."

I practically pulled him to the car only to find Stephanie had come along.

"No, you can't come ...," I began.

"Yes I can unless you want to discuss this with Mom and Dad when they get back home."

It would have taken too long to talk her out of it and maybe she would be helpful with Erin. Besides, I had a feeling I might not want to discuss this evening with my parents.

We reached the address that Erin had given me twenty-two minutes after her call. It was a big two story federal style house on a large lot in Harriman's Trace, a recent development at the edge of Montgomery County near Urbana. There were at least a dozen cars in the driveway and on the street nearby. Most of the house was dark but you could hear music on the street even with the doors closed. I passed the house, turned around, and parked heading out of the development.

Joe Franklin was a known bad guy in the senior class. Roger and Steph had filled me in on some of the details on the ride there. He was a suspected drug dealer who had almost free rein over his house. His parents were divorced and his mother was often traveling while his very successful father was now living on the west coast and sending hefty alimony checks home. Cami Donovan, a girl from Stephanie's class, lived just down the street and had shared a number of stories about other parties. Erin was not supposed to be in this kind of situation. Neither was Jamie for that matter.

"We better get her out of there as quickly as possible," said Roger.

I thought that was a good idea as far as it went but how to accomplish that feat under the circumstances was an open question. But it wasn't just the party which made me determined to rescue her. I remembered the bruises and now had a clear picture of who had done that to her. I hoped to make him pay for that someday but now forced myself to focus on more immediate concerns.

I told Stephanie to stay in the car with the doors locked and her cell phone ready to call the police. She refused, but Roger insisted, saying someone had to be safe to call in reinforcements. Stephanie finally acquiesced but she was not happy. Roger and I approached the front door. It sounded as if there were several people in the foyer so we beat a hasty retreat to the darkened side yard. We recognized that knocking and asking to see Erin might not be the best approach.

We edged around the right side of the house toward the back, ducking below a softly lit window. Since the house had a walkout basement I wanted to see if the party was going on down there too. We looked cautiously around the corner. A first floor deck on the side we were on gave us some cover. A patio was on the far side. A couple emerged from the basement door and wandered off across the back yard. Then two other couples came back and entered the basement. It was a pretty night to go for a walk though storms were expected later.

Roger whispered, "I see a problem. Assuming your plan was to just wander into the party and look for Erin that is. Everyone we've seen is part of a couple. We would stand out as a couple, even in Montgomery County."

"Besides, everyone knows Thomas," whispered Stephanie in my ear. I hadn't heard her approach. I nearly had a heart attack.

"What are you doing here? You agreed to stay in the car," I insisted.

"No, you agreed. To avoid an argument I waited to follow you. I also have a plan which you seem to need."

Staring at her with some frustration, I asked, "So what's the idea, dear sister?"

"You won't like it," she said.

"Understood, but tell me anyway."

"Roger and I will do the scouting."

"No." It came out so automatically it encouraged me to believe I could make a good father someday.

"Get real," said Stephanie. "I even know my way around in there."

"How?"

"Because it's the same model home as my friend Cami's."

"She's got a point," Roger weighed in. "These people are pretty distracted. A couple wandering around the house won't be noticeable like a single guy, especially one like you."

"What do you mean?"

"Everyone knows who you are from school and they'd be shocked to see you at a party like this one. You'd be spotted immediately."

"See, 'dear' brother? Then you can stay here and be ready to call for the police if we need them."

Unfortunately, the idea did make sense. Still, I was about to make several objections as a matter of principle when Stephanie grabbed Roger's hand and pulled him toward the back door.

All that was left for me was to stand and wait. Also to reflect on the big brave hero, come to rescue Erin, and who, upon arrival, sends his fifteen year old sister off to check out the bad guys. As a passing thought it wasn't too bad, however I had nearly twenty minutes to consider it before breathing comfortably again when I saw Stephanie and Roger coming my way. They were moving slowly, to avoid suspicion, with Roger's arm wrapped tightly around her shoulder.

"All right, tell me all about it."

Steph was smiling broadly in spite of the seriousness of the moment. "It was a piece of cake, as you might say. Roger was magnificent." He cleared his throat. Steph continued, "We wandered around trying to check out where Erin might be. We didn't want to talk to anyone so every time someone got too close we just stopped and started kissing." I stared at Roger who looked down and away. "We fit in; there was a lot of that going on." She turned serious. "It's not just drinking, Thomas, I think some of them are doing drugs upstairs."

"Erin?"

"We saw her and she saw us. She's in the living room, first floor front, far side from where we're standing. Jamie is all wrapped around her but she seemed okay. There are several other couples there, talking, smoking, and drinking. Jamie was smirking a lot."

I thought a moment. "Okay. So there's a good chance he doesn't know she's trying to escape. That makes things lots easier." I handed Steph my cell phone. Call the house number that Erin called from. Get her to the phone. Tell her to excuse herself to go to the bathroom. Then she should come downstairs, out the back door, turn right and come to us."

"It's a plan," Steph replied. She made the call. In a moment someone answered. "Hey can I speak to Erin Shea? Tell her it's her cousin Stephanie." Then to us, "He's gone to get her."

As we waited I turned and fixed my gaze on an unusually quiet Roger. "So you kissed my sister?"

"Aw, cut it out."

"And he kisses better than other guys I know, too," said Stephanie.

"How would you know?" Roger and I asked together but she motioned to us to be quiet.

"Erin, this is Stephanie O'Ryan. My brother is outside the house with me." She told Erin what to do. After hanging up, she said to us, "I think she's gonna do it. She's really scared."

We watched the back door. A couple went in from the back patio leaving it empty. Then a small figure emerged and turned toward us. She was creeping forward. I wanted to yell at her to run but resisted the temptation. Erin was ten feet from the door when Jamie emerged with an enraged bellow.

"Where d'ya think you're goin'?" he yelled. The voice seemed slightly slurred.

Erin froze and turned toward Jamie. He came and grabbed her arm.

I realized as I was running toward them that what I was about to do might not be altogether sensible. Maybe my encounter with Mr. Pierce had inspired me. Anyway, Jamie is six-three and weighs a shade under two hundred pounds, if I remember the article from the school's lacrosse column correctly. But surprise is important and I suspected that Jamie might be slowed by the results of the night's partying. In any event, I hit him just as Erin succeeded in pulling away from him. The rest was a physics problem. My lowered shoulder caught him in the chest and drove him backward, down on to the patio. He was starting to arise when the second O'Ryan sibling landed on top of him and pounded his head into the concrete. Noticing that he was still moving slightly I concluded that we hadn't killed him so I decided not to call for help. Steph scrambled up while I grabbed Erin's hand. We ran for the car.

By the time we were back in the Cutlass and headed down the street, sounds of turmoil were coming from the house.

Erin, who was sobbing uncontrollably, was in the back seat with Stephanie. Steph had her arms wrapped tightly around her and was telling her not to worry, that everything would be all right. At least we all prayed that it would be, since we couldn't find out what had happened until Erin calmed down. I drove quickly. At Lincoln Road I turned west to go the back roads home. Just in case Jamie decided to track us down I thought it best not to be on the most direct path. Plus, it would give Erin a little more time to settle down before facing her grandmother. I looked at the dashboard clock and realized I was already nearly an hour late for my date with Laurie. I had tried calling her cell while Steph and Roger were on their spying mission but had gotten no answer.

Just as we were getting to her house, Erin, finally under some semblance of control, said in a trembling voice, "Thomas, thank you so much. Stephanie, Roger, you too. I don't know how bad tonight might have been."

I pulled into her driveway, stopped the car, and asked softly, "I don't want to hurt you more, but how bad was it?"

She tried to keep her voice calm. "After we got there, and I saw what the party was like I told him I wanted to leave. He slapped me a couple of times and said that no girl backs out on a date with Jamie Schiller." Now the tears came again. "I'm such a fool when it comes to guys. Just like my mother," she cried. As she wept, none of us knew what to say. She began to calm down again and I asked if she wanted me to walk her to her door. She managed to nod her assent. So I helped her out of the car and steadied her with my arm until we were almost to her door. It was suddenly flung open by

Mrs. Shea. Descending the steps and assessing her granddaughter, she said to me sharply, "That will be quite enough of you, Mr. O'Ryan. We will see to you later. Come girl, into the house."

Despite Erin's protests Mrs. Shea had already concluded that I must be the villain in this situation. I turned and walked away.

"'No good deed goes unpunished'," Roger quoted cynically as I got back to the car. He and Steph had gotten out of the car and had heard the words of Mrs. Shea.

I didn't say anything until we were at my house. We got out and I thanked them profusely for all they had done. Stephanie looked at me, well, differently than before.

"Big brother," she had called me that for years, often sarcastically, but not this time. "I'm so proud of you. Erin knew what she was doing when she called you." She gave me a hug before motioning Roger toward his car. I couldn't speak at the moment.

I wasn't in much better shape a few minutes later in my room. But I had a call I had to make. No answer on the cell left me with one unpleasant option—the home phone. Please let it be an answering machine or Laurie.

Much worse. It was Mrs. Arnold.

"Hi, Mrs. Arnold. This is Thomas O'Ryan. May I speak to Laurie?"

"She has been expecting you for some time, I believe."

"Yes, I know, I wanted to explain that I'd been delayed."

Laurie's voice was icy. "Does your explanation involve Erin?" she asked.

"Yes, it does, but ..."

The line went dead.

I looked sadly at the box of Godiva chocolates.

On Sunday Laurie snubbed me at church. Mrs. Arnold was smiling a lot. By Tuesday word was out that Brad and Laurie were dating again.

So that was that. You might wonder that I should be so devastated when my expectations were so low to begin with. I would respond that even pessimists can be disappointed if the outcome is bad enough.

In any event, circumstances between Friday night and Tuesday provided me some new distractions from my loss of Laurie.

Chapter 21

After my unhappy phone call with Laurie, I decided to go for a walk. Though I don't believe I consciously set out to go to Jack's house, that's where I ended up. Thinking about my problems I probably didn't pay as much attention as usual to see if anyone was watching before I approached the old farmhouse. I had planned to bring the rabbit up-to-date on progress Saturday morning but this seemed as good a time as any, if Jack was available.

Mrs. Donnelly invited me to have a seat in the study. I settled into the wing back chair. The clock on the mantle showed eleven o'clock. Although I didn't yet know that Laurie had decided to go back to Brad, nevertheless I presumed I had lost all chance with her. Mrs. Shea was angry with me. Erin was hurt, emotionally, if not physically. My parents would have many questions if they found out where I had been and why Stephanie had been there and why I had allowed her to go into that house. Their final question was likely to be— "How does it feel to be grounded for six months?"

Presently Jack came in. "What have you heard from Erin? I've been hoping to hear from you ..., why, Thomas, what is wrong?" Jack showed sudden concern.

Laurie once called me a romantic. Unfortunately, it was in a tone of voice dripping with contempt. And maybe, being a romantic, explains why I had a tear or two in my eye. Maybe it was just stress. And lack of sleep. What a week.

"I'm sorry, Jack, it's just, I lost my last chance with Laurie tonight." The rabbit seemed sympathetic, though it was hard to tell. Pulling myself together, at least outwardly, I reported, "There is fascinating news from Erin."

After reporting the amazing find of the genealogical connection to Brad's cousin, Jack responded, "The climax is coming. This is the beginning of the end. We are all here because this is the time. You will never know how much I appreciate what you have done. Never lose sight of my promise to do all I can to fulfill your heart's greatest desire. What's next?"

"We wait for Brad to bring word of a meeting with Mrs. Garlington."

The rabbit quietly nodded agreement. "I agree. Now, tell me why you fear you've lost out on Laurie."

Reluctantly, I complied.

When the alarm rang the next morning I almost didn't get up. It was four-forty-five. But I had to move quickly if I was going to be in position in the woods to keep her from seeing me. Why she had to run six days a week is beyond me. All I got for my time was the chance to see her run past me several times. I didn't miss the applicability of the metaphor.

Much better was the word from another front. News of an appointment came earlier than I expected. Brad called just after ten on Saturday morning to say that we were on for that night at six o'clock. He was getting ready to go out but he would be back, ready to leave by four-thirty. I said that would be great and hung up. I tried calling Jack several times that day without success. Mrs. Donnelly was surely running errands.

I did make another phone call around noon. I dialed the Arnolds. The phone was answered by Laurie's grandmother.

"Mrs. Jernigan, is Laurie there? May I speak to her please?"

"I'm sorry, she has gone out for most of the day. She'll be back later this afternoon."

"Who did she go with? I'm sorry, that just came out. I don't have any right to ask that."

"No," she agreed, "But I'll tell you anyway. It was Brad."

I sighed.

Mrs. Jernigan, somewhat tentatively, said, "Now may I speak to you about something I don't have the right to talk to you about?"

"Why, sure." Surely I wasn't going to receive a lecture on treating Laurie better from her grandmother.

"I know this has been a busy time for the two of you. My daughter says … well, I have heard that you have broken two dates with Laurie."

"Yes, ma'am."

"Well, just don't worry too much about it." She hesitated again. "If God wants the two of you together I don't believe Laurie will refuse to follow His will. I have always ... perhaps I've said too much. Just don't lose heart."

I was genuinely touched. I managed to say, "Thank you, Mrs. Jernigan," before saying goodbye.

Chapter 22

Brad knocked on the door at four-thirty on the dot. I didn't ask where he and Laurie had gone and he didn't mention it. Unfortunately we were both thinking about it and it put a serious roadblock to casual conversation. Having something between us left both of us a bit irritable.

Brad drove to the Metro station. On the train down to the city we finally began to talk. I tried to answer as many of Brad's questions as possible with as little information as I could provide. This did not help our relationship.

We arrived at the Garlington Mansion fifteen minutes early. It occupied a corner of a very fashionable block in an upscale northwest D.C. neighborhood. I made a mental note to call my Aunt Jean to find out what something like it might be worth. Brad had told me that Penny would be waiting for us with her grandmother. "I'll let you knock," I said.

"Cowardice knows no bounds," said Brad sarcastically. It was a particularly unfair comment in light of my encounters with Mr. Pierce and Jamie Schiller that week but of course Brad didn't know about them. He knocked boldly and the door was opened by a butler. I had never actually seen one before but he looked like the ones in the movies. He led us down the entry hall and asked us to wait in what he called the parlor. The room was about twenty by thirty with an ornate ceiling, the most elaborate crown molding I had ever seen in a house where people actually lived, and more antique furniture than I could possibly describe. A Steinway concert grand was in the corner. The carpet was oriental. I don't know much about such things but I suspected it was worth more than most of my family's furnishings put together. I noticed that there was a print by Edward Hopper on the wall. At least that's what I thought until I got close enough to see the brush strokes.

I was looking at what appeared to be a painting with the signature of Mary Cassatt in the corner when Brad tapped me on the shoulder.

Penny Bradford had entered the room.

She was simply stunning. The shoulder length jet black hair styled casually but carefully. Makeup just perfect. A violet top to match the color of her eyes. Tight white jeans to show off her figure. None of this was to try and attract me—instead it was to say "You're a fool, Thomas O'Ryan, look what you lost out on." Admittedly, a jury would probably have convicted me of being a fool on the basis of that evidence without waiting to hear my side of the case. Caught up in the moment I was inclined to vote that way myself.

"Hello, Brad," she said warmly. "Hello, Thomas." Amazing how the temperature in her voice could drop so far so fast.

Sensing I was having problems getting words out, Brad said, "Thanks for setting this up. Thomas and I really appreciate it."

"Do you, Thomas?" She didn't wait for me to respond. "My grandmother will be ready to receive you shortly. She asked me to offer you something to drink. Iced tea, lemonade, cokes?" To me she said, "Or maybe you need something stronger?"

"Coke would be great." I finally said something. It would be easier with the ice broken.

"And you, Brad?"

"Make it two."

"Walter?" she called. The butler stepped out of the shadows. I hadn't noticed he had come in with her. "Two cokes and one iced tea, please."

"Yes, miss," he said and departed.

"This had better be good, Thomas. Disturbing my grandmother for no good reason would be a very mean thing to do."

Somehow, I didn't think she was being very open-minded about my visit.

Thinking that it might be a good idea to change the tone I crossed to the Steinway. "Do you suppose your grandmother would mind if I tried her piano?"

The question, somewhat out of the blue, seemed to startle Penny a bit. "I, uh, I guess it would be all right. I didn't know you played."

"He plays really well," said Brad loyally. "Nine years of lessons."

I didn't see any music so I fell back on the one composer that I most love, George Gershwin. I began with Summertime from Porgy and Bess. When I finished Brad said "Bravo" and Penny even seemed to have softened a bit. The piano had a gorgeous tone and it was obviously kept well-tuned. Somewhat emboldened I began Rhapsody in Blue though I had a suspicion that it had been too long since I last played it for me to get through it without a few mistakes. I was right. When I brought it to an end Brad and Penny were both smiling at me. Before any of us could speak though, an older voice spoke up from the doorway, "That was quite beautiful. Do you know 'As Time Goes By'?" The lady was small with her silver gray hair styled in short tight curls. I knew from Erin's genealogy that she was in her early eighties but I might have guessed late sixties from looking at her. Her eyes were clear and bright. She was dressed in a sensible but current light blue pants suit.

"I think so," I responded. And I did know it, thanks mainly to Laurie once saying she loved 'Casablanca'. After I finished I turned to see that Mrs. Garlington was sitting in a Queen Anne chair near the piano. Penny was standing at her left shoulder while Brad was standing at mine.

"Very nice, young man. It has been several months since my piano has received much use. You must come play for me again."

"I'd be happy to," I answered, which was approximately true. The actual reason why I had stopped taking lessons is that I rarely liked playing for anyone. I had gotten to the point where my teacher kept encouraging me to play in competitions and even give recitals. Instead I quit lessons and played on Christmas Eve for my family and occasionally for friends. I don't really know what possessed me to play for Penny and Mrs. Garlington that day, but it seemed to work out well. As to playing in public I was always my own worst critic. Kind comments from others make me feel patronized even when it's clear that wasn't the intent, while criticism leaves me discouraged even when it's meant to be constructive.

Penny remembered her manners and performed the formal introductions. Mrs. Garlington said she remembered Brad. She eyed me with what seemed a real curiosity.

"Perhaps we can have another selection before you leave. But first, I understand you would like to interrogate me."

I smiled, hoping it was disarming as opposed to merely goofy. "I don't remember using the word 'interrogate'. I did want to ask you about a certain medallion. I've been asked to trace it by a friend. It was in the possession of a man named Edwin Harper in the 1880's before it was stolen by an outlaw named Ben Davis."

"My, my. So you've come to accuse my family of trafficking in stolen property. I'm not sure that I should stay and listen to any more of this nonsense."

It's funny. I'm sure those were her words. When I read them it makes me think that she was angry. But I heard them, and even though she never smiled I was sure she was laughing at me on the inside.

"No, Mrs. Garlington. Your family received the medallion as a gift. Mr. Davis, many years after he stole the medallion, lost it in a wager over a game of billiards to Samuel Clemens."

"Indeed. You are at least getting warmer, young man. I do recall my mother saying she had met the illustrious writer."

"And I believe Mr. Clemens gave her the medallion."

"Why do you believe that?"

All eyes were on me. I took out the photoprint of the letter from John Parker to the editor of the New York paper. "This is why, Mrs. Garlington."

She took a moment to read the clipping then handed it to Penny. The elderly lady gave me a very serious look. Her eyes were exceptionally hard to meet.

"So, confirmed by the words of my grandfather. I would not wish to doubt his word." There it was again, just the slightest hint of mockery in her tone. "Perhaps my mother mentioned it in some of her letters. The best course may be for you to review them. They are in the attic." She rose quickly and moved toward the door, displaying a surprising agility. She paused and turned. "Well, don't just sit there. Come with me."

I wasn't hopeful that reading old letters would lead to an answer but Mrs. Garlington was certainly engaged on the problem. And why would Mrs. Amery's letters be collected here?

There was an elevator to the third floor, but since it was small Brad and I climbed up. From there, a narrow and somewhat steep stairway led to the attic.

This was my idea of what an attic should be. Ours is a hole in the ceiling above the garage. It's crammed with so much stuff that my dad claims he's afraid to park the car in the garage anymore. This one had much in it but there was still room to get around. Chests and other furniture even more antique than the pieces in the parlor were interspersed with stacks of books, magazines, and newspapers. Boxes of every sort and description were piled all around. I noticed an old telephone with separate earpiece next to what looked like a cigar store Indian. An old dressmakers dummy was next to an equally old sewing machine. And so it went.

A fading light came in from two dormers on the front of the house but happily there was adequate electrical lighting as well. This would be a great place to spend a rainy afternoon sorting through the reading material stored there. I mentioned that and Mrs. Garlington said that she would love to have me come back for just such a purpose. She was probably lonely.

In the midst of all the apparent disorder she knew exactly where the letters were. A big trunk rested beneath a variety of what I believe were hat boxes. Following directions, Brad and I removed the boxes and then moved the trunk, which was quite heavy, to a slightly open area near where Mrs. Garlington had taken a seat in an ancient straight back chair. First she answered my unspoken question.

"Allow me to explain. Many years ago my mother contacted many of her correspondents—friends, family—and asked for them to return any letters she had ever sent them that they might have kept. She wanted to write a family history and hoped to use them to refresh her memory. She began to prepare a draft of the history before she passed away. I suppose I should have engaged someone to pursue my mother's dream but there were always other more pressing matters. So I've kept these materials together all these years. Please, go ahead and open it, Thomas." So I did.

If all these were from her mother, I thought, she must have done nothing but write letters.

"Are you waiting for something, young man? Let's begin."

I sighed and handed a big stack to Brad who took them with an uncertain expression. Penny took some for herself and handed some to her grandmother. I began to review others.

As we read letter after letter Mrs. Garlington began to ask me questions. At first, I thought she was just being polite but it grew more and more obvious that she was the one conducting the interrogation. She seemed to want to know as much about me as possible. I ended up telling her about my family, my faith, my interests, my goals. I did hedge a bit when it came to girls. Brad found it boring since he already knew it all and Penny kept up an appearance of total disinterest in the entire conversation. In fact she was probably beginning to regret coming. I hadn't displayed any damage from breaking off with her two years before, she was forced to read countless dull, old letters, and, to top it off, she was getting dust on her bright white jeans.

We had been at it for over an hour and I had just finished a collection of missives from Mrs. Amery to her cousin Elaine in San Francisco when Mrs. Garlington said, "Perhaps that package, Thomas," indicating a parcel wedged in at the back of the trunk.

The parcel held about twenty letters bound by a bright blue rubber band. I paused for a moment to consider a couple of points before beginning to read through the letters. They were letters from Mrs. Amery to her mother in the 1930s.

It was the fourth letter down. I read the pertinent part out loud.

"You asked what has become of Mr. Clemens' medallion. I have set it aside in a safe place for little Evie. I look forward to telling her the story of how the famous man favored me with the unusual trinket." I scanned the rest of the letter and carefully reinserted it into the envelope.

I looked at Mrs. Evelyn Garlington. "When did 'little Evie' get the medallion and what did you do with it?"

She appraised me with the slightest of smiles. "Why do you believe I would know?"

"When Penny told you that I wanted to come and ask about a medallion once owned by your family you made time for me at once. You set this little adventure up so that you could ask me a bunch of questions to test me. You planted the letters from your mother..."

Penny interrupted, sputtering, "T-T-Thomas! How d-dare you accuse my grandmother..."

I cut her off. "Penny, your grandmother isn't offended." Turning my gaze back to Mrs. Garlington, I continued, "The dust was minimal on the trunk and the boxes even though most everything else is quite dusty. This set of letters was stuck at the back, unlike the others which were arranged in neat piles. And it was held together with a bright blue rubber band which was very flexible, just like brand new. Also, it seems likely to have been a set that you might have kept out special, since it was correspondence between your mother and grandmother. Who else but you, Evelyn, would be little Evie to the two of them?"

"Your conclusion, then?"

"You know about the medallion. You have known where it was. You may still."

She smiled broadly. "You are a very bright boy. That was the only compliment Penny gave you, and it was buried within a long series of insulting remarks." We both looked at Penny, whose face was getting quite red. "I suspected that my granddaughter held a personal animus toward you. I wanted to get to know you a bit." She arose abruptly. "I will have Walter put these things away later. You will bring the one set of letters, if you please, Thomas."

We returned with her to the parlor. Brad and I walked down to the first floor while Penny rode the elevator with her grandmother.

"Pretty slick," said Brad. "But where does this lead?"

"I think she's gonna tell us."

But not immediately. Mrs. Garlington insisted that Walter bring us fresh drinks—we'd never had a chance to touch what he'd brought earlier—and cookies. While we waited she told us many things about her mother, none of which had to do with medallions or Samuel Clemens or sorcerers or rabbits.

Walter came bringing the drinks and returned quickly with the cookies. There were at least ten varieties and they were all chocolate to one extent or another. Perhaps coming back to see Mrs. Garlington on another occasion would be a good idea. We obviously had some things in common.

"May I get you anything else, Madame?"

"No, Walter, that will be all for now."

We all looked at her expectantly.

"Now, Thomas, if you would give me the letter on the bottom of the stack."

I complied. She opened the envelope and carefully removed the letter. She noted that the date on the letter was 14 September 1938, and began to read.

"Dearest Mama,

"I have received my first letter from our darling little Evie who has begun her studies to become a nurse. I am quite proud of her as I am sure you are. Her father cannot understand why a young lady of our social class should engage in such an undertaking but he really is such a kind heart that he can forbid her nothing.

"She writes that school is very challenging and enormously enjoyable.

"She also wanted me to tell you that she wears Mr. Clemens' medallion each day and that it reminds her of both of us."

Mrs. Garlington was quiet a moment, before saying, "The letter goes on with much additional personal comment. As you have seen, my mother was very good at writing letters filled with minute detail." She fell silent again, apparently lost in thought.

"So you wore it every day?" I asked softly.

"Yes," she replied. "For many years. Until one day ... but I will tell that story in a moment. First, I suppose you would like to see the medallion?"

She laughed at the look on my face. "Don't look so surprised. This is what you came for." She carefully drew the medallion from where it had been hidden from view under her high collared blouse. "Penny, will you help me with the clasp, please?"

Penny complied without a word. Mrs. Garlington refastened the clasp and then held out the medallion to me. "Please take a close look at the goal of your search."

I think my hand might have actually been trembling as I reached for the object in her hand.

The amulet was fascinating. Barely an inch and a half across, it was more like a large coin. It may have been gold, at least in part, but what was most interesting was the design. It was the head of a lion superimposed on the head of a man. I realized that the lion's head was meant to be a crown. There were also twin moons and a number of stars. On the reverse was a design of leaves surrounding what must have been letters in what I, at least, had reason to suspect was an other-worldly tongue.

"Is this what you sought, young man?" she asked kindly.

I swallowed hard, "I hope so. The friend I mentioned is the one who can tell for sure." It occurred to me that I had not given any thought to what I should do now. Perhaps that was because, deep down, I had questioned whether we would ever find the amulet. It obviously meant much to Mrs. Garlington. I couldn't just steal it. That would have been immoral. Besides Brad wouldn't have let me.

"My friend would probably like to know what it would take to get you to part with it?"

"What would I sell it for? Is that what you mean?" She seemed amused and her eyes were quite sparkling. "I would never sell it for any amount of money. But I might give it to you if you could explain why you want it and where it came from."

I thought hard. Handing her back the amulet I asked, "May I excuse myself to make a cell phone call?"

"Certainly."

I was back in less than five minutes. There had been no answer to my repeated tries at the old farmhouse. While not surprising that Jack didn't answer—the rabbit had never answered the phone—the fact that Mrs. Donnelly was out at this time of night was unusual.

It was all up to me. If only Jack had been there when I had called. The decision was mine. I looked at Brad. He was hoping I would answer Mrs. Garlington's questions since he knew I hadn't been very forthcoming with him. I looked at Penny. She was looking beautiful, but very hostile. I hoped I was doing the right thing.

"Well, Mrs. Garlington, I will answer your questions. This is going to seem pretty crazy. It all started in Normandy in the year 1065." Her eyes widened and she seemed to catch her breath.

I told of the sorcerer coming to the town. Of the second visitor who captured the sorcerer and took him away in a burst of rainbow colors. Of Charles and the amulet and the one spell. Of the rabbit—I didn't mention Jack's name—and the thousand year chase. Of meeting Charles as the teacher—again I mentioned no names—and the discovery of the amulet's theft. By the time I was finished Brad had opened and closed his mouth a dozen times to say something but never had. Penny had started saying things a dozen times but Mrs. Garlington had told her sternly to be quiet or leave the room. At the end the older lady was quiet and thoughtful, but her granddaughter was seething.

Finally, Penny could take it no longer. "That's the most ridiculous story I've ever heard. Thomas, I am ashamed of you, trying to fool my grandmother like this. And all to get back at me for ..."

"Hush," Mrs. Garlington ordered. "Thomas is not trying to get back at you. He obviously has too good a head on his shoulders to be distracted by a silly girl like you for long." That stung Penny who reacted sharply. I could tell she had never put one over on her grandmother. "You do not understand. I believe every word of what Thomas has said."

I may have looked even more surprised at that than Penny and Brad.

"But, Nana," Penny was truly shocked this time, but her grandmother cut her off again.

"Child, I am not going insane in my old age. I have waited a long time to hear his story. Now I have a story to tell."

She examined me carefully for a moment, before speaking. "I thought for a moment, ... but I suppose not. Well, to begin, I did receive this medallion, amulet as you call it, from my mother who had received it from Mr. Clemens. It is a precious trinket to me both because of its origin and because I found myself especially drawn to its strange appearance. So I took it and wore it for several years.

"I graduated from a two year nursing program in 1940 and in a continuing effort to establish myself apart from my family I took a position with the army. My first assignment was to the medical facilities at Schofield Barracks on Oahu. It was a profound experience. Being on my own; no servants; able to do whatever I wished but totally responsible for my own actions. It was the most invigorating time of my life. Several of the nurses began to run around together. When we had the chance we would visit Honolulu. We traveled to the Royal Hawaiian for parties which…" She looked at Penny. "Which perhaps I should not discuss in detail." Even Penny smiled.

She continued to talk about her life as a nurse in Hawaii. Even though I was in some hurry to understand what this had to do with the amulet I was enthralled. The story of a now distant time and place, yet one so vital to American history was captivating. It also gave me some time to work on the cookies.

Mrs. Garlington had stopped for a moment, caught up in her memories. But before we had to prompt her, she resumed. "I want you to see and feel what it was like to have been young and to have felt so invulnerable. To believe the world was there for you. War was still far away, at least to someone as self-centered as I was then.

"One day several of us were together on Waikiki Beach. It wasn't nearly as crowded nor as picturesque in some respects as it is now. I was looking toward Diamond Head when my attention was drawn to a naval officer and a young woman walking arm-in-arm toward us. The young woman stopped at the end of the walkway but the officer stepped onto the sand and made his way toward our little group. When he got close he called out, 'Excuse me, is there a Miss Amery among you?' The other girls laughed and the men were upset that he was invading our party. But I spoke up to identify myself. He asked if I would step aside for a moment for a private word. I was happy to comply—it made me the obvious center of attention. I enjoyed that much as my granddaughter does.

"He said he had a message for me about my amulet—that's what he called it. I asked 'What amulet?' He smiled and said, 'I beg your pardon, the medallion from Mr. Clemens. The one with the lion's crown.' I wondered how he had heard of it. He wouldn't tell me. Instead, he told me to keep it very safe. And he said, 'Many years from now, when you are much older than you are today, someone will come and ask about it. When he tells you where it is from you should give it to him.' I was rather amused. I asked how I would know it was the right person. He said that the story would begin," she paused for effect, "in Normandy."

She looked around to see how we were taking the revelation. "But the reason I have always waited for this night was what he said before leaving. I felt foolish listening to anything more from this silly young officer so I started to turn away. But he reached out and took my arm, firmly but not in a threatening way, and said, 'And Evie, be very careful tomorrow.' His voice was so obviously filled with real concern that I couldn't help but take him seriously. His eyes were a pastel blue, much like yours Thomas.

"The date was December 6, 1941."

She took a fond look at the amulet which lay on her lap. She picked it up and held it out to me. "Here, take it. May God bless your purpose, Thomas O'Ryan. Free your friend. Just let me know how the story ends."

Holding the precious object in my hands I said softly, "I promise."

"I do have one more thing to show you. I believe you will find it as fascinating as I do. But first, before you go, I insist on another song. You will find some music in the piano bench. Do you know the work of Glenn Miller?"

I actually played several tunes. I was so happy with the success of the search that I was in no real hurry. But Brad was.

"I guess we better be going, Mrs. Garlington. I can't thank you enough."

"Your visit has been an answer to many prayers, Thomas. Oh yes, the one other thing. There, the small box on the mantle."

Brad was closest so he retrieved the item and handed it our hostess. She opened and displayed the contents. It was the twin to the amulet. I looked at it in Mrs. Garlington's hands and pulled the first one out of my pocket. "How can you tell them apart?" I asked.

"Hold them both at the same time," she instructed, "One in each hand."

I did as I was told, holding the first one in my left hand and the second one in my right. The chain on the second one was clearly older and more worn but the amulets were indistinguishable. There was no way to tell … but, no, they were different. The first amulet was the real one. I just, well, I just knew it. There was no explainable reason for me to know since the slight differences between the two did not tell me anything about which was the one from 1065 in Normandy. Still, I knew.

"Remarkable, isn't it?"

I nodded my agreement.

"I had the copy made some years ago. The chain on it is actually the original chain. It was getting too difficult for me to open and close. They are nearly identical though of course I can tell the difference just from appearance. But if I close my eyes and have the two held out to me I always know which is the right one just by the feeling that comes over me when I touch it."

I handed her the copy.

She was quiet another moment looking at the amulets, first the real one in my hand and then the copy. Finally she spoke, "Now go, Brad is correct, you must be on your way. Penny and I have much to discuss—she is spending the night with me."

That appeared to be the first Penny had heard about that, but she was still too intimidated by the evening's events to protest. However she actually muttered a goodbye in response to mine as we were leaving.

Chapter 23

On the Metro, riding back to Shady Grove Station, Brad began to talk about the evening. "Forget whether I believe any of your story for a moment, who was the navy officer with the message for Mrs. Garlington sixty years ago? How did he know you would start the story by mentioning Normandy? And if the guy knew about all this at that time, why didn't he get the amulet for the rabbit then?" Brad was asking the same questions out loud that I was asking internally. "That's the wildest thing. A talking rabbit? But, I know one thing. I'm glad you told me under this circumstance. Under any other I would think you had gone crazy."

"So now you think I'm sane?" I asked.

"No. Now I think we're both crazy," he said seriously, but then he laughed. "I also see why you've been acting so strange this past month. You gotta tell Laurie. She's really worried about you."

Laurie. Though glad to know she was concerned, the reality was that I was sure she had given up on me and was preparing to go back to dating Brad. I knew it as surely as if she had sent me a press release. Not that I'd been any real competition. I'd broken two of our three dates, one because of the research for Jack and the other to rescue Erin. I had to admit that it was ironic that the affair of the rabbit hadn't stopped Laurie and me from dating. Instead it was Laurie's silly jealousy of Erin. Though from Laurie's viewpoint it must have seemed strange that after I had talked so long about seriously dating her, when given the chance, I ended up spending so much time with someone else, and Erin of all people.

"Brad, the last I knew, Laurie was really mad at me for breaking a date. If she calms down to the point where she doesn't want to join Penny's 'I Hate Thomas' club then I'll think about telling her. As for your questions, I don't know the answers. All I can think of is that it must be connected to the world from which the sorcerer originally came."

I said this a bit too loud, I guess, because the person sitting in the train opposite us said, "Wow, man! You into that game too?" Brad and I were quiet after that.

When we got to Brad's minivan I began to try Jack's number again. Still no answer. "Where can Jack be?"

"Jack's the name of the rabbit?" inquired Brad.

"Yeah." I thought I might as well fill in a few blanks for Brad. It seemed to me he deserved it and by this time I just needed someone to whom I could tell the whole story. "Jack lives in the big farmhouse behind our street. He has for a long time. Mrs. Donnelly looks after him."

"So close by for all this time. That's even more amazing. Well, that explains why I've seen you heading in the direction of the old farmhouse late at night."

"You have?"

"Sure. You're not the only one out late."

That's it. Someone else must have seen me. I redialed the cell phone. This time there was an answer, but it wasn't Mrs. Donnelly. It was Jack.

"Hello?" The voice of the rabbit seemed tentative, uncertain. I froze for a moment. Jack had never answered the phone before.

"Hello. This is Thomas O'Ryan."

"Yes, Mr. O'Ryan. I was expecting to hear from you." My last name. The sign of trouble. "Do you have some information for me?"

I thought very hard. "Nothing that can't wait. I'll drop by tomorrow afternoon. Say around two."

There was a pause at the other end. Then Jack said, "It would be better for you to come tonight."

"No, I'm busy. Stop pushing. I'll be there when it's convenient for me," I said sharply and hung up.

Brad took time from his driving to glance at me quizzically. "That didn't sound like you. What gives?"

I explained that Jack's use of my last name was the sign of trouble. "We need to get to him in a hurry."

"Do you think it's Pierce?"

"Who else?" I answered.

As we were nearing our development I said, "Brad, let's park at your house and walk. I have to do something at home before we arrive at the farmhouse."

"Okay. I'll let my parents know we're going for a walk. But I thought we were in a hurry."

"I need to hide the amulet. I don't want to have it with me when we go there."

After dropping off the car and saying hi to the Elliotts, we walked along our street to my house. After thinking about the problem for a while I was no longer in as much of a hurry because I suspected it didn't matter. I wasn't quite correct.

At my house I left Brad talking to my parents—they were watching Veggie Tales with Angela. Steph was off visiting her best friend Marcie Johnson. I took some time deciding where in my room to hide the amulet. Convinced it was safe I hurried downstairs and we headed for Jack.

The farmhouse was darker than normal. The only light visible was in the kitchen. The only car around was Mrs. Donnelly's van in the driveway. I looked in the garage to confirm that no car was there. Crossing to the big porch we tried to make as little noise as possible. Confirming my fears, the front door was slightly ajar. After listening a moment I stepped inside. Brad came quietly behind. We had agreed that if anyone jumped me it would be better to have Brad to come to my rescue rather than the other way around. A dim light from the study allowed us to see that no one was in the hall, the parlor, or the study.

But in the kitchen, on the floor, with her hands and legs tightly bound, was Mrs. Donnelly.

Chapter 24

Mrs. Donnelly sipped a cup of coffee which Brad had prepared. Her eyes were red from crying but she was getting herself under control. She had refused our offer to take her to a doctor.

"He must have come in while I was working in the flower garden. Jack had gone out for the day." She cried again. "Jack was so anxious about what you would find out from the lady downtown. Some days he just likes to run and run. I think it's good therapy. It takes his mind off his ... condition."

"So Jack is really a rabbit?" Brad asked the housekeeper.

"Why, yes. Of course he's not really a rabbit but that is his appearance. Hasn't Thomas explained ...?"

"Oh, he's explained all right. But the explanation is incredible."

Mrs. Donnelly nodded. "I know it was for me. But Mr. Andrews, he's the attorney who manages Jack's affairs and recruited me for this job, was very helpful in explaining everything. And my predecessor—she's in Florida now—helped me in many ways. Also, the histories helped."

"The histories?" I asked.

"Oh, yes. The histories. So many people have written to tell of Jack's ordeal. They are so fascin-... What am I thinking? I wasn't to mention their existence to anyone." She looked distressed.

I reassured her. "That's probably not a concern anymore. We're going to break a lot of Jack's rules before this is over."

"Perhaps you're right. Oh, thank you, dear." The last was to Brad as he refilled her cup. "Look there in the cookie jar. Yes, please bring it over here. Jack would be very unhappy if I did not offer our guests the hospitality of our home. Help yourself to some milk in the refrigerator." We did what she suggested. It seemed to help her stay in control if she could see herself in the role of hostess instead of victim. Besides, the cookies were chocolate with white chocolate chips and walnuts. Even under duress you have to keep up your strength.

"You were saying about Pierce coming in?" I encouraged her to resume her account.

"Oh yes. Well, when I came back in he grabbed me from behind and put something over my mouth. I could barely feel myself start to fall. When I woke up I was tied up like you found me, only he had me propped against the far wall. The hours dragged on. The worst part was having to be so close to that man. He was at my side with a knife." She seemed much steadier now and giving her account of what must have been one of the worst experiences in her life came without too much discomfort. I knew what it was like to be tied up by Mr. Pierce and it was no treat.

"We waited for Jack to return. The phone rang a number of times. Of course he wouldn't answer. When at last Jack came in he saw me tied up and he saw the knife, well, there was nothing he could do. He was motionless. Pierce said, 'It seems I have the surprise this time.'

"Jack asked what he wanted and Pierce told him to get into the cage. He had put this large cage in the doorway to the pantry. Then he threatened to hurt me if Jack didn't do what he demanded. So Jack did." Her eyes welled up with tears again, but she kept going. "With Jack locked in, they began speaking in some foreign language. I thought it might be French, which I took in school decades ago, but it seemed different somehow. That went on for quite some time. The phone rang another time or two without them answering and they seemed to be quarreling. Then at last it rang and Pierce answered it and held it to the cage. From Jack's words I could tell it was you, Thomas. That gave me some hope."

She paused for another sip of coffee. "Pierce had bent down so he could hear what you were saying to Jack on the phone. After you hung up, Jack began talking in the foreign language again but the man seemed lost in thought for a while. Then suddenly he swept the cage with Jack inside up in his arms and left without saying another word. Jack called out for me not to worry—that everything would turn out all right. Then he was gone."

No one said anything for several minutes. I knew that they were each expecting me to come up with something. So was I. We were all disappointed.

The phone rang. Mrs. Donnelly started to answer it. But wait—maybe there was a beginning of an idea. I stopped her. "No."

She looked at me with questioning eyes.

"Mrs. Donnelly, it occurs to me that since I told Jack I was going to show up here at two o'clock tomorrow afternoon, Mr. Pierce would expect me to be here at that time unless you got free and called me earlier. If he wanted to find out if you had gotten free, the easiest way would be to call and see if you answered the phone."

"So you plan to be here at that time to catch him?"

"Actually, I'll be here considerably before that, as will Brad and someone else too if I can get hold of him. As to catching him, that's not precisely the problem. And Mrs. Donnelly, I hope you don't mind being tied up."

She got a shocked look on her face. Brad was just intense—like he was waiting for his coach to tell him about a new play.

I told them what I had in mind.

Chapter 25

When we had dropped off his car Brad had asked permission to spend the night at my house. His parents' approval made it easier for us to deal with the fact that we didn't get in until about two a.m.

Which I thought we were going to do without incident until my dad opened the door to his study as we were walking stealthily up the steps.

"Well, now," said my father cheerfully, "I thought I would stay up and inquire as to when my wife changed your curfew to two a.m.? No, that couldn't be right, since it is now five past two. She must have changed it to three. I must speak to her about that in the morning."

"Dad, couldn't we assume that Brad and I just got up early?" I asked hopefully.

"We could." He paused. "But we won't. Come in here boys."

This was not as bad as it appeared. It could have been much worse. It could have been my mother. As much as she enjoys her family she still misses litigation. I read a comment on her performance at a mock trial. The professor said she had a gift for cross-examination. As to my father, he is very reasonable and has a good sense of humor. The real trick was to get out of this without either lying or explaining the entire situation. Now, I realize I can be second guessed about not being totally forthcoming to my father, but this is just one of those decisions I made which seemed right at the time.

Fortunately, my plan of attack, a direct assault, came immediately to mind. Brad was very happy to quietly leave everything to me.

"Dad," I said, as the guilty parties settled into two chairs which faced my Dad's big desk, "We admit we were out way too late. We have a friend in serious trouble and we were checking on him. We've just had a long talk with the person who looks after him. I'm very sorry for being out so late.

Please don't punish me for this. I have a lot I need to do to help my friend. Starting tomorrow. We need to go to early service and then go somewhere instead of Sunday School."

His gaze was intense. He had taught me to look people straight in the eye and that was good for moments like these. "Hmm, so you want me to overlook your two hour plus violation of curfew which, if you had not been caught you would have had no intention of mentioning, and authorize you to miss Sunday School on the basis of an unnamed action to support an unnamed friend in some unnamed trouble, none of which you have any desire to explain. Did I summarize that correctly?"

While I thought he had stated my argument in the worst possible light I was forced to admit, "That's pretty much it."

He leaned back in his oversize chair and looked first at me, then Brad, then back at me. "All right," he said. He turned to his computer which was on a workstation at a right angle to his desk. He adjusted the volume up on the DVD he had been watching—it was Henry V. After a moment he turned back to us with a curious expression. "Was there something else?"

"Oh, uh, no," we both said as we stood up abruptly. Dad turned back to his movie and we quietly headed up to my room. I reflected, not for the first time, that it was good to have a dad who was a night owl like me.

"That was surprising," said Brad. "I thought we were really in for it."

"Parents can be hard to figure, sometimes," I agreed, thinking that I was very blessed to have a dad who would trust me. I knew from past occasions that Mr. Elliott was not so understanding when Brad had come in late.

I gave up my bed to my friend and unrolled my sleeping bag on the floor. We talked for a brief time about my plan for Sunday. But not long. Six a.m. would come soon.

Fortunately Roger always arrives at church early because his dad is in the praise team which helps lead our music. Roger has pretty well taken over the sound system responsibilities for the early service and was always there to do sound-checks at seven thirty. By now this was pretty routine and it gave me a chance to discuss what I wanted from him before church started at eight-thirty.

"You want me to do what?" he asked.

"You heard me."

"What makes you think I can track a car all over the city?"

"Because I happen to know that you once tracked Mr. Robinson's car to his friend's house to find out who she is."

He eyed me carefully. "Just who else knows that?"

"I don't reveal my sources." I had him. "I'll brag on you to Stephanie if you help me. It shouldn't be near as dangerous as the other night."

"Oh, great."

"Can you be ready to do this by lunchtime?"

"Maybe. I'll see."

"Do you use GPS …?"

He cut me off dismissively. "Do I ask you questions about history? Leave this to the pros. Okay, what do I need to do?"

Once he said yes he began to get enthused.

Before we skipped out on Sunday School Brad took a few minutes to speak to Laurie. She had made a point of snubbing me when she saw me just after arriving, but by this time that was to be expected so I didn't even bother to think about it. At least not a lot. I made Brad promise not to tell her anything about the circumstances concerning the rabbit and Mr. Pierce. To get his agreement I had to tell him about Pierce's threats and how she'd be in more danger if she insisted on getting involved. He was still not happy about cutting her out.

Brad and I reached the farmhouse by ten-fifteen. Roger would be along later. Hopefully, he would not be observed. Brad and I went over the details once more with Mrs. Donnelly. At ten-thirty, certain all was in Brad's good hands, I left.

I was really counting on this working out. Mrs. Donnelly said that there had been many more phone calls. She had done what we had told her, leaving only the kitchen and study lights on. With Brad there she would leave the front door open a crack, just like the night before. The hard job was going to be Mrs. Donnelly's. Brad, who had been in scouting for a number of years, was going to tie her up as late as possible. But we knew Pierce was likely to show up quite early. Brad would tie her legs first, then her hands at the last possible moment.

I went home and made sure the amulet was still in its hiding place. Maybe I seem paranoid but I really didn't know what Pierce was capable of doing. Then I reviewed the options. They were few in number. Time passed slowly. At least it gave me a chance to pray about the outcome. I had been praying a lot lately. Interestingly, it seemed that God was using this time to draw me away from always looking for satisfaction in others and realizing my dependency on him. Which doesn't mean that I hadn't been praying about girls, Laurie in particular. It did change the tone and substance of the prayers, though.

My family got home from church at twelve-thirty. I told Mom I was going up to the local store to get something. At the last minute Stephanie came out and hopped in my car.

"What do you want?" I asked.

"An explanation. Which I deserve. Especially since you are involving my boyfriend in whatever you are doing."

"You're calling Roger your boyfriend now?"

She smiled. "Well, after the other night I do feel a certain attachment to him. Don't change the subject."

There was no time to finesse my sister, who was not too susceptible to finesse to begin with. "Steph, Mr. Pierce has done something very wrong. We, by which I mean Brad, Roger, me, some others you don't know, are trying to hold him accountable."

"And you didn't ask me to help? You know I can't stand Pierce."

I had actually forgotten about their encounter in the fall when he had somehow offended her by something he said about athletes at an early meeting of the science club. I never thought about it again. Stephanie tends to have a longer memory.

"What can I do?" she inquired.

Earlier, when I had actually considered involving her, I had thought of something for her to do. She seemed pleased with the role. She got out of the car and went to get ready.

I drove up to the little store. My path led past the farmhouse. All looked the same. Across the street near a service entrance to the park a workman's truck was located. An electrician was fiddling with some tools or something in the back of the truck. The sign on the side said Avery Electric. I don't know how Roger had gotten permission to use it. He didn't look up as I passed.

On my way back home I drank the bottle of lime soda I had purchased at the store. I pulled in the driveway as Stephanie was leaving to go for a run. She was wearing shorts and a t-shirt with her hair pulled back. Even as her brother I had to admit that she looked cute. I suspected she would run past a certain electrician. She was also wearing a Bluetooth headset for her cell phone. She would let me know if she saw any sign of the chemistry teacher.

"Thomas, dinner's on the table," called my mom.

"Thanks, Mom, but I'm not too hungry right now. I have to meet someone at two. Could I have something later?"

"What's going on today? First Stephanie, now you."

"They'll be fine, Christy. Angela and I are ready for dinner," called my father.

My mom went on in to the dining room.

My cell phone beeped. The time was one-oh-five. It was Brad—texting. "He's here just inside front door." Brad would be in the pantry where he could keep an eye on Mrs. Donnelly and close enough to back me up if he heard me call.

I called Roger. He answered at once. "Did you see him arrive?" I asked.

"Sure did. Walking across the street from the little neighborhood on the hill." Across the street from our development was one which had been there when we moved in. It was just two streets with a couple of dozen houses.

"Okay. Back soon."

Next I called Steph. "Hope you're not too tired."

"Hah, when did you last go for a run?"

Ignoring that, I said, "Neighborhood across the street, look for Pierce's car, a silver, late-model Honda Accord."

"Yeah, I've seen it. I'll call." She was in good shape. I could tell that she was running as we talked but she wasn't breathing hard.

One-forty-seven. The phone rang. It was Steph. "Found it. Sorry it took so long. It's behind the Winters' house."

Why would he have selected that location? Oh, that's right. Kim Winters was one of his star junior chemistry students. But she and her family had gone on a three week trip to Mexico. Her father was in international marketing and took the whole family with him whenever he could. The kids had laptops and kept up their work while they were gone.

"Great, wait there out of sight for Roger. Hope he likes your outfit."

Another call. "Roger, it's behind the Winters' house. You know where that is. Be quick. Time is short."

"I'm on it."

At one-fifty-five I walked downstairs and told my mom I was going out for a while. She said that was fine. What I would have done if she had said it wasn't fine was not immediately obvious.

I pulled in the driveway of the old farmhouse. Exiting the car I took a moment to let my heart stop racing. Giving that up, I walked to the door. My watch said two-oh-three. I rang the doorbell. No response. The door was still open a crack. I called out "Jack? Mrs. Donnelly?" I waited a moment, before pushing the door open and carefully stepping inside. No sign of anyone so far. Where would I look first if I didn't know anything was going on. Probably the study. I started that way.

Now I thought I was pretty safe as I expected he just wanted to talk to me and provide a few threats. I wasn't totally right. It took a few moments to let my head clear. The dull ache behind my left ear suggested that he had resorted to more primitive methods of getting me under control. I was tied up again. It was nice to know Brad had followed instructions and not burst in without my call. Sort of. It was tempting to call for him now and let him beat Mr. Pierce senseless, but that would be counter-productive.

"Well, O'Ryan, no chance to get in a lucky punch this afternoon."

"Untie me and let's see how lucky it was." I actually didn't feel like fighting with him but I thought I should keep up appearances. But that explained the blow on the head. Pierce hadn't liked me hitting him the other day.

"Not likely," he said coldly. "We have some things to discuss. Then, after I leave, you might employ your energies to crawling to the kitchen where you will find the housekeeper in somewhat worse shape than yourself. Between the two of you I'm sure you'll find some way to get out of your bonds. But hopefully not too soon. You've been a major problem to me but perhaps that will soon be changing."

As I had noticed before, being tied up puts you at a considerable disadvantage in carrying on a conversation. Also being tied up and sitting in a chair has it all over being tied up and lying awkwardly on a floor while the other person is standing looking down at you.

Not getting any response from me he continued, "I have Jack as you call—," he cut himself short and just laughed. "Vanity and pride. Well, that's one secret I will honor. But mainly because it pleases me to keep as much as possible from you." I had no idea what he was talking about, but I didn't see much point in pushing him about it. "I will keep the rabbit until you bring me the amulet. I know you are getting close." For a few seconds he paused. "I-I c-can feel it coming close," he stammered. "I will have it again!" he shouted. His face was bright red. His eyes were suddenly wild. The look on his face was more pain than anger. If I hadn't been before, I was afraid now.

He was breathing hard but his voice was calmer when he spoke again. "You've found something I missed. You and that Shea girl. I won't bother to try to beat it out of you. Although it might be enjoyable, I might get carried away. Use the information and get the amulet. I'm sure you will. I know it somehow. Then wait for my call. The amulet for the rabbit. And also your friends' safety. Remember this; you won't always be there to protect everyone. If I think you're holding out on me someone will pay a price."

He headed toward the front door. I heard it close behind him.

I had told Brad to wait for fifteen minutes after Pierce left before coming out. For once I was thrilled he disregarded instructions. He looked in at me before stepping to the front door. Looking out through the side panels he must have been satisfied that the teacher wasn't coming back. Brad then turned and hurried off. I agreed with his priorities. Coming back he said, rather quietly, "Mrs. Donnelly is fine. She's amazing. I really learned a lot about her this morning. You should talk to her sometime."

"Very interesting, but would you mind untying me? Please?"

"I'm trying to decide if there's anything I want to ask you about while you're like this. Oh, that's right, in the fourth grade, when Mrs. Duncan thought I put the salt in her sugar jar, was it really you?"

"Brad," I snarled, "Not now."

He bent down and began to work with the cords, "I thought so. Or, if that's too much ancient history, how about this, 'Did Laurie kiss you, or did you kiss Laurie?'" By that time he had finished. I looked at him without saying anything. I stood up, rather unsteadily, before answering him.

"What's the difference? You've got her back. You know how hard this is for me. I've got other things to take care of now. It's over anyway."

Brad looked thoughtful more than chastened.

My cell phone rang. It was Roger.

"He just left. It's working fine. Steph's watching the map. He's headed toward 270."

"Okay, we're on our way." I ducked into the kitchen to tell Mrs. Donnelly we'd be in touch. She waved and said not to worry about her, that she was tough. I believed her.

At the car Brad insisted on driving. Still feeling stiff from the blow to my head I acquiesced. Besides, Brad drives faster than I do. Staying in touch with Roger we were told that Pierce was northbound toward Frederick.

Stephanie had taken the phone. "We think he got off at 85 near the Monocacy Mall. He's stopped somewhere."

"Great, we're almost there."

We arrived ten minutes later and met Roger and Stephanie in the parking lot of the Olive Garden Restaurant.

"Now what do we do?" asked my sister.

That was a very good question.

"Roger, can we find the car?" I asked

"We already have. It's parked near the end of the mall close to the two motels. But I haven't tried to close in because I wanted to know if you were ready for that. If he's around he may recognize me or the truck. Certainly he would recognize your car."

"You're right, but, I don't think we have a choice. The real question is whether he's stopped for the night or is he just getting something at the mall. Let's try the two motels close by. Brad, drop me at Simpson's then you drive over to the Holiday Inn."

"What am I looking for, Thomas?" said Brad.

"Just watch for Pierce. Roger, you keep an eye on Pierce's car to see if he comes back."

"What about me?" asked Steph.

"Why don't you go shopping?"

"Oh." She thought for a moment before realizing I was suggesting she look for the teacher in the mall, then she added, "Sure."

So we split up. My choice, Simpson's, was a new motel chain, a hundred or more rooms on three floors. The doors opened from the outside. There weren't very many cars in the lot. There also wasn't much I could think of to do next. So I just wandered around the parking lot. Which got me to thinking, if I was staying in a motel because I couldn't go home and had a rabbit in a big cage, would I want to haul it in and out of a motel, attracting considerable attention? Wouldn't it be better to leave it in a car? But certainly not a two door Honda Accord if you could even get it in the car to begin with. Probably not even a minivan or station wagon where someone could look in and see it. What about a panel truck? Now I began to find the other vehicles in the parking lot of the hotel very interesting.

I started at the lobby entrance and worked counter clockwise around the building. About two-thirds of the way around was a white panel van parked under a huge tree near the back fence. The van, an early nineties Dodge Ram, was pretty nondescript—white with no markings unless you count the patches of white on the front bumper where stickers had been scraped off. The passenger side bumper was bent in slightly. Somehow, it looked familiar, which was crazy since such vans are common everywhere you go. I mentally noted the license number as I circled around to the back where one of the rear vent windows was opened slightly. I went to the window and whispered, "Jack, are you there? Jack? Ja—"

"The rabbit will not hear you. The sedation was necessary but will wear off by tomorrow. By which time I will be in a much more secure location. I continue to underestimate you, O' Ryan. I will try not to do so again. But now I must be on my way."

When I first heard the voice at my elbow I had stood like a statue. He certainly could move quietly. As I started to turn, I once again felt a sudden sharp pain at the back of my head.

Chapter 26

The people were talking so loud I couldn't sleep. Besides, the bed felt as hard as concrete.

"Thomas! Thomas, can you hear me?" Why was Steph yelling at me and hitting my head with a hammer? Oh, wait, the hammer was on the inside.

I opened my eyes. Stephanie was leaning over me looking very concerned.

Brad asked, "How often have you been knocked unconscious lately?"

"Twice today plus being gassed last Tuesday." I sat up. I quickly lay back down. Too quickly actually. I groaned loudly.

"What's this about 'gassed'?" asked Stephanie.

"Later. Pierce got away. He had a van."

"Don't you think we need to take you to the doctor?" asked Brad.

"No. How do I explain that a chemistry teacher keeps hitting me because he kidnapped a rabbit?"

"A rabbit? This is about stealing a rabbit?" Stephanie sounded incredulous.

I forgot. I hadn't meant to bring the rabbit into it with Stephanie. "I'll explain about that, too. I promise."

Roger drove up in his dad's truck. "What's with Thomas?"

"No problem," said Brad sarcastically. "We'll keep an eye on him for 36 hours and I'm sure he won't have any permanent injury."

"Just get me home," I requested. Eventually they got me into the back seat of the Cutlass. I was glad my dad had bought a four-door those many years ago. Stephanie rode home with Brad and me. Roger drove to his house after retrieving the signaling device from the teacher's car.

We didn't say much on the way home. Stephanie kept turning to look at me with a very worried expression. I was angry that my brilliant plan for tracking Mr. Pierce to Jack had gone for nothing, but thrilled because my parents and Angela would be away from the house when we got home. They were having dinner and visiting with another family from the church.

When we got home, Stephanie asked for an explanation. I begged off, saying that I would provide her what she wanted on Monday night. I reminded Brad that he was to discuss none of what had happened with Laurie. He reluctantly said he would comply. "For now," he said.

I didn't notice till the next morning that I didn't have my cell phone. That seemed like just one more frustration. It proved a bit more than that.

I hadn't slept well again that Sunday night so I woke up irritable, with a headache. I had to drive that morning because Brad had a dental appointment. He offered to change the date but I told him not to worry about it. I noticed that he hadn't left by the time I drove past his house. A few of the neighborhood kids were at the bus stop including Stephanie. I thought about offering her a ride but we had a long standing agreement that we wouldn't speak to each other in the mornings, which had saved us a lot of arguments in the past. Besides, even though our relationship had improved over the weekend, I didn't want to deal with her questions just then. Erin wasn't there. I felt badly that I hadn't tried to catch up with her since Friday night, but of course I'd been busy.

There are two main ways from my house to John Clark High School. One route, the one we regularly use, consists of two relatively straight line segments, but you have to go somewhat out of your way on the first before turning back at an acute angle on the second.

The other route completes the triangle to John Clark, but it is very twisty. For some reason that morning I decided to go that way. It's pretty scenic with many flowering trees and shrubs. It curves and turns along a creek and by the edge of farms, some of which date from the mid eighteenth century. I had just passed the Millers' house where you have to brake quickly for the road takes a sharp bend to the left before twisting back to the right to pass under the interstate a half mile ahead.

Unfortunately, this time the brake pedal went straight to the floor to no effect. I tried to make the turn at thirty-five but at even that slow a speed the turn was too sharp. The Cutlass skidded sideways and hit the low guardrail. It flipped up and over, tumbling down the sharp incline. It may have tumbled a couple of times before landing upright at the ravine at the base of the incline. The dropoff is only about fifteen feet. I can just remember getting out of the car—the window of the driver's side door had been down allowing me to crawl out—and stumbling away with some vague concerns about fire. As it turned out there wasn't one.

The next thing I remember was the voice, and then the face, of Chuck Miller. Chuck was around twenty-five, the son of the family that owned and farmed about eight hundred acres of the county's agricultural preserve. A quiet, steady guy who went to our church, he had gotten a degree in agriculture and seemed determined to keep the farm going for at least one more generation.

"Thomas, can you hear me? Lay still. I'm calling for help." His voice was calm, reassuring.

As my mind began to clear, all I remember saying was, "The brakes weren't there, Chuck." I tried to sit up but he insisted on me staying flat on my back. He didn't have to insist very hard.

His dad came up and said something to Chuck that I didn't understand, and hurried off.

The first patrolman was someone I'd never seen but the next was Ted Prentiss, another church member. He wouldn't let me up either. At least with all the church people there we could have a prayer meeting. Which seemed a pretty good idea considering how I was feeling. I figured they had called for an ambulance but the next car to arrive was my father. He had been late leaving for work that morning and he must have been the one to take the call from Mr. Miller. As he bent down to check on me he brushed the hair out of my eyes. "I'm so sorry about your car, Dad!" I cried, but Dad just shook his head.

"Don't worry son," he said softly. "Let's just get you checked out."

"Dad, I'm fine. I didn't make a mistake, the brakes just suddenly weren't there."

Now it was his turn to choke up, but he managed to say, "Son, I should never have allowed you to drive that old thing. We'll be better rid of it."

I heard the sound of the ambulance. "Does Mom know?"

"Not yet, we'll call from the hospital."

It took a while to get me into the ambulance. They were pleased I could move my hands and feet but they insisted on taking me out on a stretcher that locked me into position to avoid any damage to my neck and back. My dad drove his car down to the hospital. By the time I was back in a room after my scans and x-rays my mother had joined us. Her eyes were red and she broke down totally the moment she saw me, which was very disconcerting since the only other time I had ever seen her do that was when her father died. She calmed down some over the next few hours. Happily, no one had called in half the church. I had specifically asked Dad not to and he had honored my request. I figured as long as my parents had each other they didn't need a lot of others around.

Eventually, after about five hours, the medical profession determined that I was not seriously injured. The diagnosis included a probable concussion, which was no great surprise to me. I did have several bruises, assorted scratches and abrasions, and I could expect to be sore for some time to come. They were confused about exactly how I had received a couple of blows to the back of the head. I didn't see any particular reason to comment on that. Even though I could walk fine, they had me sit in a wheelchair until my dad drove his car up to the emergency room entrance. The drive home was uneventful—Dad did stop and pick up some chicken nuggets and waffle fries from Chick-Fil-A for me.

When we got to the house Chuck Miller's car was out front and he was sitting on our front swing. He asked how I was doing. After replying that I was fine we went inside and asked him in. Dad had me sit in his recliner in the family room for a minute because it was obvious Chuck wanted to talk to us. My mom wasn't home yet, she had gone to pick up Angela.

"Mr. O'Ryan, there was an interesting development in the accident investigation. I don't know when the police will get around to telling you but I think you both deserve to know. On the one hand it'll make you both feel better but on the other hand it'll make you feel worse."

"Don't tell riddles, Chuck, what's the development?" asked my father.

"Yes, sir. The car was damaged."

"We know."

"No, sir, I mean before the accident. The brakes were sabotaged."

Chapter 27

I was at once relieved and angry. Relieved that my parents would now know that the accident was not my fault. Angry that Pierce was willing to go to such extremes. But this was almost inexplicable. This put anyone I would have had in my car in danger. But that's what he had said—"everyone at risk." But why would Pierce try to eliminate me when he had just said that he thought I had the inside track to recovering the amulet? The only reason I could think of was the one suggested by the look on his face when he was so agitated. Perhaps the concern over the amulet had finally driven him to totally irrational behavior.

Fortunately, my condition precluded serious discussion of this matter with my parents. After chatting a little bit longer and explaining how he had found out about the brakes, Chuck excused himself and departed. My parents knew I needed rest. Rather than try to get me up the stairs—I was not moving very well—my mother put me to bed in the small first floor guest room. Just before Stephanie was to get home my parents did come in to raise the obvious question.

"Son," my father questioned, "Do you have someone to suggest who might have done this?"

I wouldn't lie to my father, but I wasn't prepared to tell him about talking rabbits either. Under the circumstances they would be taking me back to the hospital and locking me in. So instead, I said, "It's hard to imagine anyone wanting to hurt me like that." Which was true. "Although there are some people I've had problems with over the years I'm not ready to accuse anyone of something like this. But Dad, is there anyone who might want to hurt you? It's your car."

Dad considered a moment. "That crossed my mind. I do have a couple of names to mention to the police."

I stared at him in amazement. Dad never talked with much specificity about his job. We always kidded that he might work for some secret agency, but I've seen his pay statements from the Department of the Interior.

"Oh, it's nothing serious, really," he continued reassuringly. "Just a couple of personnel problems we've had to deal with recently."

Now I was uncertain; maybe it wasn't Pierce.

"I'm very tired. May I sleep for a while?" I really was extremely worn out.

"Absolutely," answered my mom. She kissed my brow and Dad touched my hand before leaving.

As much as I tried to keep my mind focused on sorting out the problem before me I was asleep within minutes after my parents left the room. When I woke it was dark outside but a nightlight in the room cast shadows all round. The clock by the table read eleven-oh-five so I hadn't slept that long. The most startling aspect of waking up was to realize that Brad was asleep, sitting up in the corner chair.

"What are you doing here?" I asked softly.

Brad woke up immediately and was instantly alert. I've known he could do that for a long time but I'm still amazed every time I see it.

"Glad you woke up. Your mom left some medicine for you to keep the pain down, but I hadn't wanted to wake you up to give it to you."

He went to the kitchen and came back with some water and a pill. I suppose I should have refused and just stood the pain. Instead I took the pill and wondered how long before I could have the next one. The only real problem other than the concussion the doctor had suggested was that I might have a very slightly cracked rib, the x-ray wasn't totally clear on that point. But if this was what a possibly cracked rib felt like I don't ever want a truly cracked rib.

Brad sat back down in his chair. "Thomas, this has gone too far."

I winced as I repositioned myself in the bed. "I know, but there's no final proof that Pierce did this. My dad said it could have been someone from work. And it doesn't make sense that Pierce would do this when he hoped I would get the amulet. All we can do is keep trying to find Jack. How did you find out about this?"

"I dropped by after dinner to see why you weren't at school today. Your parents showed me what was left of you so I decided to stay and wait for you to wake up. They needed to go to bed. I suspect this was harder on them anyway."

I decided not to debate the point even though I had considerable empirical data on the other side of the argument.

He went on, "I'm staying the night. My mom think it's sweet that I'm helping out your parents and looking after my good friend. The real reason is that I know your mom always bakes when she's nervous."

"What tonight?" I asked.

"Two pies, coconut crème and lemon meringue. She was very nervous. I wish she could teach my mom how to make crusts."

Brad had accomplished his goal of getting me to laugh, though it had the downside of reminding me sharply about the rib. Not that he wouldn't eat a couple of slices of pie now that he was awake. My mom's pies are well-known.

"So what can we do, Thomas?"

There he had me. All I knew was that I intended to stay pretty much where I was for another day or so. But I was happy to have Brad on my side.

"Brad, one thing. No one is to know about this. Not even Laurie. Especially Laurie."

"That's stupid. She ..."

"I mean it. I don't want her around. She's chosen you. Fine. I don't want to deal with that while I'm tryin' to get better. I need to focus on thinking about Jack's situation. Besides," and I knew this would again clinch the argument, "If she comes around she may get hurt. And the more people that know, the more likely Pierce finds out the shape I'm in. He already knows that I wasn't at school."

"Maybe not. He wasn't there today either. I looked him up for a little conversation but there was a sub in his class."

Hmm. I guess that was to be expected. Even though he had surely found a safe place to hide Jack by now he probably wouldn't want to be constantly concerned about someone following him. But where was that place?

"You really don't have to stay the night."

"I know." Something in his tone suggested it would be pointless to argue. "Can I get you something?" he asked.

"Not now, I'm kinda' drowsy. I think I'll just lay here." The last thing I remember that night were the sounds of Brad in the kitchen getting a plate and fork for the pie.

I woke up in the morning and started to move. I stopped quickly and groaned.

"Are you okay, big brother?" came Stephanie's voice from the big chair.

"Yeah, sort of. Where's Brad?"

"He just went home a few minutes ago. It was so cute when I looked in this morning and he was sitting up with you. It almost made me wish I hadn't been so mean to him yesterday afternoon before we knew about your accident."

"Why were you mean to him?"

"Well, I was really mad at Laurie but Brad was walking past me in the hall. Laurie's making clear that she's back dating Brad and some of the girls were laughing at you for thinking you had a chance at her. It's just so unfair." She suddenly seemed to remember that I'd been in an accident. Her eyes grew really big. "I'm s-so s-sorry," she stammered. "I didn't really mean to say all that to you, now."

I sighed, which I found much easier than laughing. "That's okay. I do agree with you." I smiled to let her know it was okay.

She brightened, then with a stricken look exclaimed, "I've gotta' go. The bus." She hurried out the door. I stopped her long enough to extract a promise that she would not tell anyone, especially Laurie, about the accident. I knew that eventually word would get out. I really just wanted a few more days.

So Laurie had made it official by telling her friends. Suddenly my vision was a bit blurry. Probably allergies.

My mom stayed home from her part-time job that Tuesday and I was happy for the company. I eventually got up and walked around. It wasn't as bad as I had expected. A few years and everything would be back to normal. In any event I still enjoyed a day off school. The lemon meringue was better than the coconut crème, but not by much.

I called Mrs. Donnelly and told her I was still at work on Jack's case. I didn't tell her about the accident.

I established myself in my father's recliner in the family room, watching movies. I had just reached the part of Rio Bravo when Ward Bond gets shot when my mother announced my first visitor's arrival. To my great surprise it was Mrs. Shea and she had not heard about the accident before my mom told her.

"May I have a word with Thomas in private, Christine?" she asked after sitting in the chair nearest me. She was sitting straight as an arrow. I don't think she really was happy being there.

"Certainly, Harriet," Mom said, though she was obviously surprised at the request. She had taken a seat on the couch, so she had to get up and gracefully head for a different part of the house.

When Mom was gone Mrs. Shea began to speak. "I have come to apologize. I do so now. But before I say what I was going to say, I must ask if you are all right."

"I'll be fine. It's very nice of you to come by."

She started again. "By Sunday evening, Erin had calmed down enough to explain that you were, in fact, the hero of the other night. No, don't deny it, Erin rarely exaggerates in speaking to me and the word 'hero' is hers. I should have come yesterday but I am a vain and stubborn woman."

She looked at me and was clearly waiting for me to say something but I couldn't think of an appropriate response.

She went on, "I've tried to protect Erin. I thought I was succeeding."

"Mrs. Shea," I interrupted. "I don't know about failing to protect her. She made a mistake in liking this one guy. But I've known her since we were little. She's honest, kind, compassionate, hard-working. It's just that she's beginning to realize that she's also very good-looking. Instead of protecting her from that fact, maybe she just needs guidance on how to come to terms with it."

Her eyes narrowed. "So, then you are interested romantically in Erin."

"No." Since Friday I had considered why that was true. Erin was bright, cute, personable—virtually everything I might find attractive. The explanation, I realized, had two parts. First, when we were just getting to know each other we had talked about her being Catholic and me being a Baptist. We both knew that to our families that would be a big deal, even if it took us years to understand why. For a long time we had an unspoken agreement not to bring up our church differences at all. Since Erin seemed at times to be thinking about looking around theologically, I thought it best not to bring that up with her grandmother. Instead I focused on the other reason.

"As long as I've known Erin, it's been clear the only girl I've been interested in has been Laurie Arnold. Erin thinks that's kinda' dumb, but she's always known it's true. Erin's too smart, and too practical to waste her time on a guy who is so hung up on someone else. Besides, the guys she's interested in, like Jamie, are tall and athletic.

"Look, Erin just needs help in picking the right guy, not condemnation for trying to find one." That was a bit sharp but in my defense I wasn't feeling like a lengthy conversation.

Mrs. Shea took my words rather better than I expected. She gave me a very intent look. "Your explanation clears up many things, more than it's likely you know. I doubt you understand my granddaughter as well as you think you do, but I believe your heart is in the right place. As to Erin and boys generally, you and my husband have much in common. Before Friday I would have dismissed your comments as routinely as I do his. Now, I won't."

She rose abruptly. "Once again, please forgive me. I see I have misjudged you totally. You will now be welcome in my home."

"Sure I forgive you. I think it's very wonderful all you and your husband have done for Erin. You really should be proud. Oh, and you're leaving that box." I indicated the one on the table by the chair.

"Oh, yes." She reached down, picked it up and handed it to me. "Just a small token of my appreciation for you protecting Erin." She turned and left quickly before I could say another word. I opened the large tin box and smiled broadly. It was filled with Mrs. Shea's famous molasses cookies. I was touched. However, if I didn't get back to school soon I would gain ten pounds.

Thirty minutes later came my next guest. It was Erin. She had tears in her eyes. I hoped she wasn't going to break down again.

"I ran all the way here. Are you okay?"

"Absolutely," I said as reassuringly as possible. "I'm sorry for not checking on you sooner."

"You're apologizing to me? You're too much sometimes." She started to give me a big hug but my cry stopped her in mid-hug. "Did I hurt you?" she cried.

"Not at all," I gasped. Catching my breath I changed the subject. "More importantly, did Jamie hurt you?"

She thought a minute and bit her lip before replying. "Not in any long-lasting way really. Maybe a few more bruises but they'll heal." She looked away for a moment and then back at me. "I never really thought there could be something long-lasting with him. I just liked the attention and he is cute. The thing I said the other night is actually at the heart of the problem. My confidence with picking boys is back to zero. Ever since the other night I've looked in the mirror and seen my mother." She took a minute to make certain she was under control. "Of course the hardest thing to manage is the truth that the jerk she fell for was my father."

I reached over and held her hand. "You're not your mother. You're respected by all your friends. You got carried away in dating a handsome jock. That happens a lot."

She smiled, even though there were tears in the corner of her eyes, "Like Laurie, you mean."

I hadn't meant Laurie, at least not intentionally. "Brad's different. He's really a great guy."

"You're amazingly loyal." She struggled to pick the right words. "You've been ... a wonderful blessing to me. I wish I could do something for you."

"Just being my friend is enough. Besides I would never have found the amu-, medallion without your help."

"You actually found where the medallion is?"

"Better than that, I have it upstairs. I'd take you up to show it to you but I'm not ready to bound up the steps. Besides," I added without enough thought, "with my luck that would be when Laurie would drop by and see me bringing you down from my bedroom. Last Friday was bad enough."

A look of understanding flashed across her face. "Oh, please say it isn't true? You missed a date with Laurie to come for me? You did, didn't you?" She was hurt just thinking about it.

Now it was my turn to feel bad about speaking too quickly. "I'm sorry. I never meant to tell you. It just made things happen quicker than they would have anyway."

"You mean her dating Brad again. I heard today at school that they were dating again. Then, at least she actually found out that it was my fault?"

"Not your fault, Erin. I didn't tell her anything about what had gone on. She just asked if my missing the date had anything to do with you and when I said it did she hung up. I was planning to tell her that you had needed my help on something and it ran late."

She was staring at me in a funny way. "Even to keep a relationship with the girl you love you wouldn't tell her about what trouble I got myself in?" She slowly shook her head.

I was feeling uncomfortable. Not because of Erin thinking well of me; my ego can use positive strokes as much or more than the next guy's. Instead, it was her use of the word "love" with respect to my feelings about Laurie. I had always avoided that particular word both because I thought myself too young to use and mean it, and also because it scared me.

The real problem was that I heard it being used so casually as a synonym for either "like" or "lust" that I didn't want to fall victim to the same trap.

But I had wondered, often, if it was the right word for my feelings about Laurie.

But, instead of engaging Erin in a discussion of love, which would probably have been interesting since she is incredibly well-read in the classics, I said, "Enough about Miss Arnold. Thanks for dropping by and save that hug you started to give me for some time when I really need it and I don't have a potentially cracked rib."

That gave us a chance to talk about bones, another interest of Erin's ever since a ninth grade science project. She gave me a long dissertation on the importance of drinking milk instead of soft drinks. She seemed more like herself. When she finally made ready to leave she returned to the reason for her visit and to give me one more apology about making me miss my date.

"I didn't mean to even let you know. It's the medication. My mouth is moving faster than my mind, even more so than usual."

"Hah, you're the most tactful classmate I have, which isn't saying much given the level of competition. Still, I'm glad you told me, deliberately or not. It's given me an idea." She gazed at me fondly before squeezing my hand, and hurriedly leaving.

My next set of visitors came at seven o'clock. It was a pair of detectives from the Montgomery County Police Department. They had called ahead for an appointment with me and my father. As an intellectual challenge it was quite diverting to try and answer every question truthfully without being forced into a corner where the subject of a thousand year old chemistry teacher would come up. They almost had me a time or two but fortunately they were more interested in the idea that someone from my father's work held a grudge against him. Two hours later they left, having set up a time to meet my father at his office the next day.

My last visitor Tuesday evening was Brad. I had a request for him.

"Could you see if Mrs. Garlington would let us have the copy of the amulet?"

"Maybe, but why?"

"I had an idea that maybe I can pull a switch with Mr. Pierce when we try to exchange the amulet for Jack. It's the only part of a plan I can begin to put together."

He thought a moment. "Okay, for what good it'll do. I'll try to run down after school tomorrow."

Something occurred to me. "Don't you have lifting or spring practice or something?"

"Not this week," he said; which I believe meant that he had set a higher priority on helping me than on making the coach happy. Of course, there may be coaches who would make a point by punishing his high school All-America quarterback, but ours isn't one of them. He had waited twenty-five years to coach a state champion and for him Brad could do no wrong.

I went to bed in my room that night. I was staying home on Wednesday and if Mom went to work I was going to take a walk to the farmhouse. Something Mrs. Donnelly had said was troubling me and I wanted to check it out.

Chapter 28

I got my wish granted when Mom said she needed to go on to work that morning. I had already showered and dressed. The pain was much reduced thanks to the passage of time and the use of pain-killers. I could see how someone could get hooked on them.

So when she and Angela left in her car I quickly phoned Mrs. Donnelly to ask if it would be okay to come over. With permission granted I headed for the old farmhouse. I wasn't worried about leaving the amulet unsafe in my vacant room because it wasn't there. It was hidden in our basement, most of which was a storage room. Often in a marriage one party is a packrat while the other wants to clear away the clutter. In my parents' marriage they both were packrats. The gene may be recessive because all three kids have turned out that way. Our basement was like Mrs. Garlington's attic except that there's lots more stuff, it's not worth as much except to us, and there is almost no room to walk. Even if Mr. Pierce broke in and, like Jack, could sense that the amulet was somewhere around, unless his sensitivity to exactly where it was greatly exceeded Jack's, then he would need at least a week to find it in our basement.

The walk took longer that day and the inclines seemed steeper somehow. When I arrived at the farmhouse Mrs. Donnelly was waiting for me at the door.

"Good morning. Have you heard from... my word, what has happened to you?"

I had looked in the mirror and I just don't think I looked bad enough to elicit the tone I had heard in the voices of everyone who was seeing me for the first time after the accident.

"All those scratches and bruises—you poor boy, come in and sit down!"

"I'm really fine, Mrs. Donnelly, just a little car accident. But I would like to sit down."

We went to the kitchen, not the study. There was a wonderful smell in the air.

"Is that pie you've been baking?"

"Cobblers actually, peach and blackberry. Baking helps when I'm nervous." So it wasn't just my mom. "Would you like some, Thomas?"

"Yes, please."

"Which kind?"

"Both sound good."

She laughed, probably for the first time since Pierce had shown up. "Yes, teen-age boys." She bustled around getting bowls for each cobbler and a tall glass of ice-cold milk.

"This is wonderful," I said after the first taste. "You could even give my mom a run for the money and she's the best baker I know."

Between bites I got down to the reason for my visit. "You told me that there were histories of Jack's life. I know you weren't supposed to tell about them but since you have, I would like to look at them. I'm looking for some clues to how to get Jack back safely. I need somewhere to start."

She knew how to make a tough decision quickly. "I'll do it. I'll let you see them. If Jack wants to release me then that will be just fine. Finish your cobbler and we'll go to the study."

I took the chair I had always taken on my visits to Jack. Mrs. Donnelly pulled several volumes down from the bookcases and handed them to me. I selected one and placed the others on the table by the chair.

It was incredible. The oldest, and briefest, were on what I guessed was vellum. I'd read about it and seen it in museum cases but never held it in my hands. Throughout the books was the most amazing history. Jack had been protected by a society which had, from time to time consisted of some of the most fascinating people—several names I knew from history. I wanted to stop to read each detail, which was impossible in the earliest because it wasn't really the same English. Instead, when I came to passages I could read I tried to skim, looking for some additional insight, some clue concerning how the spell came about. The cursive varied from volume to volume. It appeared that throughout the life of the society from at least the sixteenth century on there had been a position of chronicler. Unfortunately, not all wrote with an easily understandable hand.

From that time on the chroniclers took upon themselves the duty to ask Jack questions about the time before the volumes began. It was in the late seventeenth century volume that I came across the first mention of how Jack came to be in the form of a rabbit. There was a lengthy interview in which the rabbit discussed the reign of Henry V. But there was also a brief mention of the spell. The chronicler recorded the conversation this way, "I then inquired as to how the sorcerer was defeated. And the protected one [apparently the way to which Jack was routinely referred in these archives], much vexed by my questions began to answer, 'There is little to tell, the stranger's sword cut the air, the sorcerer recoiled, then I clasped-, that is, the stranger clasped the invisible bonds upon the sorcerer's hands. The stranger spoke the words which I can hear even now and with barely a goodbye they departed this world in a burst of color and mist.'"

I continued to speed-read through the years, hoping desperately that I wasn't hurrying past something important.

I slowed down as I came to the 1860's. The writer of this period wrote with a firm clear hand. There was considerable interesting comment about the days leading up to the Civil War and then I came to this in 1864:

"The protected one is quite disturbed by the letter which arrived yesterday. I read it to him at once. The letter is as follows:

"'To the one searching for Charles:

"'The man is living in Maryland north from Washington and south of the Monocacy. He runs a store but is preparing to leave. If you come for him he will already be gone. I knew him as surely as the day I first saw him. But it is not my time to restrain him. As for me you know who I am.

"'You thought to hide the truth from me. But it was never so. You have paid a price but redemption is coming. Be of good heart.'

"The letter was unsigned."

It was nearly one o'clock. I had taken only a short break for lunch—a sandwich followed by more cobbler. Now I urgently scanned the remaining volumes. I looked especially for the one from the World War Two years and was rewarded by one brief note. "A letter came for the protected one. It bore disturbing but encouraging news but he does not wish me to write it down in this book. Still I might say that it suggests that time grows short for a resolution of the protected one's plight."

In one of the most recent journals it became clear that Jack had aggressively pursued the move to Maryland, well before the member of his little group of protectors had passed away.

That was all I could find. There surely was more buried in the set of materials if only I had more time to look.

"Thomas?" I looked up to find Mrs. Donnelly standing in the door. She held a small volume in her hands. She seemed to be controlling herself only with great effort. "Thomas, this is the oldest of the books. It is the one which Jack often has me bring to him. He has me open it to one special page which is marked with a piece of cloth which Jack says is most precious of all things."

She carried it to me. I received it from her carefully and opened it the same way. It was indeed very old. The binding was cracked and the page marked by the cloth was very faded. The original lettering had been inked over at some later date. The words were still clear enough to read. At least they would have been if they had been in English.

"I believe it's French of an old type," said Mrs. Donnelly. "Jack would never tell me what it says. But he would look at it and often, though it's hard to tell, I believe he would weep."

I continued to study the page. I had to see Mr. Chambers. Maybe tonight if he could come to our house. I would call him as soon as I got home.

I carefully handed the cloth to Mrs. Donnelly. "Keep this safe for Jack. I'm going to take the book for tonight. I may know someone who can help us. Is there anything else that you can tell me? Something that might help?"

She was crying, now, from the stress. After keeping the rabbit's secrets for so long it was tearing her apart to disclose everything to me even though she had reason to know I had Jack's confidence.

"Only one thing more. The other night, after you had left and Jack was aware of how you had been hurt and how you had lost that girl, he had me bring him the book and turn once again to this page. After reading a moment he said something which he had never said before. I remember the words distinctly because I asked what they meant and he refused to discuss them. He said, 'If only I had never seen the four. His admiration would not have turned to hatred. And Thomas and Brad and Erin and Laurie would all be safe and I would have been long-forgotten.'

"Then as he often did, especially on nights when he had read from this book, he had me read scriptures on forgiveness for almost as long as my voice could hold out. Then he said good night and we went to bed.

"Do you believe any of this may help, Thomas?"

"Yes, Mrs. Donnelly. I'm sure it will." 'His admiration would not have turned to hatred'. That suggested several possibilities.

Mrs. Donnelly drove me to my house. I waved to her as she pulled out of the driveway. It was almost two o'clock. After looking around the house to make sure no one had been inside I took the book up to my room. I then went to the basement, finding it harder to descend the stairs than climb them, retrieved the amulet and returned to my room.

The one obvious point was that Jack had lied to me. The real question was how much of the story the rabbit had told me was untrue. Parts of it were backed up by what had been recorded in the books. But the fact that Jack had told me less than the whole truth was very troublesome.

In any event Jack and I needed to talk. Preferably while the rabbit was still in a cage. That might not be as big a problem as I had previously thought as I had a fair idea of where Jack was. But that would come tomorrow.

The next step though was a phone call. The time was right to find Mr. Chambers in the English Department office. He almost always went there for a while after school. Sure enough; he even answered the phone.

"Mr. Chambers, I have a big favor to ask of you. Will you please come by my house this evening? I want to show you something and ask you about it."

After he asked several questions that I didn't answer directly he agreed to drop by after his church's choir practice ended, around nine o'clock

I put the book and the amulet away safely in my room and then went downstairs to watch some movies. Staying with my John Wayne theme I put The Sons of Katie Elder along with four others in our five disc DVD player. Occasionally I dozed off, which was okay since I had seen the movies before. Around four o'clock the phone rang, waking me up. It was Penny Bradford. She was angry at me again.

"Why haven't you returned my calls? And why were you impolite the one time you did answer your phone?"

I shook my head to clear the cobwebs. I never wake up as alert as Brad.

"Penny, what are you talking about? I haven't talked to you since I left your grandmother's house. I haven't gotten any messages from you and I know my parents check the voicemail every evening."

"It wasn't on your house phone, you moron, I called on your cell phone!"

Uh-oh. So I guess it hadn't fallen out in the Frederick parking lot or down between the seats of my Cutlass.

"You say I answered the phone—what did you say?"

"I asked you what you had done with my grandmother's medallion. You had promised to call her."

Now I was up to speed and I wasn't happy.

"When did you have this call with me?"

"What's with you? You're talking like you've been hit on the head." If she only knew. "This afternoon, of course."

That made it very interesting. Pierce took the cell phone. He knows I have the amulet.

"Penny, I'm sorry about the confusion. Someone stole my cell phone the other day. Did it really sound like me?"

"I don't know. Maybe. It was a little lower than your voice."

"See, it wasn't me. As to your other question, Brad's going to try and see your grandmother this afternoon or evening and will bring her up to speed. As for you, I'll simply say there's a lot going on."

"But ..."

After another ten minutes of not answering any of her questions she gave up and all but hung up on me. We did not part the best of friends. I didn't care as I had to think about what to do now. Since nothing came immediately to mind I decided to watch another movie.

Later that evening, when it was almost time for Mom to return from church with Angela, Dad was on the deck grilling hamburgers. I was almost finished with McLintock and about to decide which of the Duke's movies to watch next when I heard a car pull in the driveway. A little too early for Mom, I guessed it was Stephanie being dropped off by Laurie after practice. But the engine stopped. Stephanie hurried into the house, walking past me quickly and speeding up the stairs so I couldn't get a good look at her face. I turned back to the door to the rec room. Laurie stood there for a moment without saying a word. Her face was very red. Appearing to control her emotions only with some difficulty, she finally moved, coming over and sitting on the ottoman near my chair.

"Two days ago," she said softly. "It happened two days ago. Why did ...?" she broke off sharply as my dad came in.

"Oh, hi, Laurie," he called, "How have you been?" My dad really liked Laurie. He thought she was very special.

"Fine, Mr. O'Ryan," she answered without taking her eyes off me. After Dad returned to the deck she spoke again. "Brad went to see the car. He said it was a miracle you walked away alive. But he didn't tell me—he told Stephanie. And she only told me because she's furious at me and couldn't keep it in. Why did you tell everyone not to tell me?" Her gaze was piercing and her voice grew angrier. "Were you ever going to let me know? Or have you just decided to cut me out of your life entirely?"

Normally I wouldn't have quarreled with Laurie, but this time, probably for the first time, I got angry myself. Her attitude just wasn't fair. "Look," I said, having my own problems controlling my voice, "You picked Brad. Steph told me that you were telling everyone about it on Monday. That's fine. I can't say that I blame you. But it's not easy because ... ." I couldn't quite finish the sentence. Instead, I looked away from her. She practically ran out of the house.

The door to the rec room slammed shut.

Later that evening Mom and Dad went for a walk. Angela was listening to music up in her room. I was back in the recliner—no more westerns, I was watching The Quiet Man. Stephanie came in and sat on the ottoman where Laurie had been. I thought she was upset at dinner and now she was crying.

"I am so very sorry. I know you didn't want me to tell Laurie. But I was really mad at her. She's been so unfair to you. When I heard girls on the team talking about her getting sensible I just lost control and nearly got into a fight. Brad's your friend and all but he's nothing compared to you. Why can't she see it?" She was so earnest and so loyal to her big brother that it made me smile.

"I don't understand it either," I said with a laugh. After a moment I asked, "What exactly did you tell her?"

"Just about the accident. Oh—I get you—I didn't tell her anything about Pierce and the rabbit. Which reminds me, you still owe me an explanation about why there's all this trouble about stealing a rabbit. But," she said as she patted my knee, "I promise I won't push you till you're ready to explain."

"Thanks, Steph. Look, I appreciate what you're saying more than you might imagine. But please don't be angry at Laurie. You need to look at this from her side. I always said I wanted to date her but when she finally gives me a real chance I'm missing in action."

"You didn't tell her about rescuing Erin?"

I sighed, "Of course not. Erin was by yesterday after her grandmother was here. She's still really embarrassed. I won't embarrass her more. You know how she and Laurie are."

Steph just slowly shook her head. "Yeah, I do know that. I also know that someday one girl is going to realize how great a guy you are." She squeezed my hand and left in a hurry.

Brad came by a little later with the duplicate amulet.

"Mrs. Garlington was really worried about you when I mentioned the accident. She said to keep the copy as long as necessary. Anything to help you. You made one conquest that evening."

"Yeah. I have this thing with grandmothers."

"Like Mrs. Jernigan."

"You've noticed?"

We both laughed at that.

"I'm sorry that Steph may have caused you some trouble by telling Laurie about the accident. I didn't ask her to do that."

"I know you wouldn't do that. Hey, I've gotta' go. See you tomorrow."

It was impossible for me to be mad at Brad. It wasn't his fault that we both liked the same girl.

My last visitor of the evening was the only one I had specifically invited. He came at nine-thirty, by which time I was already up in my room. I heard him talking with my dad at the door. By the time I swung my legs off the bed and managed to stand up he had already bounded up the stairs.

"Please, sit down. Good to see John Clark's best student looking chipper after your accident. Well, at least the best male student," he added with a twinkle in his eye.

"How did you hear about it?"

"I was in the attendance office when your mother called on Monday. Since Miss Sheldon couldn't understand what your mother was saying, I offered to talk to her. Yesterday I got some more details from Brad." His face hardened suddenly. "Was this done by that scoundrel Pierce?" Only this time he didn't exactly say "scoundrel". It's easy sometimes to forget he had been a soldier.

"That was my first thought but now I'm not so sure."

We talked for a while and then Mr. Chambers asked me to explain the invitation.

"Mr. Chambers, you speak French fluently, don't you?"

"Oh, I speak it fairly well," he replied with modesty.

"And didn't you study the medieval languages of France in college when you got a minor in French literature?"

He eyed me sharply, "You do good research; I'll give you that. What's this all about?"

I handed him Jack's book and indicated the passage to which Mrs., Donnelly had always turned for the rabbit. "Can you translate this? The passage on this page?"

He examined the volume and the passage quite intently for some time. "Where did you get this?"

"A friend," I answered.

"Your friend has an interesting library."

I agreed.

"The book is very old, but the language is much older still. The vocabulary looks like Norman French, the dialect of Old French from about the time of the Invasion. But the letters are printed, not cursive, in an English script from much later, say Shakespearean times."

He studied some more. "Well, it doesn't make much sense to me, just this one page. I'm sure I won't get this quite right, but it seems to be a poem of sorts, a meditation. On temptation I believe.

"'Though wrong it was to take,' I think the next is 'without permission'— so I suppose it means 'Though wrong to steal, yet I stole.'

"'The set of four' something 'crowns of lions'

"'He knew it not but the other knew.

"'And fell' yes, that's it, 'to his own temptation, which came from me.'"

Mr. Chambers pondered the next line for a long time, "Okay, I think this is it.

"'An enchantment he gave and so I received my heart's greatest desire— but so bitter.'"

He looked very intrigued. "That's it. Very, very interesting."

He had no idea.

Later, thanks to Mr. Chambers' translation, I drew several conclusions about what I'd learned. Jack was not an innocent victim, but rather the one who had stolen the amulet. And there wasn't one amulet, there were four. The spell was meant to produce the greatest desire of Jack's heart, but it went awry. There was more to consider, but that was plenty for now.

Chapter 29

My house is two stories tall, with a walkout basement. My room is in the back corner, diagonally opposite my parents' room. I had my window cracked open a bit to get the night air. I thought it unlikely that Pierce would try to put a ladder on our deck to climb up, but the windows lock in place to make it hard for someone to pry them open the rest of the way.

I had just put down the book I was reading and turned out the light when the sounds of an altercation came through the window. I hurriedly pulled on my jeans and gingerly tried to rush down the stairs. Once out on the back deck all was quiet but I thought I saw a figure in the distance moving toward the back fence.

"Who else is out there?" I called softly.

"Just me," Brad replied from down below the deck. "Your other visitor left after I explained it was too late to call."

"Do you suppose he was really planning to break in?"

Brad had come up the steps to the deck. "I hope so. I'd hate to think I hit him just as he was comin' to apologize. If you hit a teacher is that grounds for an immediate expulsion?"

"Not if there's a good reason. Were you going to guard our house all night?"

"I didn't see anyone else doin' it. Maybe I missed someone."

I considered the situation for a moment. "Just out of curiosity, why didn't you try to catch him?"

Brad thought a moment before speaking. "For the same reason you didn't try to catch him on Sunday. What's the point? He denies everything and even if the police charge and hold him without bail, which is unlikely for rabbit-napping, we risk Jack's life. You've assumed that Pierce won't hurt

Jack for fear it will affect the spell. But if given the choice of hurting Jack or freeing him with the assurance of breaking the spell I bet he'd take the risk of letting Jack die. I guess we could torture him, but we don't know how, and it would be wrong. And as for catching him, that might be easier said than done."

Pretty neatly calculated, I thought, and exactly what I had been thinking on Sunday.

"Brad, the thing that bothers me the most is that he seems less rational the longer this drags on. Trying to get into my house with all of us here is crazy."

We stood in silence a moment.

"Go back to bed," said Brad finally. "I mean it. I'm not much on self-sacrificing. Gimme this chance."

"Okay." I grinned at him. "I still won't put in a good word for you with Laurie.'

He shook his head. "I didn't think so," he replied softly as he turned away.

I headed back up to bed.

I woke up around six-thirty though I didn't plan to return to school on Thursday. Mom had told me that I could stay home all week if I felt it necessary. I was planning to take her up on it. In a way I was taking advantage of what we kids sometimes called her 'cupcake' tendency. I wasn't taking advantage of the situation just to miss school, though. I had some very important business to take care of.

Slowly moving downstairs I arrived to find an unusual domestic situation. My father, Stephanie, and Brad were at the breakfast table reading the newspaper—we get both the Times and the Post—while my mom was scrambling eggs, frying bacon, and making pancakes. Just your average family breakfast, which never happens in my house, at least not on weekdays. Normally, Dad is gone before I wake up while Steph and I have left before Mom and Angela arise.

"Hi, Mom, where's the dress and pearls?" I smiled at her and she smiled back, albeit with a bit of a sneer, as she knew to what I was referring. Sitting at the table I asked, "What brings this happy group together this morning?"

Steph grinned but didn't speak. Brad was keeping his head buried in the sports section so I turned to my father.

"Well, son, I was about to leave for work when I discovered Mr. Elliott here asleep in the rocking chair on the front porch. While observing him the alarm on his cellphone went off and he began to make a circuit around our house. As I didn't recall retaining him as a security guard I invited him inside for a talk. He was disinclined to break a confidence with you. So we were waiting to discuss matters once you joined us. After breakfast of course, which your mother was kindly willing to prepare." My father returned to his paper. I looked at my sister.

"I want to hear your story, too," she said. "And Bradford offered to give me a lift to school later."

Brad frowned at the mention of his full name, but said nothing. The fact that she was kidding him meant that she wasn't mad at him anymore.

I took my time with breakfast trying to decide exactly how to approach my parents. After my second stack of pancakes I became aware that all eyes were on me. Brad was watching me carefully, wondering how much of the story I was going to tell. I cleared my throat. The approach I decided on was for almost full disclosure—nearly everything except the fact that Jack was a talking rabbit.

"All right. I'll explain what's been going on. Part of this will seem rather unusual, but the experiences of the past few days will bear me out. It all started earlier this month when I met someone named Jack. He asked me to help him find something which he claimed had been stolen by Mr. Pierce, one of the chemistry teachers at our school. We found that someone else actually had the item, a small medallion which we acquired and which I have up in my room. Meanwhile Mr. Pierce stole a rabbit which he is trying to trade for the medallion."

I wished that I had a camera to take pictures of my parents' faces. My mom was incredulous while my dad was very thoughtful. I could see they needed some supporting details. "Mrs. Donnelly, the housekeeper in the big farmhouse, knows Jack and can vouch for my story."

"Mr. O'Ryan," Brad finally found his voice, "I was there when we discovered the rabbit was gone and when Thomas got the amu- er, medallion. And last night it was Mr. Pierce trying to break into your house. Which is why I was here in the first place and why I stayed the night."

My mother broke the silence first, "Dan," she spoke to my father, "Can any of this be true?"

"I suppose so," he replied slowly. To Brad and me he said, "The night you were out so late ... ."

"... was the night the rabbit was missing," I finished his sentence.

Dad considered a moment. "So this teacher sabotaged the car? That's attempted ... ."

"Dad, I don't know that. You said yourself that you have some enemies at work."

"Well, the police will have their opinions, I'm sure," said my mom.

"No, Mom, please," I had known this would be the critical point. "Give us till sometime next week. I think we can make an acceptable arrangement concerning the rabbit and the medallion and then we can deal with Mr. Pierce. A few days shouldn't matter to the police and it would mean a lot to Jack if we could get the rabbit back. I promised to help make this happen and I would like you to let me try and keep my promise."

My father eyed me very carefully and said, "All right."

"Dan, you're not going to agree to this, are you?" my mom asked.

He hesitated. "I don't actually see why not. Thomas seems to have made a good argument. Chris, we've tried to get our kids to accept responsibility and make wise decisions. I trust Thomas and his decision-making as much as anyone I know." After a few seconds he added, "Maybe he's the one."

"The 'one'?" she asked.

"I mean, the one to resolve this situation."

Turning to me he said, "I'll give you till Sunday night. Then we'll talk again."

I breathed a sigh of relief. Surely that would be enough time. Pierce showing up at our house had been proof that he was getting increasingly desperate. "Thank you, Dad."

After that the breakfast party broke up. When Dad, Stephanie, and Brad had left to go their separate ways I asked Mom, "Any more batter?"

"They're already on the griddle," was her somewhat exasperated answer.

At nine o'clock Mom left with Angela. She said she would be back by three. I had to work fast. First, the phone.

"Mrs. Donnelly, this is Thomas. Can you pick me up in thirty minutes? I have an idea which may lead us to Jack." She said she would be there promptly.

The decision not to take the amulet was easy. If I could get Jack free it would be easy to bring the rabbit to the amulet. Otherwise, I was putting the amulet at substantial risk. I was reasonably sure Pierce wouldn't discover the hiding place in the basement.

But where was I going you might ask? Well …

Chapter 30

One of the great problems in analyzing data is in recognizing which pieces of data, out of the relatively vast storehouse of our minds, are applicable to the problem at hand.

In this case I knew that Charles had once lived in this area before, during the civil war, as a storekeeper. Not only had Jack told me that but it was reinforced by the passage in the rabbit's archives. Next, I knew that Jack had not merely decided to take advantage of a bequest, but rather had actively pursued coming to this area. I also knew, from Mr. Pierce's answer to my question back when I was tied up at school, that Jack's detectives had almost caught him because he had a pattern of returning to places he had been before. The easy conclusion was that Jack was here because Pierce was expected to return.

I also knew that Pierce had a nondescript van which nonetheless looked familiar to me. I had been sitting at my desk on Tuesday night when I solved that puzzle. The reason it had looked familiar was because for the past two years I had looked at a picture of it every day as it was posted on a bulletin board next to my desk.

The explanation of why the picture was there goes back to ninth grade, or 1864, depending upon how you look at it. In the spring of my freshman year I was taking an honors course in English for which I had been tasked with doing some original research. Being then, as now, very interested in the American Civil War and also hopelessly ambitious about writing assignments, at least before I start them, I decided to look for something to write about concerning the area in which I live. The connection proved to be the battle, or more precisely the skirmish, that took place at the town of Burdette on July 12, 1864.

In 1864 General Jubal Early led a Confederate army in an invasion of Maryland with the intention of threatening Washington. Delayed by General Lew Wallace's Union forces at the Battle of Monocacy on July 9, he was finally stopped by the outer defenses of Washington the following day. As Early retreated back to Virginia a small Confederate detachment headed back across upper Montgomery County. Numbering about fifty, it ran into a slightly smaller Union force at the little town of Burdette. The fighting occupied most of the morning at the cost of a combined five dead, including a woman from the town, and thirteen wounded. There were several interesting aspects to the conflict including a couple of local angles. I'm pretty proud of the paper which included references to a diary I was able to use because of some friends from the town whose ancestors were there that day.

In preparing the illustrations to support the paper, I had used my mom's old SLR to take several rolls of pictures of the town of Burdette and the buildings surviving from the civil war period. There were seven such buildings. Four were houses. Two were churches. And one was a store.

The picture I most liked was a panoramic shot of the town which showed the field where the fighting had begun, framed by one of the houses to the left and the store to the right. And next to the store was a nondescript white van with a slightly bent front passenger side bumper.

A search through the box of the other prints produced two which showed a portion of the van's license plate, confirming that it was the same one I had looked into in the Frederick motel parking lot.

The store was now a small museum dedicated to local history which was open only on the weekends. This also explained why Pierce had not taken Jack straight to a hiding place after he had captured Jack.

The night of the rabbit-napping there had been a fundraising dinner to support the museum held at the church which was next door to the store. I had actually meant to go but that desire had been overcome by events. The next two days had been the Burdette Spring Fair. Mr. Pierce, assuming he actually had planned to take Jack to the store, would have wanted to wait till the excitement was past. And one more piece of data. A review of the Burdette Museum web page showed that among the four members of the Board of Directors was one Edward J. Pierce.

So my next move was to enter the store and look for Jack. Which led to my need for Mrs. Donnelly and her car. But before she arrived I had another call to make.

The housekeeper was right on time. In fifteen minutes we were pulling into the driveway of the well-cared-for home of Mrs. Iris Brooks. She had been the recipient of my second phone call. Mrs. Brooks was chairman of the Burdette Museum Board of Directors. At age seventy-five (everyone knew her age since the community had thrown a big party for her on her birthday back in February) she was an extremely energetic chairman, determined to talk up the local history at every chance. Her late husband had been pastor of a local A.M.E. Zion church for many years before his death. They had both grown up in the area, descendants of families of freed slaves who had settled the little community of Hopkinsville two miles north of Burdette. That town had almost faded out of existence except for an old schoolhouse, but in the Burdette Museum were several pictures and mementos of the days when white and black had separate communities. Mrs. Brooks, who had taught school for forty years, would come and speak to local elementary schools about that history because, as she always reminded us, "Those who fail to remember our history will make the same mistakes again." She was one of the strong early influences who helped nurture my love for the past and what it could teach us about the present.

I knocked politely on the door. Mrs. Brooks came to the door and exclaimed, "What have you done to yourself?"

I sighed. "Just a little accident, Mrs. Brooks. I have a big favor to ask. May I have a key to the Burdette Museum. I have a project I'm working on and there's something there I'd like to take a look at."

"Why, I'd be happy to let you borrow my keys. You've always been so helpful around the Museum. Those posters you made for your report on the Battle of Burdette have made such a nice display there. Won't you come in for a moment while I get them for you?"

"No, thank you. I'm working on a short time table."

"Well, I understand how it is for you young people these days. Hurry, hurry, hurry. Let me get those keys." She bustled off toward the back of her house, returning quickly. "Now, this is my spare set, so you won't have to rush to get it back to me. The key marked one is for the main floor. Two is for the back room. Three for the cellar and four for the second floor, you know, it's just a dust covered junk room. Cleaning that up is our project for later in the summer. Maybe you'd like to come help?" she asked hopefully.

"No problem. Call me a couple of weeks in advance and I might be able to round up some other helpers as well."

"I'll do just that." She smiled happily at the prospect of co-workers.

"By the way, I didn't know Mr. Pierce was involved with the museum."

"Oh, yes, although it's always behind the scenes. He never comes to any of the events. He's forever spending time around the place, keeping it painted, working on the roof. He sometimes stays there on weekends to make it easier when he's working on some project. We turned over the garage to him for his use. It's like it was his home away from home. Oh, and he's the one who keeps the little cemetery looking so nice. He had the new marker carved for Mary Caldwell. You remember, she was the townswoman killed the day of the fight."

Mary Caldwell. For some reason I hadn't made the connection before. She had been the wife of the storekeeper.

I thanked Mrs. Brooks again for the keys. She waved good-bye as we pulled out of the driveway.

Burdette is about four miles from my house, situated on a crossroads where Maryland Route 137 cuts from west to east across the northern edge of Montgomery County and is intersected by Burdette Road which heads out to the vicinity of Sugarloaf Mountain to the north and connects back to Germantown to the south. A small convenience store with a gas station is the only real business left in town. I had Mrs. Donnelly drop me off about a quarter mile south of town. She then headed back south to carry out her part of my plan. I was happy to find out that she had a cell phone as that made communication much easier.

As for me, I had borrowed Stephanie's cell phone the night before. She was reluctant to do without it for even a few minutes but she was feeling sorry for me. I said, quite correctly, that I was going for a walk and that I might need to call someone to pick me up. I didn't explain the precise context.

I walked slowly toward the center of the town. The convenience store was on the near right, or southeastern corner of the intersection. The church was diagonally across the intersection with the store, now a museum, next to it. Next to the store and to the north was the field of the skirmish. It was owned by a local charitable trust which kept the field a wide open grassy spot where people could come for picnics. Behind the museum was a garage which dated from the 1940s. I had an idea what was inside. I bought a Coke from the convenience store and then positioned myself behind a massive oak where I had a view of the front of the old store. Now was the time to see if my calculations were correct.

With Stephanie's cell phone I punched in my own cell phone number and waited for it to ring.

"Hello?" He had probably kept the phone on the whole time, either the batteries were almost out or he had a compatible charger.

"I'm sorry for not being up to welcome you to my house last night."

Silence from the other end. Pierce was deciding whether to engage.

"Look Charles, I need to talk to you," I said, thinking that my use of his real name might get him to respond. I was right.

"All we have to talk about is trading the rabbit for the amulet." His voice was tired, with a sharp edge from something, maybe anger, or maybe pain. "Thanks to your talkative friend I know you have it. Congratulations. One more reason for you to think highly of yourself. What else is there to talk about?"

"I want to ask you why Jack had you put the spell on him."

That made him think a moment, then he laughed bitterly. "He hasn't told you much then, right?" he asked. The "He" was said with as much contempt as you can get into one syllable. Perhaps it was a friendship gone awry, I thought.

"Very little. Much of it I believe was false. He claimed it all was your fault."

"My fault?" he almost shouted. Lowering his voice again, he said, "Part was mine, most was not."

I thought he was hooked now. He wanted to tell his side of the story.

"Charles, come to Hanson's Sandwiches at Germantown in half an hour. You know I won't lay a trap for you. Brad could have taken you down last night, you know that, but we don't want to put Jack at risk."

He was hesitating, thinking it over.

"Charles," I tried to make my voice soft. "I really want to hear your side. Hanson's. A half hour."

"I—I'll consider it," he replied.

"Do that." I said and hung up abruptly.

I thought I had him. It would be very interesting to hear what he had to say. It was too bad I wouldn't be available to actually be there.

I looked at my watch. If he wanted to get there on time he would have to leave in ten minutes. Mrs. Donnelly should be almost to Hanson's by now. I watched the building carefully.

Twelve minutes later Charles emerged from the side door, carefully locking it behind him. He walked to the garage and raised the door. There was the white van. He pulled it out and, after going back to lower the garage door, drove off toward Germantown.

I let out a long breath.

Once his van was out of sight I lost no time crossing to the museum and using my newly acquired keys to enter the building. I locked the door behind me.

The building was very quiet. Enough light came through the old windows to allow me to find my way to the stairs. They creaked more than the one at Mr. Pierce's townhouse. At the top of the stairs I selected the key marked four and tried it. The door swung open.

"Jack, are you there?"

"Thomas! Oh, I am so glad to hear you." the rabbit's voice was the most excited it had ever been. "How did you ever find me?"

I picked my way carefully toward the sound of Jack's voice through a variety of old objects and boxes. Light from the front windows was filtered by both thin curtains and layers of dust and grime. "Later. We have to talk."

"Oh, be wary. Do not come very close. I believe Charles set some traps."

That made me stop immediately. Carefully, very carefully, I edged forward until I could see Jack, and the rabbit could see me. Obviously, Jack was right, at least about the cage. A series of wires were connected to it, suggesting that touching the cage would prompt some dire consequences. I had no real interest in finding myself tied up again by Mr. Pierce.

"Have you found the amulet?" Jack asked.

"Yes. It's safe at my house."

"Oh, I thought so from some of the things Charles was saying. How can you get me out of this?"

I paused before responding, "All in good time. I'm actually not ready to get you out of this."

"Wh—what?"

"Jack, I want to know how many lies you told me."

The rabbit was stunned. "Lies? How can you say this? Lies about what?"

"Everything. The amulet. The spell. Your role in capturing the sorcerer. I also want to know about the other amulets. And why you're sure you can send this one back where it came from."

Jack was very still. "How did you find out?" the rabbit asked quietly.

"I've read the histories. 'And so I received my heart's greatest desire— but so bitter.'"

The rabbit only whimpered in reply.

"Jack, I don't know how long we have."

Trying to regain composure, Jack managed to say, "And I don't know where to begin."

"Okay, let me start. You correct me when I get something wrong. You met the warrior and helped him capture the sorcerer. But you had already stolen a set of amulets—each bearing the lion's crown. How many were there in all?"

"Four," came the reply, so soft I could barely hear. Jack looked away from me.

"With the sorcerer and the warrior gone you arranged with Charles to use one of the amulets to cast a spell which would give you 'your heart's greatest desire.' But something went wrong. You got your desire but you found yourself transformed. Was it eternal life? Was that the temptation? Was that your desire?"

No response, so I went on, "No matter. The result was what it was. Charles fled with the amulet. You still had three but you were a rabbit. You waited to see if the spell would end on its own. Meanwhile the search for Charles began. It was lots more aggressive than you let on. You saw a pattern that he returned to certain places again and again. You weren't here to retire to country life, you were here expecting him to return. It makes me wonder why you didn't keep a closer eye on this store. You would have found him long ago."

"Hal said he would do it," the rabbit answered. "He failed me terribly." 'Hal' was Hal Andrews, the attorney who was out of the country. "I think he may have betrayed me."

Ignoring that for the moment I pushed on. "Oh, yeah, you heard from the warrior twice more. He was back in this world in 1864 and in 1941. Why? He had the sorcerer. The obvious answer is that he had missed something. A set of four amulets. Four amulets that were important enough to require him to return. His two appearances were to retrieve two of the amulets. But not from you. For some reason you didn't have them. You began to expect that he would come back for your amulet, the one that Charles had escaped with, but he never did. How long had you really known that Pierce was Charles? You came to me because of the visions and because you had grown impatient of waiting for the warrior to return. Impatience is not a virtue. And what of the fourth amulet? But of course, it's obvious what happened to that one."

I waited. This time Jack would speak.

"All right. I will tell you the truth."

Chapter 31

"You have everything correct, actually. I knew I was choosing someone bright and determined to help me." The rabbit sighed. "I am so sorry. Everything is entirely my fault. I thought that if I told you the truth you would refuse to help me. Why would you risk anything for someone who is the victim only of his own selfishness and arrogance? I reached for something I should never have desired. And I have been burned terribly." The rabbit lapsed into silence.

"Jack?"

The brilliant blue eyes were sad but intense. "I have lied for nearly a thousand years. Perhaps it is time to try the truth." Then Jack laughed, but it was tinged with bitterness.

"In the year 1065 all was in a state of commotion in my home in Normandy. Everyone knew that the succession to the throne of England would be in doubt as soon as King Edward the Confessor died. He had no heir. His brother-in-law Harold was the likely English successor. But William of Normandy was determined to challenge for the throne as was Harold Hardrada of Norway. Into this turbulent time came the sorcerer from the other world. Soon my father was totally under his control. And I had become a willing participant. For there was something I wanted that I was sure the sorcerer could accomplish. But he scoffed at me when I told him of my desire and sent me from his presence.

"All seemed hopeless. I went for a long walk along the river which ran near our castle. I was lost in thought, when suddenly up ahead on the path I saw a strange mist. As I looked more closely a brilliant blue light appeared within the mist. Then it flashed other colors and finally a rainbow burst and then there was a dark shape. As the mist blew away I saw, revealed before me, a warrior. He was about your height. I remember him vividly. Thomas, you remind me of him, though his eyes were brown and his voice pitched lower.

"He looked around and when he saw me he seemed unsurprised. He said, 'Your deliverance begins. Where is the sorcerer?'

"I mumbled an incoherent reply and he laughed. 'You will see much to shock you before you're done. Much you have brought on yourself.' Then he grew more serious. 'Even more will you bring, I fear.'

"Oh, how often I've remembered those words which have burned my soul. But then I could just see a way to defeat the one who had refused to grant my request. So I aided the warrior through a difficult struggle. At the last we were victorious and the sorcerer was ensnared. He was filled with hatred. He told me that he would have his vengeance yet. The warrior commanded him to be quiet. Then in the presence of my father and others of our household he stood apart with the sorcerer. He turned to me one last time. I treasure his last words to me. 'When all seems darkest I will yet aid you. Farewell, my friend.' Then he spoke the words from a distant tongue that I hold always clear in my memory. The mist enveloped them. The light, first blue, then other colors in turn, then a rainbow burst and they were gone."

The rabbit retained control with some effort. "Charles had told me that he had learned from the sorcerer a spell which would accomplish what I wanted—my heart's greatest desire. But he needed an amulet—one of the special ones the sorcerer kept put away. It was easier to accomplish than I could have imagined. Just before the warrior captured the sorcerer I was alone for a moment with the sorcerer's belongings. The four amulets with the lion's crown were mine for the taking. So I took them.

"With the sorcerer gone I arranged to meet Charles the next day. I brought one of the amulets with me. He tried to talk me out of my plan. I laughed at him and told him that he should prove his boast that he could actually cast a spell.

"So he did. And I received my heart's desire." The rabbit almost lost control again.

Trying to keep Jack focused I asked a question, "What was that desire?"

"No," the rabbit answered firmly. My question had given Jack new resolve. "If I get out of this I will tell you one day. But not now. Not even to earn your favor.

"Thomas, you must not think that seeking your heart's greatest desire is an evil thing to do. If what you seek is within God's plan then such pursuit is worthy to be honored. I know yours and it comes from a wonderful heart, not one poisoned with selfishness like mine. I do mean to see your heart's desire accomplished if at all possible."

Brushing that aside I said, "So when the spell went awry, Charles took the amulet and ran away."

"Yes. The next few days I waited in the hope that the spell would end. My father pursued Charles but he had no success. I began to consider how the spell might be broken. I became convinced that if the amulet could be sent back to the other world then the spell it bound would come to an end. Just as much of the evil of the sorcerer's acts evaporated once he left."

I picked up the story. "So you took one of the amulets apart from the other two and you used the words to send it back."

"Yes, exactly. I had to be right next to it for the words to work. I was close enough to feel the mist. The brilliance of the light at that distance was almost blinding. But when I returned to my room the other two were gone— stolen by a maidservant of our household, I believe, for she turned up missing. I cared little for the loss, though I was angry. Strange isn't it, how angry we become when others commit our crimes? Still my anger was focused on Charles. Angry at him, but even more at myself. I fell to the temptation of things which should never have been part of our world. I have paid a price with the tears of a thousand years."

"But you heard from the warrior again."

"Yes, twice, as you said. A letter in 1864 from Maryland and another, mailed from Honolulu just after the Japanese attack. As you suggested, I assumed he was there to retrieve the other two amulets. I thought that in 1864 he might have gained my amulet, because he said Charles was there but it was not to be."

"And you've expected his return for years."

"To gain the last one. But he has not returned. Perhaps he lost interest or did not survive some battle in a far-distant world."

"So you were desperate. Because of the visions of me as a warrior, you asked me to help."

"You were my last hope. But you were not an act of desperation. You are a warrior, Thomas."

I shrugged off that compliment. The one fascinating thing that I knew, but Jack did not, was that the warrior, if I was right, had known precisely where the last amulet was in 1941. But instead of retrieving it then, he only told the young nurse to keep it safe, ultimately for me to obtain over sixty years later.

A cold chill ran over me. I almost expected the warrior to arrive at any moment. He might know how to extract Jack from the cage. To me it appeared hopeless.

Stephanie's cell phone rang. I answered it. It was Mrs. Donnelly.

"You must hurry! He's almost back to the museum. I've been trying to call you but I couldn't get through."

To the rabbit I said, "Jack, I have to go. Look, Charles will propose a trade soon. I'll try to be ready. Trust me."

"Then you'll still help me?" the rabbit asked.

I paused. I actually wasn't sure what I was going to do. So I just said, "Trust me." I turned without another word. Hurrying down the steps I looked out of the window in the side door.

The white van was just pulling in the driveway.

Chapter 32

The side door was no longer a viable option. I turned down the hall and ducked into the main room. On the far side was a series of exhibits laid out on tables. I crossed to the one with which I was most familiar and hid behind it. It was the exhibit of the battle of Burdette I had made for my school assignment. It was very dark in the room as the skies had turned suddenly stormy. Rain pelted the windows with the wind howling. Lightning flashed, followed by thunder so close, that there was hardly time to begin counting. I was terrified—some warrior. With the noise from the storm outside I kept waiting for Pierce to suddenly look around the corner of the exhibit and have me trapped. I waited for twelve hours—okay it was actually forty-two minutes by my watch, but it felt like twelve hours. Just as suddenly as it had begun the storm let up to just a slight drizzle.

I risked a look around the edge of the exhibit. It was still dark and there was no sign of the chemistry teacher. Keeping low I made my way to the front door of the building. I carefully rose up just enough to put the key in the double cylinder dead bolt. Once that was turned I pulled the door open quickly and stepped outside pulling the door closed behind me. I relocked the door. Taking a deep breath I ran as fast as I could across the street and hid behind the great oak. Looking around the tree I saw what I should have feared. The van was gone.

Mrs. Donnelly was nowhere in sight either.

I finally raised her on her cell phone. She was crying.

"Oh, I've failed Jack again."

"Don't worry, just tell me about it."

Through muffled sobs the story came out. Pierce had barely gotten to the restaurant when he had an apparent change of heart. She had followed Pierce back to Burdette and had pulled in front of the gas station to avoid suspicion. The housekeeper had walked over to the same oak I had used for cover even though she was getting drenched. From there she saw Pierce emerge from the museum with a large object covered in material. She knew it must be Jack in the cage. She returned to her van just in time to set off in pursuit of our adversary.

She had followed him as best she could until she lost him somewhere in Germantown. I finally was able to get her to calm down and drive back to pick me up.

As she dropped me off at my home I assured her it was not as bleak as she might imagine. At least I hoped that was true. I knew I needed time to think.

The main question for me was whether Jack's lies made any difference. To continue to help Jack put everyone close to me at risk. That's what Pierce had said. The rabbit should have known what Pierce was prepared to do. But to leave the spell intact was to leave a stain of sorcery in a world in which it had no place. My heart said to save Jack but it was my mind that made the decision for Jack—the amulet had to be eliminated.

To write it out that concisely gives the wrong impression. I wrestled with this question until late in the evening, or rather, early on Friday morning. I spent considerable time praying about what to do. By the time I finally turned out the light I was convinced that helping Jack was the best of a bad set of choices. One thing which forced me to a decision was a phone call I received Thursday evening about ten o'clock, hours before I finally had decided to help Jack.

Steph answered the phone. Quickly she brought the portable phone to me. "I think it's him!" she whispered excitedly.

I took the phone and said, "This is Thomas O'Ryan. May I help you?"

A harsh laugh came from Pierce. "You bet you can help me. Wait by the phone tomorrow evening after dark. Have the amulet ready. Be prepared to follow my instructions immediately and to the letter. Or the rabbit will disappear for a long time. In fact maybe it's time for us all to disappear," he added cryptically, before ending the call without waiting to get a response from me.

This was not good. I would have to be as prepared as possible for anything. I needed help so I called Brad and he agreed to come by after school on Friday.

The waiting began.

Chapter 33

Time passed slowly on Friday. Early in the evening Mom and Dad took Angela to pick up Stephanie after soccer practice. They were going out to dinner but they easily accepted my decision to stay home alone. Brad had been delayed by errands for his family. He called at six-thirty with a request. Actually it was an order.

"I told Laurie to drop by at seven-thirty. If she comes, I said you'd explain what's been going on these past several weeks."

"I can't ... ," I began, but he interrupted.

"You can and you will. She deserves to hear about this. I don't want to try and explain this to her. It'd be better coming from you."

One more problem. Or maybe a solution.

It was seven-thirty on the dot when I opened the door to Laurie, but instead of letting her in, I stepped on to the porch to join her. I had put on a jacket because it was unusually cool for an evening at the beginning of May. Brad was on his way and would be there soon. We didn't say anything for a moment. Finally, thankfully, Laurie broke the silence.

"I'm sorry for getting mad at you the other day."

"That's okay. I guess I got angry, too."

She laughed; her beautiful, musical laugh. "Yeah, you did. I didn't realize you knew how." She paused a moment before continuing. "I was angry at the thought that you could have been hurt so badly and I didn't know a thing about it. Funny, just one more way I've been self-centered. It never occurred to me to look at it from your side and see how much I'd been hurting you for years. I truly am sorry."

I mumbled something and looked down at the decking on the porch.

Once again Laurie broke the silence. "I had a visitor last night," she said, almost as if she was challenging me to show some interest.

Complying with her unspoken request I asked, "Who was that?"

"Erin."

Now I really was interested. To the best of my knowledge Erin had not been to Laurie's house since the first test of ninth grade. Their earlier friendship had become a bitter rivalry.

"What'd she want?"

"To tell me I'm a jerk," she said with a forced smile. I guess I looked a little shocked because she added, "Oh, she didn't put it that way. At least not exactly. That was just what she meant. She explained a lot of things to me; like why you were spending time together and why you broke our dates, especially the last one. She said you were really brave. It never occurred to you to tell me all about it. That would have hurt Erin." She lightly touched my arm. "Envy is awful. Most people wouldn't understand but I've always envied Erin. She excelled without all the advantages God's given me. I've been so stupid. But when I thought you were choosing her over me ... well, I just got a bit crazy."

I could have quibbled about whether "a bit" really captured the true picture, but thought best of it.

"Not that I could blame you if you did after what I've done, but please don't hate me." There was a slight catch in her voice as she added, "I can't tell you how sorry I am for being jealous of you and Erin."

I wasn't sure how to respond, but I tried, "Laurie, that's okay. I couldn't explain at the time. When Brad gets here I'll fill you in about what's been going on the past month. I'm waiting for a phone call now that might get this over with. Anyway, things worked out. You're back with Brad and everything's all to the best." I was smiling at her but it wasn't easy.

The beautiful brown eyes held mine. "Do you really think so?"

Before I could reply, Brad's car turned into the driveway. He joined us and we went up to my room. I kept thinking about her question.

Thirty minutes later I had explained the situation as best I could. Laurie, it was easy to see, thought I was in need of serious professional help but Brad insisted that it appeared everything I said was true, though of course he had not seen the rabbit.

"If Thomas is crazy, it happened before the accident," said Brad. "And Mrs. Donnelly didn't tie herself up and lie down on their kitchen floor."

I held out the amulet to Laurie. Holding it close, she seemed fascinated by it.

"It's really beautiful," she said, sounding almost like Jack when the rabbit was describing it to me.

She seemed almost reluctant to give it back. When she did I returned it to my right jacket pocket. I also showed her the copy, attached to the original chain which I was keeping in my left pocket to avoid confusion. In spite of Brad's words and the physical reality of the amulet she still did not seem prepared to accept the situation.

We settled into waiting for the phone call from Mr. Pierce. In spite of all the years we had known each other I don't know if Laurie had ever been in my room before. She wouldn't have been there then if Brad hadn't been there as well. I realized there was one thing in the room which I hoped she wouldn't pay attention to. At one point I thought she had seen it and was studying it but maybe not. Brad, who had been there often, was glancing at some of my books and then saw something else which captured his eye.

"I forgot about this," said Brad. I saw he was holding my Cal Ripken autographed baseball. "You got it that time we went for the special safety patrol day." He flipped the ball to me.

I was looking at it when the telephone rang. I absentmindedly slipped the ball into the left pocket with the fake amulet.

"Hello," I said.

The voice was cold and even. "I hope you have considered all I've told you. Be at the boat landing in the park near your house in fifteen minutes ready to make the exchange. Be prepared to follow my instructions precisely and no one will get hurt."

"But I ... ." There was no point in continuing, he had hung up.

I spoke to my friends, "The boat landing in fifteen minutes."

"Let's go," said Brad.

"Wait, I don't think you should go. I don't want to put you at risk."

Brad stood up and moved in front of the door. He is imposing.

Laurie spoke for both of them, "Then you can't go either." So it was settled. We headed for the lake.

Chapter 34

The boat landing is not far from my house. As I've mentioned before, behind the row of homes across the street from my house is a park road. The shortest way to the road, and also the easiest in the dark, is to cut directly across the street between the Cunninghams' on the right and the Blakes' on the left. Laurie, Brad, and I quietly did just that, edging along the side of the Cunninghams' property while hoping that the two German shepherds were safely inside the house with Mr. and Mrs. Cunningham. Apparently they were. We reached the back corner of the fence without the sound of barking or, even more unnerving as I knew from past experience, the sounds of bounding dogs. There ahead of us was the small gap in the trees which led to the park. Unlike the bigger equestrian easement entrances which everyone in the neighborhood could use, this one was technically on private property, by only three feet. The Cunninghams jealously guarded this opening so as to deny the benefits of access to the park and their backyard to neighboring children. Whether this had anything to do with some unfortunate incidents a few years ago concerning the theft of some watermelons was unclear and, while not condoning anything which occurred at that now distant time, I prefer not to revisit that issue anyway. The opening was near the park storage buildings where park police sometimes gathered. This was another reason why we avoided this area at night whenever possible, but it was the quickest way to the road and the landing. I rarely came this way anymore but felt that the circumstances on this evening permitted the brief intrusion.

We followed the lane around the curve to the left, past the site where Pierce's car had been parked the morning he had lain in wait for Laurie. The owl that we often heard at night began to hoot from a nearby oak. A rabbit bounded away across the road, startled by our appearance. Presently we emerged into the great open parking lot which leads down to the landing. The moon emerged now and then from the clouds reminding me of the "ghostly galleon tossed upon cloudy seas" of Noyes' poem.

The boat landing consists of two parallel docks, each about six feet wide and reaching out into the lake some thirty feet. They are separated by a twenty-foot wide ramp leading into the water to launch boats from trailers.

Ahead now we could see a dark figure standing at the edge of what was from our perspective the left of the two docks. A small boat was tied to one of the pilings. Most likely it had a small but efficient electric motor. Very bright. Mr. Pierce planned to make the exchange and then escape across the lake to Germantown. Probably his car, or the van, was there, loaded and ready to abandon a life once more.

"That's close enough." The teacher's baritone resounded across the lot. "O'Ryan, I should have expected you to have your bodyguard with you, but I am surprised that you brought a girl along. For moral support, I suppose? Well, do you have the amulet?"

We had stopped upon hearing his voice, some twenty-five yards from the man, but I edged somewhat closer before calling out in response, "Yeah. Where's Jack?"

In response, the teacher stooped down and lifted a medium sized rectangular object, covered in cloth, from the boat. As he pulled the cloth away, the rabbit cried out, "Thomas! I knew you would never let me down!"

"Who said that?" asked Laurie in astonishment. I looked at her, and in spite of everything, noticed that she really looks beautiful when she's astonished.

"The rabbit. The rabbit really does talk," muttered Brad softly, "Thomas told me, so did Mrs. Donnelly, but I never really believed them."

Laurie turned to Brad. "The r-r-rabbit?" she stammered. "So the story Thomas told is true?"

"Hush," said the teacher harshly, to Jack, not to Laurie. Then, calling out to us, he said, "Let me explain how we are going to do this. I am going to take the rabbit and place it in the other boat anchored there." In the well-lit night I saw that, sure enough, there was another boat maybe twenty to thirty yards off shore, almost directly out from the right hand dock. "You, O'Ryan, and only you, will approach the dock and lay the amulet down. Then you will back away, back to where you are now, and I will approach the dock. I will pick up the amulet, making sure that you are truly giving me what is mine. When I am satisfied I will leave. You may then endeavor to retrieve the rabbit." Once he finished speaking he untied the boat from the mooring, and pushed off from the dock.

Very bright, indeed. All the work to find the amulet, with Jack almost ready to be freed from the spell, and now it appeared Mr. Pierce would get away after all. There would be no opportunity to make a swap with the duplicate amulet. He would know the false one the moment he touched it, even before taking time to examine it.

But what if ... now that was an idea, but how to make it happen? I had to think quickly, but the only bright thing to come out of my mouth to say was, "I don't like this very much."

Pierce had reached the second boat. He lifted the cage over the side and placed it carefully in the other craft. The teacher laughed acidly. "Of course you don't like this. You and the rest of your conceited friends who think that you own the school and can run the lives even of those elder to you. You should never have gotten involved in this. You have ruined one of the best lives I have had these many years. Still, it was time to move on. I will miss much about this place but there are still other destinations. And now I will have the amulet. Our friend will not find me easily—I have made many plans for emergencies. But the hour is late. Either hand over the amulet or I shall leave with the rabbit. That would not be my first choice but the time has come. Then you will be the one waiting. Hiding the amulet like I have done before and would have continued to do but for that ridiculous outlaw. Then someday when your guard is down I will find it by stealth or execute some stratagem to force you to give it to me. Let us be done with it now."

He waited a moment then called impatiently, "Well, what is your answer?"

Trying to stall for time I responded, "How do I know you won't take Jack, too?"

Pierce snarled. "Why would I want them both?" he asked bitterly.

Of course not. The man would not want Jack and the amulet. I had always assumed that Jack was in little immediate danger because the spell which bound them would make Pierce unwilling to endanger his own life by harming the rabbit. That seemed clearly right. What I suddenly realized, and what, if I had any sense I would have realized long before, was that the teacher had a great problem in making the exchange. Having Jack and the amulet close together was precisely what the teacher was trying to avoid.

All the time we had been talking I had been unconsciously squeezing the Ripken baseball in my left pocket. Once more examining the layout arranged by Pierce I had a second idea, which, when combined with the first just might make a plan. Unfortunately I didn't have the luxury of time to look for holes in the plan, of which there were several. Anyway, he had laid out a defensive strategy. My one chance was to attack immediately. I would begin by sacrificing a couple of pieces.

"All right, I'll do it," I called out.

"No!" came a wail from Jack. "You can't let this happen!" the rabbit implored. "Not now. Not when it is this close."

"I'm sorry," I called, trying to sound properly remorseful, "I've done the best I could. But Mr. Pierce is right. I can't let him take you away. We're beaten, at least for now." Only a soft whimper came across the still water.

"Just one thing, Charles," I remembered to ask the one question I needed answered. "Can the cage be easily opened? No booby traps or fancy locks like I saw at the museum?"

"I'll let the rabbit answer that," he replied.

Regaining a bit of composure Jack called out, "There are no locks. You should be able to open it easily."

Great, that was all I needed to know.

"It's now your move, O'Ryan," he called, adopting my metaphor though he didn't know it.

"Are you sure about this?" said Brad quietly, leaning over my shoulder. Laurie just stood frozen, unable to comprehend the reality of what was happening. Not that I mean to criticize—I had fainted when I first heard the rabbit's voice but then I was alone at the time.

"I hope so," I replied even more quietly. With a minimum of movement I extracted the Cal Ripken baseball and held it behind me toward Brad. "How good is your arm? Could you hit him from here as he reaches out on the dock?"

"What?" he asked in surprise as he took the ball from me. "I've never deliberately thrown at anyone in my life."

At that, in spite of the situation, I half-glanced behind me. "What about Andy Gillardi in the seventh grade?"

Brad shifted uneasily. "Okay, once in rec league but he had it coming. You know Andy made too much of that. Yeah, I can do it. Why? Do you want me to knock him out?"

I snorted. "That would be like the Lone Ranger shooting guns out of the bad guys' hands. I just want him off balance enough to cost him a little time. Can you do it?"

"What's the point …?" Brad began but he was interrupted by the teacher.

"Enough discussion! What are you waiting for? It's now or never."

"Okay, okay. Here I come." Then, to Brad, I added "When I say 'Now', throw the ball." I began to move slowly toward the left dock. As I got closer I pulled the amulet from my left pocket. I let it dangle on the chain in front of me. That would attract Mr. Pierce's attention. I walked down the slight incline of the parking lot and then stepped up on the dock, walking very deliberately out toward the end. Trying not to appear too careful I set the amulet and chain onto the dock at what I hoped would be a distance close enough for him not to complain but far enough that he would have to reach uncomfortably to avoid getting out of the boat. Then I backed off the dock and across the boat ramp. I continued away from the dock but, instead of moving toward Brad and Laurie, I moved slightly up the hill but in a direct line with the right hand dock. With my hands in my pockets and my head somewhat lowered I hoped I was the picture of disappointment.

I called across the water to the rabbit. "Jack, please forgive me, I know what you needed to do about the amulet. I'm truly sorry."

When I had reached what seemed an acceptable distance I called out, "Come on, it's your turn." My fingers closed on the item which was in my right pocket.

The teacher turned on the electric motor and quietly approached the dock. The teacher took a few seconds to reach the dock but it seemed much, much longer. Even from where I stood the amulet glinted in the moonlight. Pierce reached a hand for his prize but I had guessed the distances correctly. The amulet was too far from his reach if he tried to hold the boat in place with one hand. He looped a rope around the corner post of the pier to keep the boat steady. Then he stretched out with both hands onto the dock to grasp the amulet.

"Now!" My yell startled Pierce as his fingers closed about the ornament. But what most affected him was Brad's fastball which bounced just in front of him before skipping into his chest. Knocked off balance he almost fell from the boat. The object flew from his hands and into the water.

Meanwhile, I was running as hard as I could down the hill and on out the right hand dock. I was thinking about how close the bottom probably was at that point and hoping that my jump would not cause me to land headfirst into the lake. The water was very cold, taking my breath away as I began to swim toward Jack.

Pierce guessed my plan quickly. He freed his boat and backed away from the dock. Although, as I found out later, my friends were running full out as well, the teacher had started toward the rabbit's boat before they arrived at the end of the left hand dock to get to him. Pierce was also, as I soon realized, pulling a gun from his pocket. This was the most serious of the holes in the plan I mentioned earlier. The noise of the gunshots was as loud as anything I have ever heard. Now those sounds could be viewed as a good news/bad news story—bad that they were gunshots, good because I swam faster than ever.

Even so it was really just a math problem. As Jack's boat was anchored almost straight out from the right hand dock, this made for a right triangle. I had a shorter distance to go but Mr. Pierce would make up the delta in distance quickly. And I was hampered by a cracked rib and the small item in my right hand which hurt the form of my stroke. Four more strokes should do it, then three, then two—another explosion—another splash near my head—then one. Pierce had almost reached Jack's boat and was stretching to pull it close.

Actually, as I was swimming, it crossed my mind that this wasn't so much a plan as a wild hope. My hope was that I could reach Jack's boat and free the rabbit from the cage before Pierce arrived. In the actual event it was a virtual tie. And the teacher had a gun.

As I reached out for the boat I remember thinking that now that I was so close to Jack the teacher would surely not shoot at me for fear of hitting the rabbit. One more miscalculation on my part as a final gunshot produced a slight sting across my left arm. That was probably why I used too much force in grabbing the side of the boat, causing it to tip over, spilling the cage into the water. Fortunately, I was near enough to make a successful grab for it. By this time Jack was screaming, as much as a rabbit can be understood to scream. As I tried to tread water and not think of the wound to my arm I pushed the cage out of the water with my right hand which held the amulet while trying to manipulate the door latch with my left. Distracted by what I was trying to do I kept hoping that Pierce would take his time reloading. I was surprised to hear the chemistry teacher's sudden cry followed immediately by a terrific splash. I looked over to see that Laurie was also in the water and, without me or the teacher realizing it, she had reached his boat which she had overturned. She now kicked in my direction and with her help the cage door swung open.

"Jack," I gasped, "Can you swim?"

It was rather late to be asking but thankfully the answer came back, "Certainly." The rabbit wriggled out the door and slipped into the water. I let go of the cage.

"It does talk!" exclaimed Laurie.

As Jack swam close I managed to slip the chain of the amulet around the rabbit's neck. "This is the real amulet," I gasped. "The other was a fake."

"Thank goodness," said the rabbit. "Put it between my teeth to keep it safe."

I complied with the request and Jack began at once to swim rapidly away from us toward a point of land some fifty yards distant which jutted out into the little cove where the boat landing was. Pierce had managed to right his boat and with some difficulty was trying to climb back in.

Laurie and I swam back to the dock where, to our dismay, we found Brad sitting in considerable pain. But before we could see to him there came a burst of light from the point of land to which Jack had been heading. First a brilliant blue, then red, then green, and finally a rainbow that lit up the entire bay. The rabbit was clearly visible at the center of the light.

Then it was dark. But Jack's voice rang out joyfully across the water. "It's over, I can tell! You have succeeded! The spell is breaking! I must go, Thomas. Thanks to you and Laurie and Brad. Remember me!" A pause, then added as an afterthought, "Your heart's greatest desire—I'll do all I can to get it for you. Goodbye."

It was too dark to see Jack bounding away.

I never saw the rabbit again.

Chapter 35

The teacher appeared no longer a danger. Instead, he sat like a stone in the boat which now drifted slowly away. "It's finished," we heard him cry out, speaking to the darkness. "It's finished and I am at an end." His head hung down.

With Jack gone and Pierce floating away Laurie and I turned our attention to Brad. "What happened?" I asked.

"Nothing really," said Brad, struggling to stay sitting up. "I just stumbled on some rocks and came down on my shoulder." His left one, not his passing one. He did seem to be hurting quite a bit however, and Laurie steadied him as he rose to his feet. Once he was standing he said wryly, "Dozens of defensive linemen have tried to injure me and I do it to myself on account of a rabbit." He looked out across the lake. "Where did Jack go?"

"Back to the farmhouse I imagine."

Laurie looked at me with amazement in her eyes. She seemed unsteady herself, she was shivering badly—the water was pretty cold, but the circumstances made it worse. Her voice broke some as she said, "It's all true. The rabbit, the spell, the amulet, Mr. Pierce. I was afraid you were crazy."

"Yeah. I've been worried about that too. I'm just a little faint." I was having some trouble with dizziness.

Her eyes widened as she finally noticed the blood running down my sleeve. "He shot you!"

"I guess a little, it's just a scratch. Let's get Brad home and then we'll talk about all this. We need to leave before the Park Police come by." I looked at the forlorn figure of Mr. Pierce still sitting motionless in his boat. I couldn't think of anything to do for him or to him. Suddenly I decided to sit down for a minute.

Brad reached down with his right arm and helped me up. "Laurie, I can walk just fine but you might want to help steady Thomas."

So the mighty warrior hero arrived home assisted by the girl he once thought he had a chance to date.

My family had returned from dinner while we were in the park. When we got to my house Stephanie answered the door. That was a good thing because my sister was able to quickly take Laurie upstairs to get her into some dry clothes without anyone else noticing. Meanwhile, I went into the breakfast room to draw my parents' attention. Once Laurie was dry-clad, she drove Brad to his house in his car and explained, quite correctly, that he had slipped and fallen. Laurie returned to my house, probably having run all the way, to find it still in somewhat of an uproar. I had never come home dripping wet with a gunshot wound before. But fortunately, the precise nature of the wound never came up. Upon examining it we realized that it was the barest of scratches. So when I explained that I had gotten a cut, without providing any additional details, my Mom simply bound it up, with a mixture of affection and exasperation.

She was in the process of doing that when Laurie came into the breakfast room. Everyone welcomed her and if my parents noticed that her hair was still wet they didn't say.

That was the more difficult part to explain—the 'dripping wet' part. When Mom finally asked me point blank what I was doing I answered, "Did you ever do something as a teenager which, after it was over you really didn't want to have to explain?"

My father, who had been taking things in rather quietly, chuckled at that. "Son, were you doing anything immoral or illegal?"

"Well, I was in the park after dark and I was in the lake."

Stephanie rolled her eyes. Angela laughed. My mother and Laurie studied me intently, though I'm sure for different reasons.

Dad smiled and said, "Thanks for being honest about it. I believe that's all we need to know." He ruffled my hair, stood up, and returned to the family room and a program on the History Channel.

"But Dan," argued my mother. "This must be connected with the other difficulties with that chemistry teacher."

Dad replied, "I'm sure you're right." He turned halfway in his chair to face me at the breakfast table. "Is this related to your problems with Mr. Pierce?"

"Yes, and I think everything is resolved. The rabbit is back where it belongs. Everything's fine," I added, which I admit was a bit of an oversimplification.

He nodded thoughtfully. "Chris, I'll be going into all this in some detail with Thomas on Sunday night as I said yesterday morning. Unless," he added, "There's something I need to know right now?"

"No," I answered. "Everything's under control."

"Good," said my dad.

"If this is under control, I'd like to see what a problem looks like when it's out of control," said my mother but she didn't push it further, at least not in my presence.

After I had cleaned up and dried off I stepped out to the front porch to finally answer some questions for Stephanie. The first and most obvious was, "What actually happened out there?"

I was very glad Laurie was there as I gave Steph a quick explanation.

"The rabbit? It talked?" My sister was not buying any of my story.

"It did, it really did," said Laurie earnestly. "We all heard it."

"Then Thomas isn't crazy?"

Laurie looked at me oddly. "I wouldn't go that far," she said.

After filling Steph in on the details of freeing Jack from the cage, having played down the gunshots, I concluded with, "Jack was able to speak some words from the other world which caused the amulet to return to the place it had come from. He'd heard the words back when a warrior from that other world had come to capture the sorcerer and take him home. Long ago he had tested the words on another amulet which had been left behind." I saw no reason to bring up Jack's transgressions.

"Why couldn't you have just spoken the words yourself?" asked Laurie.

"Jack never told me what they were. I'm not even sure he would have trusted me to say them correctly. Later, when Jack had been captured, even if I'd brought the amulet to him it would have been too risky even for Jack to have said the words. Changing back to human inside that cage could've killed him."

We heard my mom call for Stephanie. "We're not finished, big brother," she said. "Not by a long shot."

When Steph had gone inside Laurie said, "Even being there tonight this is very hard to take in, you know that?" I nodded. We were both quiet for a bit. It was somewhat awkward. Over the years we had talked so often about almost everything going on in our lives but this time I had kept it all from her.

Now that she had a moment to reflect that must have been hard for her to accept. She sighed and asked, "What's Jack gonna do now?"

Strange, I really hadn't talked to Jack about that. In part it was because the end of the spell could end Jack's life. We both knew that but never discussed it.

"I don't know. I doubt that Jack does."

"And what about the 'reward'? 'Your heart's greatest desire'?

"Oh, that." This was where I drew the line, just like Jack. "Just a private joke between the two of us."

Seeing she wasn't going to get any more out of me she started to leave, then turned back. "That was pretty brave of you, especially after he started shooting."

A compliment from Laurie was something to be treasured but I said, "It's good I didn't know about the gun before I jumped in the water. Once he started shooting it was safer to keep going."

Laurie gazed at me with a funny look, "You never make a big deal about yourself do you? In all the years we've been friends, you never have."

I'm as pleased with praise as most people but under the circumstances I found her words uncomfortable. All I'd tried to do was what seemed necessary at the time. Anyway she had jumped in as well and she had never met Jack. "But you heard the shooting, too. Why'd you jump in?"

She gave me the faintest of smiles. "Because he was shooting at you."

She turned and walked back home.

After saying good night to my family and promising privately to provide Stephanie with a more complete version of the story the next day, I went up to my room. For several minutes I sat on the side of my bed without moving.

It was over—that quickly. Oh there were all sorts of details that would resolve themselves in the days ahead. But the spell was ended. Pierce had lost and Jack was free. The amulet was gone, back to the world from which it had come so long ago. Oh yes, ... and Laurie and Brad were back together.

My eyes settled on the item on my wall to which I hoped Laurie had paid no attention. I took it down to examine it as I had done many times before. I had made it the previous summer. My mom is into scrapbooking and collage making as ways to make memories. She convinced me to try one so I set out to make a collage of my friends. I went through old pictures to collect a sufficient number to use. Everything went well until I finished and showed off my work. Mom said it looked fine but Angela, in her innocent way, asked, "Why did you just make a collage of Laurie?" I looked at it again. That's exactly what I had done, though without intentionally setting out to do so. There were a few pictures without her, but not many. So I took it back to my room and hung it up in an out of the way spot. If Brad ever noticed, which I doubt, he never said.

I set it on my desk before kneeling by my bed. I had a lot to talk about.

The next morning, Saturday, thankfully, I slept late. In fact, when I came downstairs it was nearly one in the afternoon. My mother greeted me and asked if I wanted breakfast or lunch. "Does breakfast include pancakes, Mom?" I asked hopefully.

She smiled, "Pancakes it is. Remember, today is your father's big television day."

That's right. The first Saturday in May—Derby Day. The day the sports spotlight is on my dad's hometown. He always tried to get us to watch the entire day's festivities with him. For once I would do just that. While the griddle was getting hot I called the Elliotts.

"Mrs. Elliott, how's Brad?"

"Thank you for calling. His dad took him to the emergency room last night. He should be okay but they may want to do some additional tests to make sure how serious the problem is. At first look the doctors don't think it is going to be too bad. I'm sorry he can't talk right now. He's on pain-killers and is sound asleep."

I knew it had to be painful. Brad hated using drugs of any kind.

The rest of my day was spent peacefully with my family. I explained everything to Stephanie, filling in most, but not quite all, the details.

"I guess it's all pretty hard to believe but Brad and Laurie will back me up, at least for part of it. I'm trusting you with this but please don't even tell Roger."

Stephanie was quiet a moment before saying, "Okay, if you say it happened I believe you." She grinned at me. "I'm glad you're my big brother," she said and left the room before I could reply.

There was one outside interruption. "Thomas," said Stephanie, "The phone is for you. It's Mrs. Donnelly."

"How's our friend?" I asked excitedly. My heart rate was suddenly through the roof.

Her voice trembled with emotion, "Oh, everything is wonderful. Far more wonderful than we could ever have hoped. Thank you so very much for what you did. Jack has one message for you. 'Be patient.'"

The fourth fruit of the Spirit from Galatians. The one least exhibited by my life.

"And one other thing. Do not come by. Wait to hear from Jack. You'll do that, won't you?"

"Sure thing. I'll wait." I wouldn't be happy about it, though.

On Sunday Brad was wearing some sort of sling. Laurie was by his side almost all morning. Catching him when he was briefly alone I asked how he was and then thanked him profusely for all he had done to help Jack.

"I'm just sorry I didn't get to meet him. This whole thing must have been an incredible load on you these past few weeks."

"I guess so. At least summer's coming soon and I'll be able to rest up for our senior year."

Laurie came up then. She was very quiet. I wondered if, after thinking things over, she was mad that I had never told her about Jack. I walked away pretty quickly.

My conversation with my parents on Sunday evening went surprisingly well. I assured them that everything had turned out okay and that I no longer considered Pierce a problem. While mentioning Jack's satisfaction with the outcome and stressing the safe return of the rabbit I did refrain from identifying Jack as the rabbit. My parents agreed, at least for the time being, to refrain from pursuing matters further and as the summer came with no more problems they were satisfied at last. I'm sure they were convinced that a stolen rabbit was hardly reason for sabotaged brakes. The investigation at my father's work went on for quite some time.

The biggest surprise at school Monday was a note sent down from the office directing me to meet Mr. Pierce in his classroom at the beginning of fifth period, his planning time. I had not expected him to return to school and the thought did cross my mind that there had been time to reload the gun. However, curiosity overcame my good sense and I stopped in to see him. I did have Brad wait in the corridor outside.

The stage was much as before with Mr. Pierce preparing an experiment.

"Are you all right?" the teacher asked softly when he saw me. "Your cell phone is there on the counter."

"Thanks. Yes," I said. "I'm fine. How are you?"

He had been crying. "What are you going to do about me?"

Realistically there wasn't anything I could do. "I don't have any idea how the spell must have affected you. There's nothing I'm going to try to do to you. You need to work things out for yourself."

"I am so sorry for what I have done. I told Jack—yes I spoke with... with Jack yesterday by phone. I made that apology." He walked to his desk and sank into his chair. "I sat on that boat for hours going over and over all that I have done in my life. Well, maybe not everything, that would take too long." He looked up pensively at me. "Do you suppose God could forgive me? I don't suppose I will ever forgive myself."

Forgiveness can be a tough thing. For me to forgive Mr. Pierce, the shooting wasn't the problem. The problem was the car and the brakes, which I was convinced was another product of the teacher's rage over the missing amulet and which could have hurt any number of people. Still, if I couldn't give it, why should I receive it? It was easier than I might have expected to say, "I forgive you. I believe God wants to forgive you, too, if you ask him."

Thinking that I needed to show him I was trying to understand, I picked a subject from the past that he might need to talk about. "I'm sorry about Mrs. Caldwell. She was your wife wasn't she? Mrs. Brooks said you put up the new marker for her grave."

He began to cry again but he managed to nod his head in confirmation. "In all these years, she was the only one ... the only one I loved."

I saw Brad look in and wave once he figured all was well for him to go on to class. Mr. Pierce and I talked for the rest of the period. In an earthly sense there was no practical way to bring him to justice. Kidnapping a rabbit? Shooting at me to prevent me from getting the amulet close to a rabbit? Justice? I don't think so. Maybe the only thing was to let him find grace instead.

When we were finished, I turned to go, but I had one more thing to ask, forgiveness notwithstanding. "Mr. Pierce, when you were so determined to get the amulet from me and you thought I might have it, why did you try to kill me?" At his confused expression I described the sabotage which had been done to my dad's car.

The chemistry teacher looked very concerned. "I've done many terrible things. But I remember every one of them. Each is burned in my memory. I never did anything to your car."

Now I was more than a little troubled. If Mr. Pierce had not sabotaged my car, I needed another suspect. If my dad's work didn't supply one, maybe it was someone closer to home. Perhaps Jamie had been so angry about the way we had freed Erin that ... hmmm ..., he would need to be watched.

I also saw Laurie that day for a brief moment. I had refined my theory about why she was acting the way she was. While still convinced that she was upset that I had not told her about Jack earlier, I also thought there might be something else. Even though happy to be back with Brad, she was also feeling sorry for being jealous about Erin, especially since she now knew how much pressure I had been under. When I got home I decided to write her a letter. Not a text message, or an e-mail, but a good, old fashioned letter.

It read:

Dear Laurie,

I think I am making your life more complicated and more stressful than it needs to be. Don't let me. Enjoy the prom. Brad's a great guy. I know you said it would be different this time. I'm afraid you feel badly that it's turned out not to be different at all. But I understand. I want you to know that was a wonderful date we had, but that's all it was—a date. You do not owe me anything.

If you ever need me I'll be there for you. Remember how in second grade we decided we would always be best friends.

Thomas

The first six versions ended "Love, Thomas". I finally decided that would be adding pressure and run counter to my point in writing the letter at all. Besides, if I ever decided I had to tell Laurie I loved her I would do it in person. I made the long walk up to the post office and dropped the envelope in the box.

Later that week came the reply, on flowered stationery which she had probably borrowed from her grandmother:

Dear Thomas,

I'm sorry. Again. I'm also very confused. Pray for me. Thanks for being you. I do remember second grade. I always will.

Laurie

Nine days later was the junior-senior prom. That evening a white Cadillac limo showed up at the Arnolds where the four couples going together would meet for pictures. One of the couples was Stephanie and a senior from church. They really were "just friends" —he just didn't want to miss his senior prom. After much soul-searching Mom and Dad decided to let her attend. Roger, it should go without saying, was not happy.

Steph looked very pretty in a mint green dress. I told her so and she beamed. My Mom looked almost ready to cry. Maybe I'll understand that someday. I could have walked down to see everyone off. But I didn't. I did step out on the front porch once and glance down toward the Arnolds' house.

Just at that moment Laurie stepped out of her front door. Her dress was canary yellow. Even from a distance she took my breath away.

Quickly stepping back in the house I went to the living room. I sat at the piano and began to play. Sometimes I can get really caught up in playing and that time I barely noticed Mom, Dad, and Angela returning. Then I felt Mom at my elbow for a moment. She never said anything but she sighed as she turned away.

The rest of the school year was busy. With the class of '03 leaving we were now the seniors, but we still had finals. I tried to give Laurie plenty of space and when we did talk it was just casual stuff. I never even asked how she was getting along because I figured if she wanted to discuss it she would bring it up. I doubted she would ever look at me quite the same way after the experience of the talking rabbit.

I did have one pleasant outing. I owed Mrs. Garlington in many ways, including the fact that I had lost the duplicate of the amulet. When I called to tell her what had happened she insisted on me coming to explain in person. So, on a bright May Saturday, I took the Metro down to the beautiful mansion in northwest Washington. Much to my surprise Penny was there. Even more surprising was the fact that the lunch and an afternoon of talk and piano proved very pleasant. Penny, for once, was dressed conservatively in jeans and a sweatshirt and we actually seemed to be friends. I promised to return when I had more news of Jack.

I saw very little of my two best friends that summer. Laurie was away for ten weeks—on a touring team for a while and then at a special summer soccer camp (no cell phones, no e-mail, just soccer). We exchanged a couple of letters but from the looks of them her heart wasn't in writing. She got back to town late on the Friday night before school started and left the next morning for a weekend with her parents.

Brad was working at Giant in the evenings and on weekends while I was working early days at the golf course. By mid August he was in two-a-days to prepare for football season. His shoulder was fine. He never mentioned Laurie but he wasn't dating anyone else and the Arnolds took him up to see the closing game of the soccer camp (the football coach gave him a special exemption—it's nice to be a star).

One happy consequence of the springtime adventure was that Stephanie and I had become friends. We saw several movies together, a couple with Roger. Family activities were more fun too, without the constant quarreling.

Even with those outings, I was lonely. I did check on Erin a time or two. Mrs. Donnelly had mailed me a cashier's check for two thousand dollars to pay Erin for the research. Erin was thrilled. Then one day she called me excitedly to tell me that she had received an all-expenses paid scholarship, plus a monthly stipend, to any school she cared to attend. She had never heard of the sponsoring foundation, the Philippe de Normandy Fund, but her research on the web showed it to be legit. The name was quite familiar to me. Jack had told me that when it became apparent the net worth of all the funds established by the protectors was well more than was needed, a charitable foundation had been set up to allow the rabbit to contribute to worthwhile causes. Like, as it turned out, sending Erin to college. Of course she could have gotten a full paid scholarship to a lot of places based on her academics but the stipend was a cute idea which would mean that she wouldn't have to work while in school. I would have called Mrs. Donnelly to thank Jack but the housekeeper had left the old farmhouse a week after the spell had ended and had not returned as far as I knew.

The one day I did walk over to the old farmhouse was because I saw a construction crew there. They were beginning to add a glassed-in room across the back. It was a good sign my friends were planning to return but there was no sign of Mrs. D., and if Jack was there I wouldn't have known since I had no idea what the rabbit-turned-back-to-human looked like.

At least my life had calmed down. Except for the dreams, that is. Every week or so I was having the same one.—a knock on a door followed by me calling out 'come in' but no one ever did.

The high point of my summer came in early August with a postmark from New York City.

"Dear Thomas,

"I cannot tell you how exciting it is to be writing this to you with my own hand. I hope that this is legible. As I never wrote in English before, I have had much to learn. God has been so gracious to me to provide deliverance from the evil which I suffered as a result of my own selfish desires. I know I was forgiven long ago but today I'm at last able to fully appreciate the new beginning of my life. Someday I will tell you about those desires. You will laugh at me I am certain.

"To you and your friends I owe so very much, but especially to you. In spite of my lies and deception you risked your life for me. Words cannot properly express my gratitude.

"I must apologize for leaving so abruptly. You deserve an explanation. Upon speaking the words in close proximity to the amulet, it began to glow and colors flashed as I'm sure you saw from the landing. I was thrilled to see the amulet vanish as I was sure that sending it back to its own world would cause the spell, bound by the amulet, to end. I knew that the departure of the sorcerer long ago had brought an end to the magic he had wrought while here, but I was not prepared for the immediate sense within me that the spell was breaking. After calling to you I quickly ran away for an extremely practical reason. Rabbits, as you may have noticed, do not wear clothes. I was determined to get back to the farmhouse and Mrs. Donnelly as quickly as possible. I raced through your backyard and at almost the same place we first met, alongside the creek, the transformation back to human took place. I continued the rest of the way with mixed feelings of fear that someone would see me and the inexpressible joy of feeling the reality of my human body, just as God created me to be. Mrs. Donnelly was first unwilling to believe it was really me, but when she did she provided a joyous homecoming to the human world.

"I have spent the time since I left preparing to serve whatever purposes God has for my life. There have been amazing new experiences every day.

"The past will always be there but I am resolutely determined to focus on the future.

"Mrs. Donnelly sends her love and appreciation.

"One last item—about your "heart's greatest desire"—my plan is coming together better than I would have believed possible. I hope you will be pleased. I expect to see you by early autumn at the latest.

"With the greatest of love and appreciation, I sign this with my own hand,

"Jack"

I wondered whether Jack was taking time to interview possible girls for me. I didn't expect anything to come from the mentions of my "heart's greatest desire" but it was a kind thought.

One night later that month, I went for a walk about eleven o'clock. I headed down past the clubhouse and through the back gate. The creek was a bit noisier than usual due to some recent rains. No rabbits disturbed me as I sat on the rock where I had first met Jack.

There were some questions which lingered. First, when exactly would Jack come back? With Mrs. Donnelly gone I didn't even have anyone to ask. Early autumn seemed a long time to wait.

Second, what forces had helped resolve the mystery of the amulet's whereabouts, especially the warrior who spoke to Mrs. Garlington at Pearl Harbor so many years ago? Why hadn't he taken the last amulet then? Why hadn't he appeared to intervene this past spring?

Third, who had sabotaged my car? If it was Jamie, was that the end of it or would there be more trouble?

Fourth, why had my dad been so understanding about all my odd activities? I'm not complaining, but somehow I think I'd demand a lot more information if my kids start coming in at all hours, especially when dripping wet.

My list of questions went on and on.

And one was the most important of all to me. Was there a way I could have avoided losing Laurie? Not that I ever really had her of course, but I did have one brief glimmer of hope. I still thought about her question the night we rescued Jack. Also, the line in her letter which said she was confused. Confused about what?

The sky was clear. Many stars were visible. Perhaps the answers to some of my questions were out there on a distant world of warriors, sorcerers, and amulets; a world called Merindelon.

I wondered.

Chapter 36

At last, the first day of school of my senior year. I was up very early, thanks to my recurring dream, which had finally changed. I would consider that later, after I got home.

I drove to school in a brand new Ford Focus. My dad had been unsure what to do since the Cutlass was not repairable. But a guy showed up and offered him an unreasonable amount of money for the wreck. He said he had a pair of 1980 Cutlasses and he needed a source of various obscure spare parts. Dad was thrilled. I suspected the stranger worked for a certain charitable foundation. Anyway, Dad put the money together with some I had been saving from my summer jobs and some presents from the grandparents and I had a new car with manageable payments.

I passed Laurie in the hall only long enough to say hello on the way to first period, which for me was to be an honors course in medieval European history. I really was looking forward to it because Mr. Grimes, the teacher, was very highly regarded and the class was pretty popular. Admittedly this may have been because he didn't require a major term paper.

I was first in the classroom and chose a seat near the center, mid-way back. I was looking at my notebook—it was something of a joke among my friends that I still looked forward to assembling school supplies for the new year. While true as far as it goes, there is no truth to the rumor I still buy crayons.

Praj, who had taken the seat behind me, let out a low whistle and said softly, "Wow, look at her." I glanced up and knew at once to whom he was referring. She was standing in the doorway to the room. A vision. Shoulder length, softly curled, golden blonde hair. Drop-dead gorgeous in a royal blue dress. She caught me staring at her and I reflexively looked down. But I noticed that she walked over and took the seat directly in front of me. I don't know much about perfume but the one she was wearing sure smelled nice.

Since she was obviously new to our school it was only right that she should be welcomed. So, after gathering up all my courage, I said, to her back, "Hi, welcome to John Clark High School. My name is Thomas O'Ryan."

Turning only slightly, she said, "My father hoped for a son. He was planning to call him 'William'." Her voice was a soft and musical soprano. She turned slowly and raised her eyes to mine. They were the most incredible blue. The look on her face was quite serious as she said, "Since I was a girl he left naming me to my mother. She decided on Jacqueline." She smiled, and it was as if the sun had burst through the clouds. "But you can still call me Jack."

Made in the USA
Middletown, DE
12 February 2020

84462820R00118